"Will remind readers what chattering teeth sound like."
—*Kirkus Reviews*

"Voracious readers of horror will delightfully consume the contents of Bates's World's Scariest Places books."
—*Publishers Weekly*

"Creatively creepy and sure to scare." —*The Japan Times*

"Jeremy Bates writes like a deviant angel I'm glad doesn't live on my shoulder."
—Christian Galacar, author of GILCHRIST

"Thriller fans and readers of Stephen King, Joe Lansdale, and other masters of the art will find much to love."
—*Midwest Book Review*

"An ice-cold thriller full of mystery, suspense, fear."
—David Moody, author of HATER and AUTUMN

"A page-turner in the true sense of the word."
—*HorrorAddicts*

"Will make your skin crawl." —Scream Magazine

"Told with an authoritative voice full of heart and insight."
—Richard Thomas, Bram Stoker nominated author

"Grabs and doesn't let go until the end." —*Writer's Digest*

I

BY JEREMY BATES

THE CATACOMBS

World's Scariest Places 2

Jeremy Bates

THE CATACOMBS

PROLOGUE

They were dead. All of them. Pascal, Rob, and now Danièle—dead.

I tried not to think about this as I fled down the crumbling and rock-strewn hallway. I kept the torch ahead of me and above my head so the smoke didn't waft back into my face. The flames bounced shadows off the stone walls and filled the air with a sickening tar-like stench. The only sound was my labored breath-ing and my feet splashing through the puddles that dotted the chalky gray ground.

A passageway opened to my left, a gaping mouth leading away into blackness. I veered into it, hoping to zigzag ever farther through the underground labyrinth, praying it didn't lead to a dead end. If it did, I would be trapped. My pursuers would catch me. Smash my skull into bits like they did to Pascal. Set me on fire like they did to Rob. I couldn't fathom what they did to Danièle, but judging by her screams, I suspect she got it the worst.

I wanted desperately to believe that this wasn't the case, that Danièle wasn't dead, and for a moment I allowed my imagination to run wild with fanciful speculation, because I hadn't actually seen her die...

No—I *heard* her. She was gone, she had to be, and I was next, as doomed as the rest of them.

Still, I kept running, I kept putting one foot in front of the other. I was too afraid to accept the inevitable and give up and die, too hardwired to survive, even though there was nothing left to live for.

I opened my mouth and yelled. I hated the sound of it. It was shrill and broken and full of pain, what might come from a mon-grel dog beaten to within inches of its life. My disgust with my-self lasted only a moment, however, because seconds after the wretched moan tapered off, a riot of savage cries erupted from behind me.

So goddamn close!

The cries rose in a crescendo of frenzied bloodlust. Terror blasted through me, but I couldn't make my legs move any faster. They were cement blocks. I felt as if I were running in the oppo-site direction on a moving walkway.

Suddenly the ceiling and walls disappeared and a vast dark-ness opened around me. While looking up to gauge the size of this new chamber, I stumbled over unreliable ground, lost my footing, and fell upon a mound of rubble. The torch flew from my grip and landed a few feet ahead of me. I stared at the pol-ished rocks illuminated in the smoking flame until I real-ized they were not rocks but bones. Human bones. Skulls and femurs and tibias and others. I grabbed the torch by the handle and thrust it into the air.

Bones and bones and more bones, for as far as I could see.

I shoved myself to my feet, took several lurching steps, as if wading through molasses, then sagged to my knees. A centur-ies-old femur splintered beneath my weight with a snap like dead-wood.

The sounds of my pursuers grew louder. I refused to look back over my shoulder. Instead I clutched at the bones before me, my fingers curling around their brittle lengths, pulling myself forward, my legs no longer responding at all.

Finally, beyond exhaustion, I flopped onto my chest and lay panting among the thousands of skeletonized remains as a sleepy darkness rose inside me.

They don't smell, I thought, bones don't smell, funny, al-ways imagined they would.

And then, absently, in a back-of-the-mind way: *I don't want to die like this, not here, not like this, not in a mass grave, I don't want to be just another pile of nameless bones, forgotten by the world.*

That video camera.

That fucking video camera.

PARIS

40 Hours Earlier

CHAPTER 1

I was seated at a pavement terrace in Paris's 3rd arrondissement, waiting for my steaming cappuccino to cool down and thinking that I was a long way from home. I was born in Olympia, Washington, but my family moved to Seattle when I was ten because my father was sacked from his job as a camera technician at Canon and decided he could find better work in a bigger city. He ended up selling used cars at a Ford dealership. He was never very good at it, not a natural salesman, and took orders from someone twenty years his junior until he retired. My mother, the head librarian at a private high school in Olympia, found administrative work with the King County Library System in Seattle. Though she took a salary cut in the move, she didn't complain. She'd always been a team player, putting others ahead of herself. This was especially true for family.

A lot of my adolescent friends went to Seattle University or U Dub or one of the smaller colleges in the state. They wanted to stay close to home so they could live with their parents to save cash. Where's the adventure in that? I'd thought, and relocated across the country in New York City to study journalism at NYU. I wanted the college experience, and for this you had to get away from home. I remember my grade twelve English lit teacher telling the class one day how college was going to be the best three or four years of your life, so you better make the most out of it. In my case he had been right. It wasn't that college had been ridiculously fun—though it did have its moments—it was that things had been pretty shitty for me ever since my younger sister, Maxine, died two years after I graduated.

As I braved a sip of my cooling coffee, I decided the 3rd arrondissement reminded me of Manhattan's Soho neighborhood. It had a young vibe, with all the pubs and designer boutiques and vintage shops and brasseries-turned-hipster hangouts. The main difference, I'd say, was that here nobody seemed in any real hurry to get anywhere.

The tables around me had filled up with the after-work crowd, the men in dark suits, some without neckties or blazers, the women in institutional skirts and plain blouses. As seemed to be the fashion in this city, everyone sat facing the street, nonchalantly judging the people walking by.

I returned the white mug to the saucer with a delicate clank of porcelain and judged too. A woman dressed in lipstick colors and high heels held my attention. She was willowy with sharp cheekbones and a hooked nose, not the type of lady you'd approach for directions. A pair of big sunglasses covered much of her face. That was something else here. Everyone had great eyewear. No cheap prescription Lenscrafters, or pharmacy-rack shades with colored lenses and fluorescent frames. Only high-end designer stuff. I bought myself a pair of Ray Ban Aviators a while back. I also started wearing a lot of neutral tones. Nowadays I stuck mostly to black, and I guessed I looked about as French as you could get.

Just then I spotted Danièle halfway down the block. She was riding toward me on a pink bicycle with fenders the color of pearl and a wicker basket mounted on the front handlebars.

I stood and waved. She pulled next to the table, scissor-stepped off the bike's seat, propped the kickstand, then bent close for a double air kiss—social protocol for both hello and goodbye. I haven't gotten used to this yet, it wasn't me, but whatever. When in Rome, right?

"Sorry I am late, Will," she said in her French-accented English. "Do you want anything to eat?"

"I'm good," I said, and retook my seat while she entered the café. I watched her through the large bay window. With her jet-black shag, pixie face, dark mascara, sooty lashes, and pale lips, Danièle reminded me of Joan Jett in the "I Love Rock 'n' Roll" days. She wore a butterfly-print summer dress that clung to her thin body as she moved, a silk scarf looped chicly around her neck, and knee-high green suede boots.

How long had I known her now? I wondered. Two months? Two-and-a-half? Something like that. I'd been in Paris for at least a couple of weeks then, got tired of pantomiming my way around the city, so decided to give learning French a shot. I placed an ad for a language exchange partner on the France version of Craigslist. The site was used mostly by American expats. Apparently the French haven't taken to it because of their difficulty pronouncing "Craigslist." Even so, I received several replies. I chose to partner with Danièle because she came across as open and friendly in her initial emails.

We've gotten to know each other fairly well since then. She was born in Germany to a German father and French mother. They divorced when she was six, and she moved to France with her mother and older sister. She graduated from L'Ecole des Mines two years before. It was a prestigious engineering school, the MIT of France. She could have interned at any company she wanted. But, according to her, she wanted to take it easy for a while, so now she spent her days working in a florist shop and her nights exploring the network of catacombs that snaked beneath the city.

We got together twice a week, usually on Mondays and Fridays. She would teach me French one day, I would teach her English the other. Actually, I didn't really "teach" her anything. She was pretty much fluent. English had been a prerequisite for admission into Les Mines, and she'd studied it extensively as an adolescent. She told me she just wanted someone she could speak the language with so it didn't get rusty on her.

She liked me—romantically, I mean. She was fairly obvi-ous about it too. I should have been flattered. She was good looking. I'd thought that the first time I saw her. But I hadn't come to Paris searching for a relationship; I'd come to get away from one—at least the aftermath of one. My ex's name was Bridgette Pottinger. We'd met at NYU. In our senior year we moved into a tiny flat together off the Bowery near China-town. I got a job as a copy editor for the *Brooklyn Eagle*. She was accepted to the law program at Columbia. I popped the question a year later at the top of the Statue of Liberty. I know, cheesy, but at the time I'd thought it was romantic. The wed-ding was planned for the following July at a lodge on Lake Placid.

The night before the ceremony my younger sister, Maxine, and my best friend, Brian, died in a boating accident. The wedding, of course, was cancelled. My life was thrown into chaos. My parents blamed me for the death of Max. My friends blamed me for the death of Brian. Bridgette and I began to un-ravel too, and we decided it would be best to take a break. I had moved on from the paper to a travel writing gig, assisting with the guides for the Mid-Atlantic states. I was close with my boss, both professionally and personally. He knew what I was going through, knew I needed a fresh start. He told me head office was looking for someone to revamp a few of the European editions, and he put my name forward. A month later I was in London, getting the lowdown for a revised Paris guide. The other correspondents in Paris were covering the cafés and restaurants and hotels. My brief was to cover the nightlife scene. They wanted to jazz up the guide to appeal more to the younger crowd.

And so far, so good. My new boss liked the copy I was turn-ing in, and I liked doing what I was doing. I spent my nights checking out different bars and clubs, and my days writing up an opinion of them. There was a lot to do, and the deadlines were tight, but the work kept me occupied, kept me from thinking too much about my old friends, family, and most of all, Bridgette.

Still, I'd be lying if I said I'd gotten over Bridgette. I hadn't. In the back of my mind I had a plan. After a year or so away, I would return to the States, I'd be a little more worldly, a little more mature, and Bridgette and I could start things anew.

I winced. *Danièle's birthday party*. Christ. How the hell did I get roped into that? Danièle's friends—an eclectic mix of bohemians and young professionals—had been pleasant, the drinks kept coming, and everyone got piss drunk...and then... then everything blurred together.

When I woke in Danièle's bed Saturday morning, I could barely remember how I got there. Filled with guilt, I did the asshole thing and left without waking her. I spent the entire weekend at my laptop whipping my latest bar and club notes into some sort of coherent form. I didn't answer my phone when Danièle called Sunday afternoon, and we didn't communicate again until earlier today when she texted me to confirm that the lesson was still on.

I almost cancelled, but I knew how obvious that would look.

Danièle returned from the café proper with a cappuccino now. She sat across from me, took off her sunglasses—Fendis —and smiled hesitantly. I cleared my throat. I had already decided to act as if this was any other lesson, and I said, "French or English today?"

A flash of surprise crossed her face before she turned her attention to the spoon stirring her coffee. "Friday was French," she stated. "So today is English, if that is all right."

"Good with me," I said. "So..."

She lifted her eyes. "Yes?"

"I'm thinking of a topic to discuss."

"How about the weekend?" she suggested coyly. "You always ask me about my weekend on Mondays."

"Did you get up to anything on Sunday?"

"On Sunday?" More surprise, maybe some disappointment. She shrugged. "No, I stayed home all day. What about you,

Will? Were you hung over both Saturday and Sunday? Or did you do anything special on Sunday?"

"I made chicken Provençal. Have you tried it?"

"Of course I have. I am French. What else did you do?"

"Nothing really. Work. That's about it."

"I see."

I frowned. "You see?"

"You do not want to talk about Friday night. I see. That is fine with me."

"I had a fun time."

"Did you?"

"Yes."

"*All* night?"

I wondered if I was blushing. "Yeah."

"You were gone when I woke up. I thought…"

"I know, I— What time did you get up?"

"You are very good at avoiding this topic."

"What topic?"

"Us."

"I'm not avoiding it."

She nodded silently.

I lit a Marlboro Light to give myself something to do. The trio at the table next to us were sharing a bottle of wine and laughing loudly. This made the silence between Danièle and me seem all the more protracted and uncomfortable.

I decided it was stupid to try to ignore what had happened between us, to pretend this was nothing but another lesson.

We had slept together. We were having coffee now.

That made this a date, didn't it?

At least in Danièle's mind it did.

"I liked your friends," I said, segueing back to Friday.

She smiled. "They liked you too."

"Except for one guy. What was his name? Patsy…?"

"Pascal?"

"He had a wool cap."

"Yes, that is Pascal. You do not like him?"

"He's fine, I guess. He just didn't seem like he wanted to talk to me."

"Because he has a crush on me," she stated matter-of-factly.

"A crush?"

"Yes, for many years. We were in the same freshman class at school. He was with me during my initiation."

Danièle was referring to her university initiation. She had told me all about it on numerous occasions. You could enter her favorite stomping ground, the catacombs, any number of ways, including Metro tunnels, utility systems, church crypts, and the basements of homes, hospitals, lycées, and universities (apparently there was even an entrance in the bowels of Tour Montparnasse, one of Paris' first skyscrapers). Like most of the other buildings in the old Latin Quarter, L'Ecole des Mines had its own secret access points, and it was a tradition for seniors to drop freshmen into the underground maze and have them find their way out again.

I said, "Do you guys still go into the catacombs together?"

"Many times. As a matter of fact—" Her phone rang. "Just a moment, Will," she said, and answered it. The voice on the other end was male. My French was still piss poor, and I was only able to gather that she was meeting this person later in the evening.

"Big date tonight?" I asked when she hung up.

"Would you be jealous if it were?"

"Immensely."

"I do not believe you."

"I would be."

"You know, Will, I thought we had a good time on Friday."

"We did."

"Then why...I have the feeling you...regret it."

I looked at my cigarette. "I don't regret it."

"Then why are you acting so strange?"

I was about to tell her I wasn't acting strange, but I held my tongue. I suppose I was.

I took a final drag on the smoke and stubbed it out in the

ashtray. "Look, Danièle. I like you. But we have been friends for a while now. And then...you know, just like that. Boom. I—it's a bit overwhelming."

She considered that, nodded. "Okay, Will. I understand. You just tell me when you are ready."

I studied her. The delivery was so pokerfaced I couldn't discern if she was being sincere or sarcastic.

"Anyway," she said, "that was Pascal."

"Speak of the devil," I said, happy to change topics. "What did he want?"

"He is confirming our plans tonight."

"What are you guys doing?"

"We are going into the catacombs."

I raised my eyebrows. "Seriously?"

"Why is that surprising?"

"Only the two of you?"

"No, someone else is coming as well. You see, tonight, it is very special. I have something I want to show you."

She moved her chair around the table, so she was sitting beside me, our knees brushing. I could smell her perfume, a light citrus scent. She extracted her laptop from her handbag and set it on the table before us. She opened the lid and pressed the power button.

While we waited for it to boot up I said, "In what world do people use the semi-colon more than the full-stop?"

She frowned. "Huh?"

I nodded at her keyboard. "Don't you find it a pain you have to press the Shift key every time you want a period?"

"Hmm. I never thought of that. Perhaps you should have brought a computer from your country, Will."

"It was stolen, remember."

"Yes, you left it on the table when you went to use the restroom. That was very foolish of you."

The computer finished loading. Danièle used the trackpad and navigated to a folder filled with thumbnail-sized videos. She opened the last one in a media player and resized it to fill the screen.

A point of view shot appeared: a video camera light illuminating a grainy corridor the color of slag iron. The ceiling was low, the walls smooth stone. The crunch of footsteps was the only sound.

"That's the catacombs," I stated, surprised.

Danièle nodded. "This woman is very far in, very deep."

"How do you know it's a woman?"

"You can hear her in the other video clips. She mumbles a few times."

The woman stopped at a side passage and looked inside. It was a small room. She played the camera over the floor. It was scattered with a half dozen different sized bones.

A shiver prickled the back of my neck.

"Those are all human bones," Danièle told me. "There are rooms everywhere like this one. She has already passed several others."

The woman continued along the corridor, but stopped again to film an arrow on the ground. It had been formed using three bones. Ten feet later she came to another bone-arrow.

"Who made those?" I asked. "Other explorers?"

"Yes, maybe." But she didn't sound convinced.

The woman pressed on. More grainy gray walls and crunching footsteps. She arrived at a T-junction and paused.

"She is confused," Danièle told me. "She obviously does not know this part of the catacombs well."

"Why would she go down there by herself?"

"We do not know she went by herself. Perhaps she went with others and became separated and lost."

The woman chose left and followed a winding passageway. She stopped for several seconds to examine a wall painting of some sort of stickman. It was at least six feet tall, painted quickly, almost frantically, the limbs spread eagle.

Danièle said, "Watch closely now. She becomes very scared. Maybe it is this painting that scared her. Or maybe she heard something. But, look, she has begun to walk faster."

Indeed, the woman was now moving at a trot. The footage became jumpy. Her breathing was loud and fast.

Not from exertion, I thought, but fear.

Twice she whirled around, as if to see if anyone was behind her, the camera moving with her.

"She keeps going, faster and faster," Danièle said in a soft voice, "deeper and deeper, and then..."

All of a sudden the woman dropped the camera. It landed with a bang and kept filming.

"...she just drops it. See! She does not stop to pick it up. You can see her feet disappearing, splashing in the puddles. And then—nothing."

The footage continued to roll, filming a close-up of pebbles and the ripples in the nearby puddle.

"What happens next?" I asked.

Danièle held up a finger: wait. She used the trackpad to skip a slice of footage and pressed Play. The image was exactly the same.

"What—?"

"Listen."

A harrowing scream erupted from the tinny speakers. It sounded distant, coming from deep within the black tunnels. It escalated to a banshee-like fever—

The screen went blank.

"What happened?" I demanded.

Danièle looked at me. "The camera went dead. That is it."

CHAPTER 2

"**W**hat do you mean, 'That's it?'" I said, frowning. "You saw," Danièle said. "The battery died."

"And?"

"And nothing."

"You don't know what happened to her?"

"How could I? Nobody has ever seen her again."

"How do you know that?"

"Well, I do not," she admitted. "But she left the camera there. She never came back to retrieve it. And you heard her."

I sat back. My stomach felt unsettled, as if I had just downed a shot of paint thinner. "Is this for real?"

"Of course, Will."

"How did you get the camera?"

"Pascal found it."

"Why was he so deep in the catacombs?"

"That is what he does. He explores, even more than me. He has visited the catacombs hundreds of times before."

I looked at Danièle, then the laptop, then Danièle again.

"So you weren't with him?" I said.

"No, I was not."

"Where's the actual camera?"

"Pascal has it. I copied the files to my computer."

"Maybe he's playing a joke on you?"

"Why are you so skeptical, Will?"

"Why? Because this seems like something out of *The Blair Witch Project*."

"Pascal did not make this up."

"Then maybe the woman did."

"Why would she do that? The catacombs are very large. As I told you, the camera was in very deep. The chances of someone finding it were small. Also, there is no footage of her. Not on any of the video clips. Just her voice. The camera could never be traced back to her. She would never have any idea who found it, if someone did. Why would she make a joke like that?"

"She was running, right?" I said. "At the end she was running. She was scared. She thought something was coming after her. But she keeps filming? Would you do that? They only do that, keep the tape rolling, in those found-footage movies."

"No, Will. She was not filming. She was using the video camera's LED light to see ahead of her. If she turned the camera off—it is perfectly dark down there."

I chewed on that. "So what do you think happened? She believed someone was behind her. Did someone run past the camera in pursuit?"

"No."

"So who made her scream?"

"I have no answer for that."

I knew Danièle well enough to discern whether she was pulling my leg or not. Looking at her now, I didn't think she was. Right or wrong, in her mind she was convinced this was genuine footage. A woman had gotten lost in the catacombs, and she had the unfortunate luck to run into someone who had done something terrible to her.

And why not? I thought. Why was I so adamant this wasn't the case? Bad shit went on in the world every day. A lot of bad shit. Some truly horrible shit. You could pretend it didn't, but you would only be fooling yourself.

"Have you given a copy to the police?" I asked.

"The police?" Danièle's eyes widened in surprise. "Of course not."

"But if this is real, then something happened to that woman. You need to tell the police."

"And what do you suppose they would do, Will?"

"I thought you told me once that there are police who patrol the catacombs?"

"Catacops, yes. But they only patrol the popular areas. They make sure no one is breaking things or stealing bones. They do not perform manhunts. They do not go into the unmapped areas. The catacombs are hundreds of kilometers long. There are many levels."

"I still think you need to tell them."

"We are doing something better. We are going looking for her."

"Tonight?" I said. "You're going looking for this woman tonight?"

She nodded.

"And you think you're going to find her?"

"We have no idea. But we are going to try."

"That camera could be years old."

"The video was time-stamped only three weeks ago."

"Aren't you...I don't know...scared?"

"You heard her screaming, Will. If we find her, it will probably be just her body. Whoever attacked her, he will be long gone."

"And if he isn't?"

"There will be four of us."

"Four? You said—"

She took my hand. "I want you to come with us."

I blinked. "You're kidding?"

"I want you to experience this with me."

"There's no way I'm going traipsing around the catacombs, Danièle, looking for some lost woman, and I think you should reconsider going as well."

"I am not reconsidering."

"This isn't a game. For all you know that woman might have been murdered. You don't want to get involved in this."

"Then come with me—protect me."

I tugged my hand free. "Jesus, Danièle. Didn't you just see the same video I saw? What you're planning on doing, it's dangerous and irresponsible."

"If the woman had been filming aboveground, in an alleyway, and she dropped the camera and screamed, would you refuse to search the alleyway for her?"

"That's not the same thing."

"I am perfectly comfortable in the catacombs."

"Have you been this deep, where Pascal found the camera deep, before?"

"I told you, Pascal—"

"Not him. You."

"No, I have not."

I shook my head. "Okay, take the whole crazy killer out of the equation, the killer who might have gone back down there. What if, like that woman, you get lost? What if you can't find your way out again?"

"Pascal knows—"

"You're putting a lot of faith in that guy."

"He is my friend. He is the most experienced cataphile I know. I trust him completely."

I didn't say anything.

"So?" she pressed.

"No, Danièle. Absolutely not."

"It will be fun."

I stiffened as that statement took me back to the night on Lake Placid. *Let's do it, dude*, Brian had told me minutes before his death as he tossed me the keys to the Chris-Craft. *It'll be fun.*

"Is there anything I can say to convince you not to go?" I said.

"Is there anything I can say to convince you to come?" she said.

"Don't be a goddamn idiot, Danièle!" I snapped, glaring at

her.

She stared back, surprised and confused. Then defiant. Abruptly she closed the laptop, stuffed it in her bag. She withdrew a pen and scribbled an address on a napkin.

"If you change your mind," she said stiffly, standing, "I will be at this location between eight and nine o'clock tonight."

She climbed on her bicycle and pedaled away.

▼

My apartment building was located on a quiet street close to the St. Germain district and the Jardin des Plants. St. Germain was lively and full of restaurants and bars, though I often avoided the area because I didn't know many people in Paris, and I wasn't the type to dine or drink by myself, at least not outside of work. The botanical gardens were a different story though. I spent a lot of time in the free sections, walking the trails for exercise or reading a book on a patch of grass or on a bench in the shade of a tree.

I climbed the front steps of my building's stoop and checked my mailbox. It was one of six organized into two vertical columns of three each. A locksmith service advertisement was stuffed inside it. I received several of these a week, from different locksmiths. It made me wonder if Parisians locked themselves out of their homes in disproportional numbers compared to people in other metropolises. Next to the bank of mailboxes was a placard that read: "*2e étage sonnez 2 fois.*" Ring twice for the second floor. I lived on the second floor, but no one had ever buzzed me. Well, except the pizza guy. I ordered from Dominos two or three times a week. The pies in France were smaller than the ones you got back in the States, and some came with weird cheeses, but they were still good.

I entered the foyer and made my way up the squeaky wooden staircase to the second floor. I was halfway down the hall when a door opened and my neighbor, Audrey Gabin, called to me. She was a stooped, frail woman pushing ninety. She wore smart black-rimmed eyeglasses and had luxurious brown hair that had to be a wig. As always, she was impeccably dressed. Today she sported a pumpkin-orange ensemble, a purple brim hat, and a matching purple scarf.

She caught me walking past her unit nearly every day. I had a theory that she had either memorized my routine or she sat near the door, patiently waiting for me to arrive home. I thought of her as a Miss Havisham type. While not a spinster or vengeful, she was lonely and heartbroken, and she hermitted away inside all day. In fact, I wouldn't be surprised to learn she had all her clocks stopped at the exact time her husband died nearly two decades before.

"*Bonjour, Madame Gabin,*" I greeted.

"So beautiful the day, do you think?" she said out of the left side of her mouth. The partial facial paralysis, she'd told me, was the result of a stroke she'd suffered while on a train to Bordeaux to attend her sister's funeral some time back.

"It's lovely," I agreed, a little louder than conversational because her hearing wasn't great. "The perfect temperature."

"*Un moment.* I 'ave something for you."

"No, Madam—"

But she had vanished back inside her flat. She returned a few moments later carrying a plate of pancakes. She always had some dessert or another for me.

"You must try real French *crêpes,*" she said. "I add little…" She seemed to forget for a moment. "Ah, *oui.* I add *un petit peu de Grand Mariner.*"

I took the plate from her, which had begun to tremble in her hands. "You're going to make me fat."

"I 'ope so! You are *très* thin. You must eat."

The elderly loved to give this advice. My grandparents had told me the same thing every time I saw them while I was growing up. And I had seen them a lot. They had lived a few blocks away from my family in Seattle. Even in my late teens, when my six-four frame had peaked at two-hundred-plus pounds, my one surviving grandmother would give me chocolates whenever I visited her at Bayview Retirement Community, telling me I had to put some fat on my bones.

Madame Gabin, however, had a valid point. I had lost a lot of weight recently and could be described as gaunt for the first time in my adult life. I simply didn't find myself hungry of late. I didn't know whether my suppressed appetite was because I had started smoking again, or because I was struggling with the rats of depression. I guess it was a combination of the two.

"I'll eat everything," I assured her. "They look delicious."

"Roland, he loved his *crêpes*. I made them him every mornings."

Roland Gabin, her long-deceased husband, had flown Spitfires in World War Two, then spent the next forty years as a civil servant until his heart gave out at the age of sixty-four.

I said, "He was a lucky man to have you."

Madame Gabin nodded, but her eyes had clouded over, as if she had lost herself in the past. Poor woman, I thought. She had nobody. At least I had never seen anyone visit her since I became her neighbor. No children, no grandchildren. If, or more probable, *when* she died inside her apartment, she would likely remain there undiscovered, rotting in her bed or in her chair or wherever until someone—me?—detected a funky smell. It was an undeserving fate for a lady I suspect had been as ravishing and charming as a film star in her prime.

"Well, thanks," I said, raising the plate.

She blinked. "*Oui. De rien.*"

I started toward my unit, then stopped. Madame Gabin remained standing out front her door, staring at some middle distance.

"Madame Gabin?" I said.

She didn't reply.

"Audrey?"

She turned her head slowly toward me.

"What are you doing tomorrow evening?"

"Tomorrow?"

"I've been practicing my French cooking lately. I think I'm getting the hang of some dishes, but I would love some feedback. Would you like to come by for dinner?"

"Oh, *non merci.* I—I don't think…"

"I'd like to hear some more stories about your husband."

"*Vraiment?*" She lit up. "Well…yes, *oui*, if it ees okay?"

"How about seven o'clock?"

"Yes, seven o'clock. I will bring dessert."

Smiling in her sad-happy way, she hobbled back into her unit while I continued to mine.

▼

My cracker-box studio had a lack of idiosyncrasy so jarring it became an idiosyncrasy all of its own. It was drably furnished with brown wall-to-wall carpet, a swivel-egg armchair older than me, a small wooden desk, and a metal-frame bed so short my feet dangled over the end. A television sat in the corner on a low table. It only got a few channels and I rarely used it. The walls were mustard and pitted with the holes from screws and nails which previous tenants had used to hang pictures. My only additions were an iron and ironing board because the dryers at the Laundromat a block over didn't work sufficiently, leaving my clothes damp and wrinkled.

Nevertheless, I was okay with the place. It wasn't much smaller than the one Bridgette and I had shared off the Bowery. Also, there was an oven, which was great for cooking frozen pizzas when I was too impatient to order one in, and a balcony, which Danièle told me was uncommon in Paris.

I grabbed a beer from the refrigerator, then opened the window that overlooked the small courtyard to let out the foxed-paper smell that permeated the entire building. The air was springtime fresh, and the landlord was edging the garden with a hoe, making some sort of drainage line. I rarely saw any of the tenants down there. In fact, aside from Audrey Gabin, I rarely saw any of the tenants anywhere, anytime.

I sat in the armchair, flipped open my laptop, and accessed the internet. I typed "paris catacombs missing person" into the search engine. The first page of results mostly referenced the section of catacombs beneath Montparnasse's Place Denfert-Rochereau. This was the tourist attraction open to the public. For a fee you could descend one hundred thirty steps underground and walk along a dimly lit circuit passing macabre alleys and pillars artfully constructed with tibias and femurs and punctuated with vacuous skulls.

I tried a number of different keyword combinations, but didn't come across anything involving a missing woman or a lost video camera. I had been hoping to find the video Danièle had shown me, or at least a reference to it. This would have proved Pascal was full of shit. It was something he'd downloaded, a hoax, that was all. Unfortunately, the fact there was no mention of the video indicated the guy had likely been telling the truth about finding it on his own.

Still, I kept searching and got sucked into learning about the catacombs' long and storied history. They began as limestone quarry tunnels dating back two thousand years to the first Roman settlers. They were greatly expanded during the cathedral boom of the late Middle Ages, honeycombing beneath the arrondissements of the Left Bank and the suburbs south of the city proper. In the late eighteenth century, long after the quarrying had stopped, Paris had become a crowded city. It had a burgeoning population clamoring for housing and burial plots. Churches maintained their own graveyards, but they were overcrowded and unsanitary. To free up valuable real estate, and to get rid of the health hazards created by corpses buried ten deep and literally bursting through the walls of people's cellars, officials ordered the graves dug up— all of them. Over the next several decades the skeletonized remains of six million dead were dumped into the abandoned quarries, forming the largest mass grave on earth.

For safety reasons access to them had been banned since the fifties, most of the entranceways closed off, though this hasn't deterred people such as Danièle and Pascal. They called themselves cataphiles, a colloquial name for underground urban explorers—

My cell phone rang suddenly, breaking the studious trance I had fallen under.

Danièle?

I took my phone from my pocket and glanced at the display. A blocked number. I pressed Talk.

"Hello?"

No reply.

"Hello?"

"Will?"

My heart skipped. "Bridgette?"

"Will, can you hear me?"

"Yeah, can you hear me?"

"I can now. I guess we were lagging." A pause. "How are you?"

"I'm good," I said, getting to my feet for some reason. A warm breeze came through the window, smelling of freshly cut grass. The landlord was now mowing the patch of green lawn with a push mower. I glanced at my wristwatch. It was 7:10 p.m. "What time is it there?" I asked.

"I'm on my lunch break."

Bridgette and I had emailed a few times since I left New York, and I had given her my new phone number, but this was the first time she had called it.

I opened my mouth to reply, but I realized I had nothing to say. I felt how you do with a stranger in an elevator. It jarred me how Bridgette and I could go from being so close, to sharing everything together, to becoming less than friends. And that's what we were, wasn't it? Less than friends. Because friends, at least, had things to say to one another.

"Are you enjoying Paris?" she asked.

"It's a nice city."

"It's been...how long now?"

"Nearly three months."

"And the guide?"

"It's coming. It'll probably take me another couple months."

"And then?"

"I think they want me to revise the Barcelona one."

"Spain! Very nice. I'm glad you're happy."

I wanted to tell her I wasn't sure I was happy, but I didn't.

"How about you?" I said. "Everything okay?"

"There's something I need to tell you, Will." She hesitated. It might have only been for a second or two, but it felt to me like an eternity. In that moment I was positive she was going to tell me she wanted to get back together. She said, "I met someone."

A hot flash zinged through me. I continued to stare out the window, though I was no longer seeing the courtyard. Everything but Bridgette's voice had become ancillary. "You mean a boyfriend?"

"Yes."

I still didn't move. I was numb. Emotionally numb.

Why the fuck was she telling me this?

"A lawyer?" I asked, surprised at the normalcy in my voice.

"He's a police officer."

"A cop?"

"Yes."

"Huh. Well—"

"Will, we just got engaged."

I'd always thought it was melodrama when people tell you to sit before hearing certain good or bad news. Now I believed it to be a justifiable forewarning, because my knees literally gave out and I collapsed into the armchair.

Bridgette said, "I didn't want you to find out on Facebook or whatever..."

"I don't use Facebook."

"You have an account."

"How long have you known this guy for?"

"We met in March."

"Two months? That's it? And you're engaged?"

"We...I'm pregnant," she said. "It wasn't planned," she added quickly. "But...then...I started feeling sick in the mornings, and I took a test. And...and we decided it would be best to get married."

I was listening but not listening. My thoughts were a thousand miles away, fast-forwarding through the years I had spent with her. How good she had been to me. How she had stuck by me when nobody else had. How much I had loved her. How I would have done anything for her.

How could she be engaged with someone else and pregnant with his child?

She was mine. She had always been mine.

I was back on my feet. Anger churned within me, burning me up from the inside out. My jaw was clenched, my free fist pumped open, closed, open, closed. I wanted to throw the phone as far as I could out the window.

Instead I shut my eyes and tilted my head back. I took a silent breath. What was my problem? Fuck, I had slept with Danièle just the other night. Bridgette had every right to do the same with someone else. She hadn't planned on getting pregnant. It happened. So what did I want her to do? Have an abortion? Stop seeing the guy? What would any of that accomplish? We were done.

But we weren't. I was going to come back. We were going to start over...

"Will?" Bridgette said. "Are you there?"

"Yeah, I'm here."

"I know how all this must sound..."

"I understand. And...congratulations. I'm happy for you."

She didn't say anything. The line hissed with long-distance static interference.

Then: "Thank you, Will." Her voice was croaky, and I thought she might be crying. "That means a lot to me."

A chorus of voices sounded in the background.

"I should go," she said.

I didn't protest. There was nothing more to say.
"Will?"
"Yeah?"
"I love you. I always will."
"I love you too."
I didn't hang up immediately. Apparently she didn't either, because the line noise continued for another five seconds.
Then silence, perfect silence.
She was gone.

▼

Sometime later, as the late dusk settled and shadows lengthened outside my window, I started packing a bag.

CHAPTER 3

The name of the pub Danièle had written on the napkin earlier was La Cave. The façade was nondescript, and I walked straight past the wooden door and small neon sign on my first pass down rue Jean-Pierre Timbaud.

The interior had all the intimacy, intrigue, and secrecy of a speakeasy. Red cone lamps suspended from the barrel-vault ceiling cast butterscotch light over the button-tufted sofas and armchairs and low wood tables. The bar was tucked into one corner. Behind the fumed-oak counter a chalkboard listed a variety of cocktails. In another corner sat a white claw-footed bathtub, filled with ice and green bottles of what looked to be home-made beer. Good-natured old-timers schmoozed next to crowds of younger hipsters, voices and laughter raised in a cacophony of merriment.

I didn't see Danièle anywhere and checked my wristwatch, a six hundred dollar Hamilton that Bridgette had splurged on for my twenty-fourth birthday.

It was a quarter past eight. Danièle had said she would be here between eight and nine. Had she changed her mind and left early?

"Excuse me?" I said to a waiter wiping down a recently vacated tabled. He was a clean-cut guy with a back-in-fashion mullet, rolled-up cuffs, and a black apron. "Have you seen a woman, short black hair, a lot of mascara?"

"Why don't you use your eyes and look for her yourself?" he

snapped, turning away from me.

I stared at his back, pissed off, but letting it go. People say the French are rude, but I've found that stereotype mostly applied to the service class, who could act as hoity-toity as pop stars; they certainly had no regard for the Anglo-Saxon maxim, "He who pays the piper calls the tune."

I continued searching for Danièle, and after five minutes without success, I was about to give up and leave when I spotted a staircase that descended to a basement level. I went down a set of steep, narrow steps that emerged in an expansive area styled similar to the first floor, only the walls were brick instead of paneled wood and there were no windows. I immediately spotted Danièle and Pascal and a third guy off by themselves, at a corner table.

"Will!" Danièle said, springing to her feet when she saw me approach. We did the air kiss thing, then she turned to the others to make introductions. "You remember Pascal?"

"Hey," I said, sticking out my hand.

Pascal shook, but didn't stand. He was a handsome guy, dark-complected, with thick eyebrows, brooding eyes, and long brown hair. He had gone chic-bum with a wrinkled linen T-shirt and a tweed jacket with brown elbow patches. The tee was wide-necked and showed off too much hairless chest which a loosely knotted scarf failed to conceal. It was the kind of overthought getup you saw aged rock stars don to prove they still had their thumb on the pulse of the times. He was wearing the same black wool-knit cap he had on at Danièle's birthday party.

"And Will," Danièle said, "this is Robert."

"Just Rob, boss," Rob told me, standing and shaking. He was a short bulldog-looking guy whose body was not only compact but tightly muscular, like a college wrestler's. He had a spray of freckles that hadn't faded over time as mothers always promised would, lively gray eyes, and a balding crown shaved close to the scalp. I guessed he was the oldest in our motley crew, maybe thirty.

"You're American?" I said. Pascal's silent greeting had made me feel unwelcome, and it was nice to know I wasn't the only outsider.

"Nah, Canadian, but what the fuck, right?"

"We have just ordered," Danièle told me. "But do not worry. There is enough for you."

"I'm not hungry," I said.

"You should still eat. You will not get another chance until morning."

"I brought some snacks."

"Okay, Will, do not eat, but sit down."

I took a seat beside her, across from Rob and Pascal.

"So Danny says you're a travel writer or something?" Rob said. He had a husky voice, as if his throat were corroded with rust. "How you like the frogs?"

"Why do you say that, Rob?" Danièle demanded. "We are not frogs. Where did that come from? I never understand that."

"You eat frog legs, don't you?"

"Maybe I should call you 'rosbif?'"

"Ross what?"

"Roast beef?" I offered.

Danièle nodded. "Yes, because you Canadians and Americans eat so much red meat—and you are all so fat, like cows."

This cracked Rob up. He jumped to his feet and crouched-walked around the table, carrying in his hands an invisible belly, which he began thrusting at Danièle from behind. The action resembled a stubby stripper grinding a pole.

"Get away!" Danièle said, swatting him. "You are so gross. Stop it!"

Still laughing, Rob sat back down. "Fucking French," he said. "Can't take a joke. Got assholes so tight they squeak when they fart."

"Where're you from?" I asked him.

"Quebec City."

"The French-speaking part?"

"Quebec's a province, bro. Quebec City's a small city in that province. But, yeah, the French-speaking part. Moved to Toronto when I was ten. Actually, moved to Mississauga. But nobody knows where the fuck that is, so I just say Toronto."

"What are you doing over here?"

"I'm a translator, sort of. I do the subtitles for movies."

"Hollywood stuff?"

"Other way around. I translate French films to English. You've probably never seen any of the ones I've done—because French films suck."

"They do not suck," Danièle said.

"If you like pretentious art house crap."

"Pascal, why did you invite Rosbif? He is so annoying sometimes. Did you forget we have to spend nearly ten hours with him?"

Pascal said something in French, paused, then added something more, making a curlicue gesture with his hand. Rob nodded and shot back a reply.

"Do you speak English?" I asked Pascal.

He leveled his gaze at me. "Do you speak French?"

Mr. Mullet appeared with a huge tray of food. We had to clear the condiments from the center of the table so everything could fit: oysters, soufflé, pork belly, garlic sausage, and a platter of cheese.

While everyone ate, and I nibbled, Danièle said, "So this is the plan, Will. We will arrive at the entrance to the catacombs around ten o'clock. We will continued for four hours, then rest for one. Then it is another two hours or so to the spot where the camera was found." She consulted Pascal. "Is that right?"

He nodded without looking up from his food.

"Which means we finish around 7 a.m.," she added. "Still enough time to get to work."

I was surprised. "Work?"

"You must work tomorrow, yes?"

"I figured I'd write the day off."

"Then you do not need to worry."

"You're working tomorrow?"

"Of course. But I do not start until nine."

"Lucky you," Rob said, sawing a piece of pork. "I start at eight."

I did Danièle's math in my head. "If we start at ten, walk for four hours, rest for one, walk for another two, that's seven hours in total. That will take us to five in the morning. Seven hours back, it won't be noon until we resurface."

"No, Will," Danièle said. "Pascal knows a different exit close to where we will rest. We will leave that way."

I looked at her, wondering if I had to state the obvious. Apparently I did, and said, "Why don't we just enter through that exit?"

"Because that is not what we do," she stated. "The catacombs, it is an experience, every time, even for Pascal and me. It is not something to rush through. You and Robert will see. You will understand."

CHAPTER 4

ROB

Rob Stratton cast another passing glance across the table at Danièle's friend Will, trying to get a read on him. He wasn't your typical American expat, not loud, not wanting to be the center of attention. Not all American expats were like that, of course; they ran the spectrum like expats from any nationality did. But Yanks could be loud. Yanks, then Aussies, then Spaniards—especially the senoritas. That's how he'd rank them all on the loud meter. The worst of the lot weren't only loud but didn't adapt. They brought their native country with them wherever they went.

Rob was thinking about a friend of a friend in particular, a Texan in the import-export business who'd made a fortune selling Chinese junk to the French bourgeoisie. He didn't wear a cowboy hat around, that would have made him the laughing-stock of Paris, but he did wear these fancy-ass pointed-toe cowhide boots. You could hear the Cuban heels click-clack across the cobblestone streets from a block away. And if this fashion faux pas wasn't bad enough, the sad fuck shouted everything he said. "Y'all" this and "I'm fixin' tuh" that. It made you want to smack him one.

Anyway, generalizations aside, Rob wanted to like Will, he was trying to, but it was tough, knowing how much angst—albeit unintentional—his presence was causing poor Pascal, who'd held a flame for Danny for as long as Rob had known him.

If Rob were Pascal, he probably would have popped Will one right in the kisser by now. But Pascal was a lover, a romantic, whatever you called dudes with more heart than testosterone. He didn't have it in him to hurt a fly.

When Pascal rang Rob two days ago, and explained the pathetic situation, he had been trying to act blasé about the whole deal, but it was obvious he was crushed. Initially Rob declined his invitation to come along; he knew Pascal was only asking because he didn't want to be the third wheel at his own party; also, the wife had some work thing, and Rob had promised to watch the girls.

Nevertheless, the little bugger wouldn't let up, even offered to pay for a babysitter, and Rob finally relented. Why not? he'd thought. Pascal and Danny had been going on about the catacombs for years now, and he figured it was about time to find out what all the fuss was about.

CHAPTER 5

PASCAL

Pascal Gayet slurped an oyster from the wide end of the shell, doing his best to ignore Danièle and the American Will. He still couldn't believe he'd missed out on his chance to hook up with Danièle yet again. He'd wanted to ask her out ever since they'd first met years earlier at Le Mines. However, he'd been in a relationship then, and by the time he got out of it, she was in one. Ever since, it'd been the same thing: whenever she was single, he wasn't, and vice versa. Eventually she'd gotten serious with a tattoo artist named Marcel, and for the next three years he had to listen to Danièle complain about what an asshole the guy was to her. Pascal told her repeatedly to dump him, but she never listened. Then, a few months ago, he dumped her for a TV actress who had a part in some kid's show about a family trying to run a Bed and Breakfast. Pascal figured this was finally his chance. He and Danièle were both single. He'd give her a couple weeks to get over Marcel, then he'd tell her how he felt about her.

Before he could do this, however, she began going on about this American she was doing language exchange lessons with. She obviously liked him. She didn't shut up about him: *Why doesn't he like me? Do you think he's gay? Do you think he has a girlfriend? Should I ask him out? Do American women do that?* By the time of her birthday party Friday evening Pascal had expected some Fabio-type to stroll through the door with her. To his satisfaction, Will was no Fabio. He had short scruffy black hair, seemed to be in good shape, girls probably found him attractive. But Fabio? Not a chance.

Still, that didn't stop Danièle from fawning over him. At one point she hopped right onto his lap, her arms hooked around his neck, throwing her head back, laughing. Eventually Pascal couldn't stand it anymore and left the pub with Danièle's friend Fanny. She wasn't attractive, he didn't have sex with her, he didn't want to. He just wanted company—that, and he wanted Danièle to find out, though if she did, she never mentioned it.

Across the table Danièle was sitting ramrod straight, her hand out before her, fingers splayed, as she told of the time she had met the Russian ambassador to France at Place de la Bastille. She was up to the point when she had pretended to be Russian to gain access to the VIP room, where all the diplomats were knocking back free champagne during the ballet's intermission. Obviously she was trying to impress Will, who was listening stoically beside her, staring into the beer he'd ordered.

Pascal slurped a second oyster from the shell and entertained himself for a bit with all the different ways the American could meet a grisly demise in the catacombs tonight.

CHAPTER 6

Outside the restaurant, rue Jean-Pierre Timbaud was alive with lights and bustle and noise. We walked two blocks, turned down a side street, and walked another half block before arriving at Pascal's ride: an old, beat-up Volkswagen campervan. Pascal and Rob got in the front while Daniel and I climbed in the back through the sliding side door. We sat next to one another on a bench seat that I suspected folded down into a bed.

Was this Pascal's Lovemobile? I wondered. Did he drive girls to the top of Montmartre, booze them up, then shag them back here?

To my left was a long counter with knobs protruding vertically from the surface. I lifted one, which raised a section of countertop, and discovered a sink beneath.

As Pascal pulled onto the street and made a tight U-turn, Rob swiveled the front passenger seat around so he was facing us and opened a cupboard below the counter, revealing a mini fridge. He snagged three Belgium beers and tossed one to Danièle and one to me. "To the catacombs fuckers!" he rasped.

We popped the tabs, toasted.

Rob swiveled forward again and turned up Bob Dylan on the stereo.

"So this is fun, right?" Danièle said to me, leaning close to be heard.

"Sure," I said.

I peeled back the tatty chintz curtain and looked out the window. I had never traveled Paris by car, and as we rattled down a wide avenue lined with chestnuts, I watched the stream of closed shops float past.

Nearly everyone had a similar idealized image of Paris in their heads. A mecca of culture and history populated by beautiful architecture, stylish women clad in Gautier or Givenchy, and mustachioed mimes carrying easels under one arm and baguettes under the other. I guess this was sort of true —aside from the mustachioed mimes—but already the gloss had begun to wear off for me, and it had become just another steel-skied, rambling city.

"What are you looking at?" Danièle asked me.

I dropped the curtain. "I've never been this way before."

"You have not seen much of Paris, have you?"

"Just the bars and clubs, mostly," I said.

"Why not sightsee more?"

"I haven't gotten around to it."

"You know, Will, you are a hermit crab."

"A hermit crab?"

"You like to be by yourself."

I thought about tweaking her analogy, but didn't.

A hermit crab. Fuck. I sort of liked it.

I said, "What's wrong with being a hermit crab?"

"What made you change your mind tonight?"

"About coming out?"

"Yes, you were so against this idea."

"I still am."

"Then why are you here?"

Because the alternative was sitting around my apartment all night thinking about Bridgette and her cop boyfriend and their yet-to-be child...

"I wanted to hang out with you," I said—and this was true. I hadn't wanted to be alone, and I'd always felt comfortable around Danièle.

She stared at me for a long moment. I waited for a sarcastic zinger. In the front Rob and Pascal were joking back and forth in French. Dylan was warbling about how the times were a-changin'.

Then, suddenly: "Oh, Will, look!" Danièle pointed out my window.

Far in the distance, visible between a break in the buildings, the iron lady rose into the sky, lit up in a twinkling light show.

"You must come to the Trocadéro with me," she added. "We will go early in the morning, before the tourists come. It feels like you have the Eiffel Tower all to yourself. What do you think?"

"Sure."

I caught Pascal watching us via the rearview mirror. His eyes met mine, then he looked away.

Rob swiveled his chair around again, opened the mini fridge, and grabbed a second beer. "Anyone?" he said.

Mine was still half full. "No, thanks."

"I will," Danièle said cheerfully, and she caught the one he tossed her.

Tabs popped again. Carbonation hissed. Cans foamed over.

"I take it you saw the video?" Rob said to me.

I nodded.

"What do you think?"

"It's something."

"What do you think got her?"

I had considered this a fair bit since I decided to come on the excursion. My revised conclusion was not as ominous as the one I had initially jumped to. I said, "I think she snapped."

"Went crazy?"

I nodded. "If you assume she was lost down there for days without food or water, she would have been weak and dehydrated. She would have been exhausted, mentally and physically. So she snapped."

"Why'd she start running?"

I shrugged. "When you go crazy, you go crazy. Maybe she

was hearing voices and stuff in her head."

"And the scream?"

"She dropped the camera. She no longer had light to see by. She was lost in absolute blackness. That was the last straw."

"You know, Will," Danièle said, touching my knee, "that is a good deduction. Maybe you are right. See—you had nothing to be scared of to begin with."

Pascal chortled from up front.

"I was never scared," I said. "I was concerned—for you."

"Is that not the same thing?"

"What do you think?" I asked Rob.

"Sounds like you were scared, boss."

I ignored that. "I mean, what do you think happened to her?"

"What you said makes sense," he agreed. Then, with a campfire grin, he added, "But on the other hand, maybe there *is* something down there. A mop-wielding Toxic Avenger mutant that stripped her, fucked her, ate her, then tossed her bones to one of those rooms with all the other bones."

Danièle rolled her eyes at this. Rob winked at us and chugged his beer. The van tooled on through the night with Dylan singing in his campy, folky voice.

▼

Later, somewhere in the southern suburb of Port D'Orléans, Pascal pulled up to the curb twenty feet shy of a dark street corner and killed the engine.

Danièle said, "We are here."

CHAPTER 7

On the sidewalk outside the campervan Pascal and Danièle pulled on hip waders. Rob was on his butt, swapping his shoes for a pair of Wellingtons.

"I didn't know I needed any of this stuff," I said, feeling suddenly foolish standing there in a black pullover, black jeans, and powder-blue Converse All-Stars.

"There is water in some places," Danièle told me. "But do not worry, you will be fine. Most important is a helmet."

"I don't have that either."

"Pascal and I have extras. You and Rob choose."

Rob opened the large navy canvas bag before him, which reminded me of my equipment bag when I played prep football. He withdrew two safety helmets, one red and one white, both with LED headlamps strapped to them. "Red or white, boss?" he said.

"Either."

He tossed me the red one. I caught it and turned it in my hands. It was well-used and scuffed. On the back was a fading sticker of a grim reaper flicking off the world with his bony middle finger. Along the brim, written in black marker, was: CHESS. "Who's Chess?" I asked.

"That is Pascal," Danièle said. "It is his catacombs name."

I would rather have used Danièle's spare helmet than Pascal's—I didn't want to feel indebted to the guy—but if I asked Rob to trade I'd probably have to explain the reason for my request. "Catacombs name?" I said.

"Every cataphile has an aboveground name and a catacombs name."

"Dorks!" Rob said as he plunked on his helmet and rapped it with his knuckles to check its integrity.

"Why the aliases?" I asked.

Danièle shrugged. "In the catacombs, the above world does not exist. We do not speak of it. You are free of your old life, free to reinvent yourself any way you like. With that new identity comes a new name."

I had to admit, after all the shit I'd been through over the last couple of years, this sounded rather appealing. "So what's your catacombs name?" I asked.

"In English it translates to Stork Girl."

Rob howled.

"What?" Danièle demanded, planting her fists on her hips.

"Danny, that's the stupidest name I've ever heard."

"You are the stupidest person I have ever met," she declared. "And, if you must know, I did not make up the name. Pascal did."

Rob said something in French to Pascal. Pascal said something back, pantomiming a big head.

"He thinks when I wear a helmet," Danièle explained to me, "it makes my head look big. This makes my neck appear small and long, like a Stork's."

"I like Stork Girl," I said.

"Thank you, Will."

And I did. It was cute. Definitely a better moniker than Chess. I imagined Pascal came up with that one on his own too. It was pretentious while masking the pretentiousness. Sort of like saying, "I'm a master manipulator, a strategist, a genius in my own right, checkmate asshole" while at the same time, if asked about its meaning, allowing him to humbly confess he was just a simple guy who enjoyed a game of chess.

"So what's my dork name?" Rob asked.

"Rosbif," Danièle said immediately. "And you, Will, I do not know yours. I will think about it."

A middle-aged man turned the corner at the end of the street and approached us. He was walking a brown dachshund on a leash. Pascal clipped a ragged utility belt around his waist from which dangled a 6D Maglite flashlight and Leatherman hand tools. He retrieved the last two helmets from the bag, handed one to Danièle, then tossed the bag back inside the campervan and locked the door.

Everyone stepped aside so the man and his dog could pass. I expected him to stop and ask us what we were doing. He only nodded politely and continued on his way, tugging the sausage dog along to keep up.

"He doesn't find us strange?" I said when he was out of earshot. "We look like sewer workers or something."

Danièle shrugged. "He is aware of what we are doing. Many people dressed like us come and go this way."

I spotted a covered manhole in the center of the road. "Is that the entrance?"

"No, it is this way. Follow me."

She started away, her helmet tucked under one arm. I shrugged my backpack over my shoulder and followed. We crossed a vacant lot and came to a crumbling dry stone wall. It was as high as my chest and thick. I gave Danièle a boost, then heaved myself up, so I was sitting on the capstone next to her. We shoved off together, landed on spongy dead leaves, and scrambled down the slope of a steep, forested ravine. When we burst free of the vegetation, we were standing among a pair of abandoned railway tracks.

"Where are we?" I asked, turning in a circle, seeing only shadowed foliage surrounding us on all sides. The earth was carpeted with more dead leaves and lichen. Everything smelled lush and fresh.

"The Petite Ceinture," Danièle said. "It was a railway track that used to circle Paris, sort of like a defense, yes? The trains moved the soldiers from one point to the next quickly. It has not been used for a very long time."

I flicked on my headlamp.

"No, not yet," Danièle said. "We do not want to attract attention."

I frowned. "Who's going to see us here?"

"Not yet," she repeated.

I turned off the light just as Rob and Pascal joined us. Rob was cupping his left eye with his hand, cursing inventively. "Pissing branch," he complained.

Danièle smiled. "You must be more careful, Rosbif."

"Fuck off, Stork the Dork."

Still smiling triumphantly, as if she had been the one to poke Rob in the eye, Danièle headed off along the tracks. The rest of us fell into line behind her, single file. The rusted rails and rotted wooden ties were nearly overgrown with weeds. I began playing a game in which I was only allowed to step on the ties. If I missed one, and my foot touched the crushed stone that formed the track ballast, I had to start my count from the beginning. On my third go I was up to one hundred sixteen when Danièle stopped suddenly. I bumped into her from behind and saw several flashlight beams maybe a hundred feet in the distance.

Pascal brushed past me and conversed with Danièle in serious tones.

"Who are they?" I asked.

"Other cataphiles," Danièle said.

"Oh." I had thought they were the police. "So what's the problem?"

"There is no problem. Most cataphiles are friendly, but some..." She shrugged. "What you are on the surface, you are underground."

"So a tool's a tool," Rob said. "Who gives a shit? What are they going to do? Looks like there's only three of them."

Danièle said, "I think we should let them enter the catacombs first, then we will follow afterward."

Rob snorted disapproval. "And what if they don't move for an hour? We're on a schedule, right?"

Danièle looked at Pascal. He nodded.

"Okay," she said. "We will go. But Rosbif, Will, do not speak English."

"Why not?" I asked.

"Even friendly cataphiles, they do not like foreigners coming and going. The catacombs is their world. They want it to remain secret, as much as it can. If they hear you speak English, they will know you are a foreigner."

"And?" I said.

"And nothing. But it is better to be safe."

"Do not be scared," Pascal told me.

I leveled my gaze at him. He turned promptly, and we continued toward the cataphiles, four abreast. Rob had been right. I counted three flashlight beams, three guys. They stood at the mouth of what appeared to be a train tunnel, speaking loudly and laughing.

When they noticed us they went quiet.

Pascal said, "*Salut!*" and began conversing with one of them.

They were all dressed in boots, blue coveralls, and white gloves. Their ages ranged from twenty-five to forty, give or take. Two oxygen tanks, fins, and an assortment of other diving gear rested beside them.

The guy Pascal was speaking to was the oldest. He had beady eyes and a hangdog face with the loose jowls of an aristocratic banker. Greasy black hair, parted down the center, gave him a Dickensian air. His voice was gruff, atonal, sort of pissed off.

The other two complimented each other only in that they were opposites. One was short, Rob's height, but much skinnier. He had a bad case of acne, and he seemed nervous, staring fixedly at a spot on the ground in front of him. His buddy, on the other hand, cleared six feet. I couldn't tell if he was as tall as me because he wore his hair in a volcano of dreadlocks, but he would have been a good thirty or forty pounds heavier. Judging by his barrel chest and knotty neck and broad shoulders, he subsisted on a diet of eggs, meat, and protein shakes.

His face had that young Arnie look, all thick slabs and bony protrusions. His coveralls were stained with clay, no doubt from previous descents into the catacombs.

He was ogling Danièle in a way I didn't like. He sensed my eyes on him, turned toward me, and said something.

When I didn't reply, he scoffed and reached for my helmet.

I batted his hand away. "Fuck off."

Surprise flashed on his face. Then a toothy, Neanderthal smile.

Pascal and the old guy stopped talking. Everyone's attention turned to Dreadlocks and me.

"You American, huh?" he said, stepping toward me. His size made it feel as though he was crowding my personal space. "You go catacombs?"

Either he was as dumb as he looked, or that was a rhetorical question. I waited for him to continue.

"You take many photographs, huh?"

"I don't have a camera."

"You going to paint your name? Paint a pretty picture?"

"Why would I paint a picture?"

"That's what you *touristes* do. You come here, you paint pictures."

"Not today."

He licked his lips. He had either exhausted his English, or he was thinking of something else to say. He nodded at Danièle. "She your girlfriend, huh?"

"Why do you care?"

He sneered at her. "You *touriste* too?"

She fired off a string of French. He chuckled, though not in a friendly manner, and replied. Their back and forth devolved into a heated argument.

For a moment I was absurdly proud of Danièle for standing her ground.

Pascal was keeping his distance. Rob was grinning amusedly, maybe even manically. His hands were balled into tight fists. I had the feeling he was about to throw himself at the big guy.

I stepped between him and Dreadlocks and said to Danièle, "Let's go."

Dreadlocks gripped my shoulder and spun me around. I stepped on one of his boots and shoved him in the chest, removing my foot so I didn't break his ankle as he dropped, arms pin-wheeling, to the ground.

Sitting on his ass, he appeared momentarily dazed. Then his eyes stormed over. Roaring, he lunged at me, thrusting his meaty hands in my face. Everyone in both parties got into it, yelling and pulling us apart.

Danièle tugged me free. I was panting, not yet done. Dreadlocks continued to hurl curses, towering above his two buddies, who were doing their best to hold him back. Blood smeared his hammered forehead.

"Will, enough!" Danièle said. "Stop it!"

It took most of my self-restraint, but I reluctantly turned my back to the fight. I snatched my helmet, which had fallen off my head, and drew the heel of my hand across my lips, which were numb from a blow the fucker had landed.

Pascal was already walking away into the tunnel.

Both Danièle and Rob placed a hand on my back, urging me to follow.

I went.

▼

Darkness folded around us like great black wings. Ahead Pascal turned on his headlamp. Rob and Danièle and I did the same.

"What a fucking knob jockey," Rob said as Dreadlocks' taunts faded behind us. "Him and his asshat friends too."

Danièle looked at me. "Why did you speak English?" she demanded. "We told you not to say anything."

"He tried to grab my helmet," I said. "What was I supposed to do?"

"You should have ignored him."

"What was he saying to you?"

She didn't answer.

"Talking smack," Rob offered helpfully.

"Yes," Danièle said, "but Will did not have to push him."

"He grabbed me," I reminded her.

"You cannot do that anymore," she said, and in the bright LED lights of our helmets I saw she wasn't angry, only concerned. "If something happens when we are deep underground…"

She didn't have to finish. I understood.

"They had scuba gear," I said, wanting to change topics. "What was that about?"

"There are some spots, some shafts, in the catacombs that have filled completely with water. They likely want to see whether they lead anywhere."

We walked on, our headlamps shooting zigzags of light around the cavernous arch. Gusty trails of graffiti covered the walls, curving onto the bricks overhead. The ground was chunked with rocks that glowed pale gray, the color of Paris, the buildings.

A few minutes later Pascal called a halt. He swung his Maglite to the left. Where the graffiti-covered wall met the earth was a hole—or, more accurately, a chiseled craggy break in the rock, no more than two feet wide. Spreading away from it was what I assumed to be cataphile refuse: empty beer cans, juice cartons, candy wrappers, white paste from carbide lanterns. A junked foam chair sat off on its lonesome. I wrinkled my nose; the stench of urine was strong.

"This is the entrance?" I said. I had been thinking it would have been more clandestine. This screamed: "Come on in, we're open!"

Danièle nodded. "Some cataphiles, they are such slobs."

"Don't the police—the catacops—know about this?"

"Of course. This is the main entrance nowadays."

Rob said, "So why don't they seal the thing up?"

"They have before," she continued, "but cataphiles open it again. Also, it is not an easy situation for them. They are scared they may trap inexperienced cataphiles inside. But, you know, I think it would be a good thing if they somehow closed it for good. Because then the people who make the trouble, the vandals and drug-users and tibia-collectors, they will get bored and find other things to do."

"Yeah," Rob said in an *uh-duh* way, "but wouldn't that screw you too?"

"Me?" Danièle seemed insulted. "I am not an amateur. Pascal and I know ten other entrances."

The ever-silent Pascal got to his knees and ventured first into the hole.

"He doesn't say much, does he?" I remarked when he was no longer in sight.

"His English is not so good," Danièle said.

"Fuck me," Rob said, peering into the fissure. "I can't see shit."

"It is okay, Rosbif," Danièle told him. "You are so small, you will have no problem fitting in there."

"Bite me," he said, then lowered himself into the opening. When only his legs were visible, poking out of the rock mouth like a half-eaten meal, he let rip a fart. His laughter floated back as he crawled forward.

"Ugh," Danièle said, waving her hand back and forth in front of her nose even though the smell had yet to reach us and couldn't be much worse than the stink of urine. "I really hate that guy, you know?"

"After you," I said.

"No, you must go next so I can push you in case you get stuck."

I stared at her. "In case I get stuck?"

She smiled. "You will be fine. Now go. Just watch your hands for glass."

I waded through the rubbish and stood in front of the main entrance to the catacombs, which was little more than a crack. Cool air sighed out of it.

Setting aside my reservations, I slipped off my backpack, pushed it into the shaft ahead of me, and followed it into the blackness.

CHAPTER 8

THE SUNDAY TELEGRAPH,
JULY 29, 2011

Three British Men Feared Lost in Paris Catacombs

Paris police headquarters have reported that three British nationals went missing in the Paris catacombs late Monday while exploring with friends.

When they didn't return to the surface, their friends alerted police, who have spent several days searching for the missing men without success.

Gaspard Philipe, of the police unit that monitors the ancient quarry tunnels, said on RTL radio Friday that anyone considering entering the tunnels should understand the dangers.

"It is not only off limits to the public, it is dangerous. You can get lost. There are cave-ins. You don't know who you might run into. If you want to see the catacombs, there is a section open to the public as a museum for a very reasonable admission fee."

The network of tunnels beneath the capital is said to extend more than 300 kilometers (186 miles) and reach depths of 30 meters (100 feet), too deep for phone coverage. Some passageways are large enough that ten men can walk abreast and not touch the sides, while others are so small that those who enter them must squirm forward on their bellies.

CHAPTER 9

I t was a tight fit, and Christ if I didn't have to squeeze my shoulders together so I could progress forward. I flashed on those scenes in movies in which you see someone struggling through a ventilation conduit, only here the passage was unpredictable and dirty and potentially deadly.

Then it twisted and angled downward. At first I was able to control my descent. But the pitch dropped suddenly and steeply, and I found myself skidding on my stomach, the way kids hydroplane on a Slip 'n Slide. I must have gone fifteen or twenty feet before friction slowed me. Ahead I saw light other than mine. I dragged myself out of the small opening, my ribs aching, spitting dust from my mouth.

Rob pulled me to my feet. "Thanks," I told him, looking around. The inky-black tunnel was maybe four feet wide and equally high. Rob stood stooped over. I had to pretty much squat. The passage had collapsed to the left of us, leaving a jumble of large boulders and smaller rocks, so there was only one direction in which to go. The air smelled of mold and dampness, making me think of waterparks. It was cooler than it had been outside, maybe fifty-five or sixty degrees.

"Rascal went on ahead," Rob told me.

"Rascal?" I said distractedly, brushing chalky beige dirt from my clothes.

"That's what I've always called him. I never heard of that Chess shit before tonight."

Danièle's LED light winked from inside the hole, drawing our attention. A moment later she slipped out more gracefully than I had. I helped her into a crouch. She smiled. "Fun, yes?"

"A hoot," I said.

"Good. But I am serious when I say we must all stay close. You must not stray. This place, it is not like a labyrinth. It *is* a labyrinth."

"Have you told Pascal that?"

"He will be ahead in the rest room. We should join him."

"In the restroom?" I said.

"What is wrong?"

"Maybe he wants his privacy."

"Do not be silly."

She duck-walked ahead. Rob and I exchanged glances and followed.

We found Pascal fifty feet onward. I had misinterpreted Danièle. He wasn't in a restroom with a toilet and plumbing—of course he wasn't, I thought; not here, not twenty feet underground—but a room with carved limestone benches where cataphiles apparently rested before they set out on their journey. The walls were smooth and whitewashed a pig-blood pink.

Pascal folded the map he'd been studying into a small square and squeezed past us into the shaft again, leading the way bravely onward.

"After you, Frogster," Rob said to Danièle.

She poked him in the chest with her index finger. "If you call me Frogster or Froggy or Frog-anything one more time, I will kill you. Can you understand me?" She pivoted on her heels and followed Pascal.

Rob shook his head. "In-laws, eh?"

▼

Walking single file in a troll-crouch wasn't ideal for conversation, so I set aside the genealogy questions I had for Rob and focused on keeping up with the fast pace Pascal had set. Because of my hunched-over position I didn't see much of the tunnel except for Rob's backside and the ground, which was a powdery mix of sand and crushed gravel.

I had been down here all of five minutes and I hated it. My back and neck ached, claustrophobia had set in like a too-small second skin, and I was already looking forward to when this night would be over.

Finally, however, we entered a new shaft. The ceiling was higher here, and for the first time I was able to stand almost to my full height. This made me feel substantially better. I had been worried I would be troll-walking the entire nine or so hours we were supposed to be down here.

Freed from staring at my shoes, I could now pay more attention to the palimpsest of colorful graffiti that had been scribbled and spray painted everywhere on the honey-colored stone walls. Most of it consisted of bright hip hop tags and punk rock anarchy symbols. One English entreaty read: "Lost in the catas! Help!" Given how close we were to the exit, I assumed it had been a joke. I *hoped* it had been a joke.

Up ahead Pascal and Danièle had stopped. When Rob and I reached them, Danièle pointed to the left wall. An inscription was etched in carbon black onto a cornerstone. She said, "That is the street address directly above us."

"Who made it?" I asked.

"Les Inspection Générale des Carrieres. It was their job to make sure Paris did not sink."

"Paris was sinking?" Rob said dubiously.

"That is what I said, Rosbif. Most of these tunnels were made in the Middle Ages. At that time they were outside the city limits. But as the population grew, the city expanded south over the tunnels. No one realized how bad the foundation was until one of the chambers down here collapsed. It swallowed the entire neighborhood above it. The main street was called rue D'Enfer. It is funny because that means—"

"Hell Street," Rob said.

"Yes. So the king at the time, the one who would get his head cut off in the revolution, he created what I told you, Les Inspection Générale des Carrieres, to strengthen the tunnels. If the inspectors saw a crack or a falling roof, they prepared a reinforcing wall or something like that." She pointed to the inscribed street address. "They also mapped everything. The result was a mirror reflection of the streets above, a Renaissance Paris frozen in time."

"So that street still exists?" I said.

"It is there, yes, but wider now. It has become a boulevard, I think. And this is interesting." She pointed to the fleur-de-lis carved above the street name. "That is the symbol of the French monarchy. Here it is intact. At other locations it has been scratched out by revolutionaries."

"Revolutionaries?" I said, surprised. "They used these tunnels?"

"Yes, both in 1789 and the student protests in 1968. You know, even the Nazis built a bunker down here in World War Two. It is on our way. It is where we will rest for one hour."

From somewhere overhead came a faint, continuous rumble, like the sonorous drone of the ocean. We paused to listen. It lasted for about ten seconds before silence returned once more.

"That is the Metro," Danièle explained. "There are tracks nearby."

Late-night workers returning to their homes and families, younger men and women heading out to meet friends. In other words, life going on as usual. These mundane images made burrowing beneath Paris in the dark and dirt seem all the more surreal.

Pascal, who seemed anxious to keep moving, said, "*Montez la garde,*" and continued on.

"Yes, be careful," Danièle told us. "The ceiling height varies. You must watch your head. And watch your feet. You do not want to step into a crevice or a well. Some can be very deep."

"How deep?" Rob asked.

"I do not know, Rosbif," she called over her shoulder. "I have never seen the bottoms."

CHAPTER 10

DANIÈLE

The trick was to remain close behind the person in front of you, so you could see in their backsplash of light, and Danièle remained so close to Pascal she could reach out and touch him if she were so inclined. She was not kidding when she told Will and Rob to watch where they stepped. Last December a couple of cataphiles reportedly broke through a wall in the remote western portion of the tunnels and discovered never-before-seen galleries, one of which featured a series of life-size statues carved from the limestone. While on an excursion to see the statues for themselves, Danièle and Pascal came across a man sitting by himself in a small chamber. He was weak and delusional due to dehydration. A single candle burned next to him. It was his last one. After it went out, he would have been plunged into total blackness. They gave him food and water, and when he was lucid enough, he showed them his ankle, which he explained he'd broken when he'd stepped in a two-foot-deep crevice. The ankle had swollen to the size of a cantaloupe and was marred with splotchy purple spots. His friend had left to get help but never returned. The man didn't know when that had been, he could barely remember what day he'd entered the catacombs, but given his deteriorated condition, it was likely it had been several days before. It was also likely his friend had not been an experienced cataphile and hadn't been able to find his way back again.

So, yes, the dangers were real down here, she thought. But if you were smart, if you had a guide as experienced as herself, or Pascal, chances were you would be fine.

CHAPTER 11

For the next fifteen or twenty minutes I forgot about the graffiti and returned my attention to the ground, watching for the apparently bottomless crevices and wells Danièle had spoken of. I didn't see any, but I did spot discarded water bottles, candy wrappers, and other sundry items. At some point the monotonous crunching of our footsteps was joined by the dripping of water.

Pascal kept up his fast pace, and the rest of us followed close as he turned one corner after another, passing numerous branching hallways, each surely leading to others, and those to others still, hinting at the enormity of this underground realm. Danièle had not been exaggerating when she called it a labyrinth. It was a chaotic maze of more than—what had I read—two or three hundred miles in aggregate? If you stitched the tunnels together into one long Frankenstein worm, they would surpass the width of the state of New York. This got me wondering about their construction. Who were the men who had dug them, likely with nothing more than pickaxes and shovels and wheelbarrows? Convicts who couldn't get employed elsewhere? Destitute farmers looking for regular work that didn't rely on the seasons or the climate? Whoever they were, they likely would have toiled away underground in the dust, humidity, and sometimes pitch dark for their entire lives—if they weren't first crushed to death, buried alive, or knocked off by infections and disease.

From ahead Pascal hollered "*Ciel!*" While I was trying to figure out what that meant—*wham*. I came to a standstill, dizzy, my ears ringing.

"You okay, boss?" Rob said. He'd turned back to look at me, his headlamp shining in my eyes.

I took off the helmet and touched a fiery spot high on my forehead. No blood, not yet. A tender bump throbbed.

"Will, what happened?" Danièle asked, slipping past Rob and stopping before me.

"I hit my head."

She parted my hair. "There is no cut."

"I'm okay."

"I told you to watch out. Remember, I said the ceiling height—"

"I didn't see Rob duck, so I didn't either."

"Yes, but he is much shorter than you."

"I realize that now, Danièle, thanks."

"I am sorry. I should have explained. *Ciel* means 'sky'. We call it out when the ceiling juts down."

"Got it," I said.

After once more reassuring her that I was fine, that I didn't need to rest, we continued on. When the tunnel widened enough to walk two abreast, I moved up beside Rob. He glanced sidelong at me and said, "You know what this place reminds me of?"

"What?"

"Vaginas."

I smiled, sort of. What had I expected him to reference? Tom Sawyer's spirit of adventure? Verne's *Journey to the Center of the Earth*? Jonah and the Whale?

"I'm serious," he added. "Everywhere I look I see one. This is vag land, nature porn. Tell me you don't see it."

"You have a point," I said as I thought about all the metaphorical psychobabble regarding caves and wombs and Mama Nature and fertility. Also, I had to admit it wasn't a stretch to imagine, if you were so inclined, the entrance to the catacombs that we'd passed through as vulvaesque, Pascal's rest room as a uterus, and these tunnels as fallopian tubes.

Rob said, "Now I understand why Rascal spends all his time down here. What a perv."

Ahead Pascal reached into a little gully in the wall, felt around, then kept going.

"What's he looking for?" I asked.

"Dunno." Rob called out in French. Pascal answered back. Rob laughed. "He said someone once had a stag party down here. They left a calling card in the wall with the date and directions. You find it, you're invited. He wanted to see if there was anything new."

"A stag party?" I said.

"Apparently all sorts of crazy stuff goes on down here. Cops found a movie theater once. Yeah, I shit you not—lights, sound system, projector, fully stocked bar. It was right under the Trocadéro, a stone's throw from the Eiffel Tower, one of the most famous fucking landmarks in the world. There was a whole security setup too that included a motion detector that set off a recording of barking dogs to scare people away."

I wasn't sure if Rob was having me on or not, but I asked, "How was all this stuff powered? With batteries?"

"Electricity, boss. They siphoned it from underground power lines. And get this. A few days after the police discovered the place they came back with guys from Électricité de France, to shut it down. But they were too late. Someone had already unwired everything. Disappeared with all the electronics and booze. What used to be a cinema was a plain old rock chamber. The only thing left behind was a note that said, 'Ne cherchez pas.' Don't search."

"Don't search for who? Cataphiles?"

"That's what I figured. That's what most people in the media figured. It was big news for a while. But Rascal says cataphiles don't do stuff like that. They're misfits mostly. They just go underground to hang out, party, explore."

"So who made the cinema?"

He shrugged. "Nobody knows. Rascal talks about this big group with a hundred members or so, supposedly organized and wealthy, sort of like an old boys' club. They use the catacombs, but only to get around Paris undetected. They have keys to everywhere in the city. They'll hold poetry readings in the basement of the Paris Opera, or booze it up on the roof of the Parthenon, or whatever."

I didn't reply as I contemplated this. It sounded neat. It also sounded completely farfetched.

"You mentioned Danièle's your in-law?" I said. "What, sister-in-law?"

"Yup. Dev and Danny Laurent. The Double Ds."

"Why don't you guys get along?"

"Me and Danny? You mean 'cause of the French jabs?" He shrugged. "It began with me and the wife. Dev makes fun of me all the time because I'm French Canadian. Calls me Queeb, Beaver Beater, Poutine. She's actually the one who started the whole frog thing, calling me Frozen Frog. I call her shit back. That's just us, our relationship. I found it funny how insulted Danny always got when she was around, so I started calling her Frenchy shit too. I don't think she cares as much as she lets on. What about you?"

"What about me?"

"You and Danny. What's your deal?"

I glanced ahead at Danièle. She was speaking with Pascal, her voice flat and muted. Sound didn't carry well down here. The soft silence was like being in an old library or root cellar or attic.

"We're just friends," I said.

"Come on, bro. She invited you to the catas. It's always just her and Rascal. She even put up a stink about *me* coming tonight, and I'm fucking family. So what's the word? You shagging her?"

The question caught me off guard, and invoked memories of Saturday morning. Waking in Danièle's poverty-posh bedroom to the half-light creeping beneath the fuchsia blinds, the smell of the Kashmir Rose incense she'd burned the night before, the sensuous curve of her spine, from the nape of her neck to where her tailbone disappeared beneath the sheets...

Rob, I realized, was watching me closely.

He snorted. "Just friends, my ass."

CHAPTER 12

ROB

S o they really were fucking, Rob thought. Couldn't say he was surprised. Like he'd told Will, Danny didn't invite just anyone to the catas. Not only that, Danny's been all over him since he arrived at the pub.

Once again Rob felt bad for Pascal. He could tell her flirting was eating the sad fuck up inside. At the same time, however, he was happy for Danny. After that prick Marcel, she deserved to be happy again.

Marcel.

His name alone pissed the fuck out of Rob. It wasn't just his cheating. That was almost the norm over here. Men cheated. Women cheated. A coworker of Rob's thought her long-term boyfriend was cheating on her, or at least thinking about doing it, so she cheated first, to beat him to the punch. And look at the guy running the country. He began an affair with a woman twenty years his junior during the presidential race. A few weeks after the story broke, he divorced his wife, the First Lady, and carried on with the sex kitten. You ask the average Parisian what they thought about it, you'll probably get a shrug and a "*C'est la vie.*"

So it wasn't the cheating. It was the way Marcel had treated Danny, bossing her around, keeping tabs on everything she did. Often when she went out he'd call her every ten minutes demanding to know what she was doing. But when he went out, he'd be off the radar until he returned at two or three in the morning. Danny would call Dev on these nights, bawling her eyes out. Rob would usually be nearby with the girls, listening to Dev's end of the conversation. He couldn't get his head around why Danny stuck with the fucker. She was usually so strong, so independent. It was like she became a different person when she was around him. Yet no matter what Dev told Danny, she wouldn't ditch him.

Then, a few months ago, Dev ran into Danny at Les Quatre Temps, a shopping mall at La Defense metro station. Danny had a dark bruise along the left side of her face. The makeup job would have fooled a stranger, but not Dev, and Dev got the entire lowdown from her.

Marcel did it. They got in a fight while she was cooking dinner the evening before. She didn't want him to go out. He punched her and went anyway. And this wasn't the first time this had happened. Once Danny got talking, she spilled the beans. He'd been beating her for almost as long as he'd known her. He usually hit her on the body, so she could cover up the evidence, and when he struck her face, he did it in such a way he rarely left a mark. Danny tried to tell Dev that Marcel only hit her when he was drinking. Her denial was mind-numbing. The guy smacked her up on a regular basis, and she was trying to protect him?

Rob got home from work late that day. The girls were sleeping in their bunk bed, and Danny was sleeping in the guest bedroom, surrounded by all her stuff she and Dev had collected from Marcel's flat, where Danny had been living for the last year. Dev told him what happened and wanted to call the cops. That probably would have been the best thing to do, but in the moment he was seeing red and wouldn't listen to reason.

Rob drove to Marcel's apartment building in the 12th arrondissement and waited across the street in his car for two hours until the fucker returned sometime past midnight. Then he pushed his way into the lobby behind Marcel before the door locked and beat the Frenchman with a steel pipe to a whimpering, bloody pulp. He wasn't proud of this, but he didn't regret it either.

Danny stayed at the flat for a month until she found the studio she was in now. To Rob's knowledge, she hadn't seen anyone else since Marcel. Will was the first. And, fortunately, Will was proving to be an all right sort. Rob just hoped he treated Danny well.

For her sake.

And his own.

CHAPTER 13

While Rob and I had been talking, clear, still puddles had begun to appear on the ground here and there. Pascal, Danièle, and Rob stomped through any in their way, while I sidestepped or hopped over them the best I could. Gradually, after numerous twists and turns, the entire passageway became a mushy gray paste that sucked at the soles of my shoes.

Pascal and Danièle stopped again. I came to a halt behind them and peered over their shoulders. The tunnel was flooded with glassy smooth water that stretched away far beyond the reach of our probing lights.

Pascal said something and shrugged. Danièle translated for me: "He says sometimes the water is here and sometimes it is not. It depends on the weather conditions aboveground. He thought it would be dry today. He is sorry."

I looked at him. He didn't appear sorry at all. He appeared indifferent and smug.

"When was the last time you were here?" I asked him.

He barely looked at me. "Last week."

"And it was dry then?"

"No, it was like it is now."

"And you thought it would be dry today?"

He shrugged. "It is difficult to know for certain."

"We will backtrack," Danièle stated. "There are many ways to go—"

"Doesn't matter," I said. "It's just water." I dropped to my butt and took off my shoes, one after the other, then my socks.

Danièle frowned. "That is not a good idea, Will. What if there is glass in there? We do not know."

"We're not backtracking."

I stuffed my shoes and socks into my backpack, rolled the cuffs of my pants up as far as they would go, Huck Finn style, and stood.

Pascal smirked at my bare legs and feet. Then he and Rob strolled breezily into the water, splashing and chatting. Danièle and I went next.

The water was ankle-deep and not as cold as I would have thought, maybe fifty degrees. This surprised me. I thought it would be colder, given it had never been touched by sunlight. Unlike the puddles we had passed earlier, it was an opaque gray. I couldn't see the bottom.

At first I felt tentatively with my lead foot before exerting my full weight. But after a number of steps and no encounters with razor-sharp glass or daggered rocks, I gained confidence and proceeded more naturally.

"It is okay?" Danièle asked.

"No problem."

"Make sure you do not trip."

"I won't."

"Motherfucker!" Rob shouted from ahead. "Deep here. Over my boots."

He was right. Soon the water was shin-high, then knee-high, wetting the tapered folds of my pants. It swirled around my legs like miso soup.

"How much farther?" Danièle called.

"Almost there," Rob shouted back. Then: "Holy shit!"

The panic in his voice made me freeze mid-step.

"What is it?" I said.

"Something just brushed my leg!"

"Fuck off."

"Swear to God! It was long and slimy."

A chill shot down my spine as I thought of fanged eel-like creatures and poisonous snakes.

Rob was maybe thirty feet in front of us, little more than a silhouette. I couldn't see Pascal.

"Arg!" Rob cried. "It touched me again!"

He began running, splashing madly.

"Go!" Danièle said, pushing me forward.

I took her hand and ran, or at least I tried to; it was more of a pigs-on-ice madcap dash. The water dragged at my legs, my helmet chafed the ceiling, the knuckles of my free hand skinned the wall. I kept waiting for a prehistoric monstrosity to latch onto my calf or snip off a toe.

Then the water was back to shin-level. Rob and Pascal were shouting, urging us on. My eyes darted between the frothing water and Danièle, my headlamp jerking every which way, until we stumbled onto the mushy ground. I keeled over, as if I'd been poleaxed in the gut. Danièle fell to her knees, a light patina of sweat on her forehead.

Rob and Pascal tittered like loons.

It clicked for me, then Danièle as well. Her eyes flared. "*Ta gueule!*" she shouted, scrambling to her feet. She smashed into Rob, pounding him on the head with her fist. Pascal attempted to pull her away unsuccessfully.

I might have laughed at this absurd theater, but my feet were in too much pain. I'd stubbed my left big toe on a rock, and it was already swelling and bruising. I'd broken the same one a few years back in New York, catching it on a door frame, making me wonder if I'd re-broken it. I'd also sliced the pad of my right heel. I couldn't tell how deep the cut was, but it was bleeding freely and stung like a son of a bitch.

Nevertheless, I hadn't brought a first-aid kit, and I didn't want to ask the others if they had one, so I pulled on my socks and shoes, then stood, wincing. Danièle had stopped her assault and was now chewing Rob and Pascal out.

"Loosen up, Danny," Rob told her. He'd moved a safe distance away and was dumping water from his boots. "Can't you take a joke?"

"You do not think! What if we fell and cracked our heads open?"

"Gimme a break."

"It could happen!"

"And so could getting locked in a sauna and getting lobstered alive. Or rolling your ride-on mower and getting chewed like summer turf. Or walking past a construction site and—"

"Oh, shut up!"

"If you think like that—"

"Really, Rosbif. Shut your mouth. I do not want to hear your talk."

"My talk?"

She was turning red.

"*Allons-y*," Pascal said quietly, putting his arm around Rob's waist and leading him down the passageway.

"I will kill him," Danièle stated when they were gone.

"He's not that bad," I said.

"He is such a loser."

"He's sort of funny."

She glared at me.

I held up my hands. "I said 'sort of.'"

"Because you only have to see him for a few hours. You know, he is married to my sister? I have to know him my entire life."

"Yeah, I heard."

"He told you?"

"In passing."

"I will kill him," she repeated, shaking her head. She picked up her backpack and shrugged it on. "We should go. We are almost there."

I frowned. "Almost where?" We had been in the catacombs less than an hour. Based on what I'd been told, there was no way we could be anywhere near the video camera with the mysterious footage.

Before I could ask for clarification, however, Danièle started away, leaving me to bring up the rear.

CHAPTER 14

O ur destination, it turned out, was called La Plage—
the Beach—a vast series of connecting galleries
and caverns with sand-packed floors, from which I
gathered the area had gotten its name. Almost every inch
of available wall space was covered with the omnipresent
graffiti, but also impressive murals. They depicted everything
from Egyptian gods to magic mushrooms to surrealist Max
Ernst-like portraits. One large rectangular support pillar had
been transformed into SpongeBob SquarePants. Some of the
paint smelled fresh.

We wandered from room to room, no one saying much, our
headlamps sweeping the way before us. In the ghostly silence
I saw countless cigarette butts, makeshift chandeliers sitting
on rock-cum-tables, crushed beer cans, and strange metal rods
and hooks protruding from the ceiling. These, I imagined, had
at one time accommodated power cables.

My eyes kept returning to the murals. They were multi-
generational, built up over decades, the new painted over the
old in an ongoing cycle. The sheer amount, the variety, was
incredible.

I stopped in front of an especially striking painting of a six-
foot-tall naked woman that reminded me of the Statue of Liberty. It was clearly old, one of the few works of art that had
stood the test of time without being vandalized or replaced.

Rob appeared next to me. "Nice tits," he said approvingly.

Danièle joined us and said, "She is famous for cataphiles because—how should I say this? She represents all of us. Can you understand, Will?"

"Not really."

"It is like what I told you before. In the catacombs, the above world no longer matters. I do not care if you are a janitor or a company president. Here, there are no bosses, no masters. We are all free. We are all naked."

"And cataphiles just like to get naked," Rob told me with a nudge and wink. "You should hear about some of the mad orgies they have. Sick fucks, they are."

"We are not sick," Danièle said. "You are sick."

"You know, Danny," Rob said, "I don't know if it's a language thing, but I've heard better comebacks from preschoolers."

Danièle brushed past him and went to the next room.

"Seriously," Rob said to Pascal and me. "You guys don't agree? I keep waiting for her to bust out, 'I don't shut up I grow up and when I look at you I throw up!'"

"And your mother, she lick it up," Pascal said.

Rob grinned. "Right on, bro! But it sounds sort of gay with your accent."

Pascal shoved him. "*Ta mere suce des queues devant le prisu.*"

"And yours sucks bears in the forest."

Leaving them to swap mother barbs, I went looking for Danièle. At first I had no idea which way she went, then I spotted the afterglow of her light around a corner.

I joined her in the largest room yet—and came to an abrupt halt. Three of the four walls were covered by a massive, continuous mural, a reproduction of *The Great Wave*, one of the most famous works of Japanese art in the world. It depicted an enormous white-capped wave roaring against a pink sky, seemingly about to swallow Mt. Fuji whole.

Bridgette and I used to have a print of it. She had picked it up at a garage sale, along with a number of old black-and-white Hawaii photos: a surfer standing next to a redwood board in the 1890s, the luxury ocean liner *Mariposa* at Honolulu Harbor, six-year-old Shirley Temple singing "The Good Ship Lollipop" on Waikiki Beach, the *China Clipper* landing at Pearl Harbor. We had framed all of these and hung them in a horizontal line above the sofa in the living room.

Danièle interpreted my stunned reaction as awe and said, "It is amazing, right?"

I nodded, but I wasn't really listening. Bridgette was inside my head, and I couldn't get her out. She'd been wearing a yellow cotton dress with a fat black belt that day of the garage sale. I remember because I'd teased her by calling her "Bumblebee." Along with the print and the photos, she had two bags of groceries from the Asian supermarket down the street, and we ended up making a green Thai curry for dinner, which we ate with a bottle of relatively expensive wine. I'd just gotten the job with the travel book company a few days earlier, and we had been celebrating all week.

After dinner we'd been goofing around on the bed and she had said to me, "Should I go off the pill?"

"The pill?"

"Do we want a baby, Will?"

I was thrilled. "Really?"

"We're getting married in three weeks. If we start trying now..."

"We'll have been married for about a year by the time he's born."

"He?"

"He, she, whatever."

She beamed. "So?"

"Yeah, I want to... I mean, if you want to."

"Of course I want to!"

And we had rolled around and play wrestled, our clothes coming off piece by piece...

Pascal and Rob had entered the room behind me, causing me to start. Pascal started chatting with Danièle, while Rob slumped onto the chiseled limestone bench that lined the walls. He dug through his backpack, produced a couple beers,

71

and asked me if I wanted one.

I turned my back to the mural, and the past.

"Sure," I said.

▼

Danièle and Pascal produced some tealights from their backpacks and placed the small candles around the cavern. Then they took off their helmets and turned off the headlamps, presumably to save batteries. They instructed Rob and me to do the same.

When everyone was settled on the limestone bench, I studied the can of beer Rob had given me suspiciously. The label read: "Bière du Démon."

"Strongest blonde beer in the world, boss," he told me.

I didn't doubt him; it boasted a twelve-percent alcohol content.

"You drink this often?" I asked.

"Never tried it. But thought it would be appropriate for tonight. And they were only a buck a can at the Super U near my place."

I popped the tab, brushed the froth off the top, and sniffed. It smelled of fusel alcohols and bitter yeast. The taste, a skunky sweetness, wasn't much better—and then the burning of cheap vodka kicked in.

Rob made a disgusted face—I imagine I was making a similar one—but said, "It's not that bad." To prove he meant this, he took another sip.

I smacked my lips. The aftertaste was an unwanted gift that kept on giving. I thought I could detect a hollow fishiness, and not in the delicate sashimi type of way.

Nevertheless, the demon grog was drinkable, and drink it I would. I wanted to forget that damn mural and forget Bridgette—Bridgette who was now married and pregnant.

I took another, longer sip.

"You like it?" Danièle asked me, surprised.

"I've had worse."

"It is for hobos."

"I probably look like a hobo right now with all this muck on me," I said. "By the way, where's all the sand from?"

"The ocean," Danièle replied. "Millions of years ago Paris used to be under a tropical sea. And I should tell you," she added, "that this is one of the most famous places in the catacombs for parties. If you come on a weekend, Friday or Saturday, you will likely see many cataphiles. Everybody drinks, smokes. It can be a lot of fun. Do you smoke, Will?"

"Pot?"

She nodded.

"I don't buy it." I shrugged. "But if it's around..."

"Good. I will get you high later."

I didn't know if I wanted to get high down here, but I didn't say anything.

"Any chicks at these ragers?" Rob asked. "Or is it one big sausage fest?"

Danièle scowled at him. "You are married to my sister, Rosbif. You should not care if there are 'chicks' present or not."

"I'm asking for Rascal's sake."

"Pascal does not need woman help from you, do not worry."

Rob and Pascal began bantering back and forth in French.

"Do you know most of the other cataphiles you run into?" I asked Danièle.

"Some. But there are always new people."

"What if assholes like those scuba guys show up to one of these parties?"

She shrugged. "Usually everyone is friendly. The people you have to be careful about are the meth heads and drug dealers. But you do not see them very often. And if you do, there are more normal people than weirdos. So if you stay together, you are okay. Do not go anywhere on your own. That is the second rule of the catacombs."

"What's the first?"

"Bring backup batteries."

"No, no, no," Pascal said, shaking his head. "The first rule is to get out again. The second is to come back. And the third is to do whatever you like."

"You know what would be awesome?" Rob said. "A stripper pole, right over there, in the center of the room." He had moved off the bench and was stretched out in a recumbent position on the sand, his head in one hand, his beer in the other. He would have been right at home with a couple palm frond-fanning, grape-dangling servants hovering over him.

"At one of the parties," Danièle said, "a woman gave everyone who wanted one a lap dance. I do not know if she was a stripper, but if she behaves like that, probably."

I said, "What's the strangest thing you've seen down here?"

"Oh, so much!" She made a thinking face. "There used to be a group of women called the catachicks. They walked around in their bikinis and nothing else."

Pascal said something.

Danièle replied, shaking her head.

He persisted.

She shrugged and looked at me. "Pascal wants me to tell you one of our stories," she said. "I can do this. But I have to warn you it is very scary. Maybe you do not want to hear it."

I set aside my beer, bumped a Marlboro from my pack, and lit up. "Go for it," I told her, exhaling a jet of smoke away from her.

"Okay...but do not say I did not warn you." She cleared her throat. "So, it happened a few weeks after Pascal and I were sent into the catacombs for our initiation at Les Mines. We wanted to visit the tunnels again on our own, but we knew nothing then, we had no maps, so we found a guide online. His name was Henri. He charged us two hundred euros." She confirmed this with Pascal, who nodded. "Yes, two hundred," she went on. "When we met him, he was with another couple, a guy and girl our age, Etienne and Mari. They were very sweet. So it was the five of us. We explored for maybe ten hours. Then suddenly—and this is crazy—all our lights went."

"At the same time?" Rob said.

"It is true, Rosbif. We do not know why, but it happened. And no one had matches or lighters. You do not know what it is like down here without any light. The darkness, it is so incredible. Wait—you must experience this. Pascal, put out the candles."

I stiffened, then berated myself. There was no reason to be afraid of the dark. If we couldn't relight the tealights for whatever reason, we had our headlamps right next to us.

I took a final drag and stubbed out my cigarette while Pascal went around the cavern, snuffing the candles one by one. I don't know what I had been expecting, but when Pascal extinguished the final flame, a darkness like I had never experienced enveloped us. Only it wasn't a darkness; it was a blackness. Black-hole black. I blinked, but that changed nothing. It was like being in some sort of sensory deprivation chamber. I couldn't see anything, couldn't hear anything, couldn't smell anything aside from the omnipresent dank musk, like time stored in a bottle.

And Danièle had said her lights—everyone's lights—had failed them? She had been plunged into this nothingness without the reassuring knowledge she could leave it anytime she wanted? That would be a psychological nightmare. Obviously she had escaped. But what if she hadn't? I tried to imagine what it would be like to walk alone in utter blackness, with only your hand on the wall to guide you, your mouth dry from dehydration, your throat and lungs burning from the rank air and the countless hours of screaming for help, your feet weeping with blisters, your legs jellied with exhaustion, nothing around you but tunnels and more tunnels, ad infinitum.

At some point it would hit you that you weren't getting out of there alive. And then what? Did you give in to your despair and slump to the cold hard ground? Or did you keep pressing on, driven by the naïve hope of salvation, the sheer will to survive? Would you eventually turn on the others with you?

Would you begin knocking them off one by one, either out of primal hunger or insanity? Or would the insanity not come until later, when you were little more than skin and bones, when the rats grew bold enough to sample your living flesh, when you were counting down the hours and minutes until the end?

"Amazing, yes?" Danièle said softly.

I started at the abrupt sound of her voice.

"Yeah, great," Rob said. "Now I know what it's like to be dead. Thanks, Danny. I've always wondered."

"Will?" she said.

I found it strange to be speaking in complete darkness. It was sort of like speaking on the phone to someone, even though they were next to you.

"Freaky," I said.

"I am going to finish my story in the dark. Is that okay?"

"Seriously?" Rob said.

"It will not take long." She cleared her throat. "So—Pascal and me were down here with our guide and those other two people and our lights went out. It was just like this—only for real. At first we tried to get our lights to turn back on. When they did not, Henri told us he knew a manhole exit close by. He said he could lead us there, even in the dark. We walked for ten minutes, and it was the longest ten minutes of my life. I thought we were going to die, I really did. But then we saw light, a pinhole coming through the manhole cover twenty meters up. We climbed the ladder. The cover was not sealed, and we pushed it open. We were right in the middle of a street, but it was late, and there were no cars, so we climbed out."

There was a long pause.

"That's it?" Rob said.

"No, that is not. Etienne was missing. Mari said she had been holding his hand the entire time. Then, at the ladder, she said he told her to go up, he would be behind her. But he never came."

"You're full of it," Rob said.

"I am not, Rosbif. Ask Pascal."

"*C'est vraiement,*" Pascal said.

"So what did you do?" I asked.

"We called down to him. There was no answer. Henri bought new batteries from a nearby store and put them in his flashlight. It worked and he and Mari went back down."

"You and Pascal didn't go?"

"Are you listening to me, Will? I was so scared. We waited at the top for them to return. They did, with Etienne. But he was all...messed up. He was like a zombie and would not say anything at all. We took him to a café, we gave him food and water. He finally spoke a little. It was in a flat tone, like he was not aware he was speaking. He told us he remembered walking in the dark, then all of a sudden he became very cold. He did not recall anything after that. Nothing. Not until Henri and Mari found him again, curled up in a ball on the ground."

I frowned. "But you said he was holding his girlfriend's hand all the way to the manhole."

"Yes," Danièle agreed. "And he told her he would climb up behind her. That is the thing, we have no idea if she was lying, or if..."

"Or what?" Rob said.

"Or..." I could almost sense Danièle shrugging. "I cannot answer that."

"Bullshit!"

"It is true, Rosbif. We exchanged contact information with the couple, in case they needed to get in touch again. They did not. But *I* did. I needed to know if they had been playing a joke on us. So I sent an email to them about one month later. Only Mari replied. She told me she was no longer with Etienne. Apparently after that day in the catacombs his mental condition got worse and worse until his parents could not care for him and were forced to admit him to a psychiatric hospital. To this day, Pascal and I have no idea what really happened to him."

Another long pause. The silence that ensued was deep and ominous. I wanted to turn on my headlamp. Danièle's story might have been laughable had she told it aboveground. But hearing it here in the catacombs where it happened, in the unprecedented blackness, was borderline terrifying.

A quick snick. A flame appeared.

Pascal went around the cavern, relighting the candles.

I looked at Rob, then Danièle. In the candlelight Rob seemed half confused, half amused, like he'd shit his pants and didn't know what to do. Danièle's eyes were bright and intense —and not a hint of deception in them.

"Fuck me blue," Rob said, chugging the last of his beer, crushing the can, and opening another. "That's something, Danny."

I said, "This Etienne guy must have had some sort of nervous breakdown."

"Obviously, boss. Why do you think he got locked up in a mental asylum."

"I mean while he was in the catacombs. He didn't think he was getting out. His mind snapped."

"But who was holding the girl's hand all the way to the manhole?"

"He must have been."

"Then he wanders back into the tunnel and curls up in a ball?"

"Rosbif is right," Danièle said. "That makes no sense."

I said, "So we're talking about ghosts now?"

She shook her head, shrugged. "Anyway—you wanted to know the craziest thing that happened to me. That is it."

"But you still come down here all the time?"

"I did not come again for maybe six months. But eventually I did, yes. I cannot stay away. This place...it is magical for me."

Pascal returned to us and withdrew three objects from his backpack. At first I thought they were really old flashlights before realizing they were juggling torches. The handles appeared to be made of spiral-wound plastic. The upper portion of the dowels were shrouded in aluminum.

He set a bottle of kerosene on the ground and held a torch

for me to take.

"It is easy," he said in that French way of his with equal stress on each syllable. "You try."

I looked at him, but couldn't tell whether he was being friendly or not.

I said, "I can't juggle."

"Just one. Like this." He flicked the torch into the air, then caught it again. "See, easy." He smiled at me—his smug GQ smirk.

No, not friendly, I decided. "I told you—"

"Okay, okay, I know, you cannot do it, no problem."

He doused all three wicks in kerosene and lit them with his lighter. Orange flames whooshed to life. Still grinning— now like a showman—he began to freestyle, tossing the fiery torches from one hand to the other in a jaunty, cascading fashion.

Danièle clapped to an inaudible beat. Rob joined her. I didn't. Pascal was really beginning to get on my nerves. I've been trying to cut him some slack. I knew the attitude he was giving me stemmed from the fact I was with Danièle. To be fair, I didn't blame the guy for that. He had apparently liked her for several years, couldn't find the balls to do anything about it, then some American rolls into town and hooks up with her, and he gets delegated to yesterday's news. If I were in his position, I wouldn't like me either.

But he wasn't giving it a rest; it was one snub after another. And now this: offering to let me juggle only to prove to everyone he could do it better. He reminded me of a reporter at the *Brooklyn Eagle* who always caught me in the kitchenette while I was making coffee. He was a nerdy, know-it-all sort, and he would ask trivialities like, "Do you know how the Greek Thales measured the height of the pyramids?" And after you gave him an inane answer or passed, he would tell you in an off-hand way, like he was an unsung genius, that Thales measured the shadow the pyramid cast on the ground at noon. He was a phony and an attention-seeker, and so was Pascal—or Chess—

in his own subtle way.

Pascal reversed the direction of the torches, now cycling the lead one over as opposed to under the others. He carried on juggling for another full minute, accelerating his speed, performing different tricks, at one point balancing one torch on his chin while flourishing the other two with his fingers.

For his finale he tossed the three torches so high they almost touched the twelve-foot ceiling, pirouetted one-hundred-and-eighty degrees, caught them in descending order, and bowed—all in one fluid motion.

"*Très bien!*" Danièle cheered. "*C'est épatant!*" She cupped my knee with her hand. "Unbelievable, Will, right?"

"Maybe he should join the cir—"

A distant shout cut me off.

CHAPTER 15

We listened. The only sound was the flickering of Pascal's torches.

"Put those out," I told him quietly.

He did so. I thought I could hear some sort of chanting.

"Who the fuck's that?" Rob said.

"It must be other cataphiles," Danièle said. "They are goofing around."

"They're coming closer."

"Yeah," I agreed. The chant was getting louder.

"Guys, it is no big deal," Danièle said. "We always see other cataphiles. There is no need to worry—" She frowned.

"What?" I said.

"It sounds like German."

She was right, I realized. "Are they sieg heiling?"

Danièle and Pascal began conversing with what seemed liked great seriousness.

"Nazis?" Rob said. "Really? You're shitting me."

"Whoever they are, they're going to be here soon." I interrupted Danièle. "Is this going to be a problem?"

"It depends on who they are," she said with a shrug, but her expression revealed a quiet trepidation. "Pascal thinks it might be Le Diable Peint."

"Who?"

"The Painted Devil," she said. "There are many stories about him... I thought they were only stories."

"You've never met him before?"

"No, never. Not once. You are very bad luck, Will."

Pascal was shoving the torches into his backpack.

"Yes, hurry," Danièle said. "We should leave."

"And go where?" I said. "They're going to be here any second."

Pascal stuffed his folded map down the front of his pants. He passed Danièle his lighter. She tucked it down south too. There was no time to ask them what the hell they were doing, for a moment later three men marched into the room, chanting and saluting in rhythm.

CHAPTER 16

DANIÈLE

T
he men halted at parade rest: chins up, chests out, legs apart, arms behind their backs. They were in their mid-forties and dressed identically in high leather boots, military-style peaked caps, trousers, and tunics. Everything was black except the red arm bands emblazoned with the swastika and the white runic insignias patched onto their collars. They each carried 6D flashlights.

Pascal was right! Danièle thought. It's them—the Painted Devil and his henchmen. It has to be. Who else dresses up in SS uniforms?

Fear shot down her spine like a bullet as she wondered what they had planned, and they surely had something planned, because this meeting was no coincidence. They had not been surprised to see her and Will and the others when they entered the room, which meant they had heard them and had come specifically for them.

Pascal, she was sure, would not say or do anything stupid. He knew how dangerous these men were. Not Rob and Will though. Rob was a brawler by nature. Back when he and Dev were still courting, he used to get into bar fights on a regular basis. He was like a ferret, fearless. He would antagonize men twice his size for no other reason than to pick a fight. But becoming a husband and father seemed to have put some sense into him. She couldn't remember the last time he'd lost his temper. She prayed he could keep it in check now too.

And Will?

Danièle didn't know. He had always been so laid-back, soft-spoken. That's why she was so surprised when he got into that full-out fistfight with that over-muscled rhinoceros on the train tracks. He had been swearing and swinging and so intense—yes, that was the word, *intense*—that he had scared her a little.

She glanced at him now, trying to catch his eye, but he was focused fully on the Painted Devil.

And he was smiling.

▼

As I studied the three men in the Nazi uniforms before us I couldn't help but think of my Pi Kappa Alpha fraternity initiation at NYU. All the pledges, which had included myself, had been blindfolded and taken to a hotel ballroom. When the blindfolds came off, we found ourselves surrounded by candles, robed, chanting frat members, and various alumni. I kept things together well enough until I had to kneel in front of the frat president while he read the secret oath from a large embossed book. That's when I broke out in giggles; I couldn't help it. The guy was a good friend of mine. I hung out with him all the time under more ordinary circumstances. Seeing him in his getup, reciting Latin, which I knew he didn't understand, was a gag.

It was one of those times when something that was supposed to be serious came across as ridiculous.

Like now.

I mean, these three geezers from equally mediocre gene pools went around the catacombs trying to scare harmless cataphiles?

Fuck them.

The one in the middle had birdish features and resembled

the actor Ed Harris. His blue eyes locked on me and narrowed. He barked something that had the inflection of an order.

"I don't speak German," I told him.

"Ah!" He raised his plucked eyebrows in surprise. "American, am I right?"

He might be outfitted as a Nazi, but his French accent was clear as day.

"You guys like playing dress up?"

"Will," Danièle cautioned me.

I looked at her, wondering what she was worried about. There were four of us. Douchebags like these three were all bark and no bite. I doubted they would start anything unless the odds were squarely in their favor, which they were not.

"I asked you a question," Ed Harris said to me.

"Yeah, I'm American. He's Canadian. These two are French."

"I love America," the man said, flashing a bright white smile. "Especially your movies. Batman, what a guy."

His buddies had yet to do anything more than stare myopically ahead. One had a wormy red scar that followed his left smile line. The other had a drooping mouth corner.

Danièle said, "*Nous partons—*"

"Shut your mouth, whore," Ed Harris snapped. "I wasn't speaking to you."

I blinked, shocked into silence.

"Yo, whale shit," Rob snarled. "That's my sister-in-law. Watch your mouth."

"Are you threatening me?" Harris said calmly.

"You better believe it."

"You do not know who I am, do you?"

"You're a joke," I said.

Danièle touched my arm. "Will, stop."

"Yes, you know who I am, don't you, *chérie*?" Harris said to her.

She nodded. "Le Diable Peint."

"*Merci, mon amour.*" He glared at Rob, then me. "Maybe if *you* and *you* knew what your friend knows, you would show more respect. For I should warn you, *messieurs*, that I am not partial to the aegis of ignorance."

I turned my back to the guy. Danièle and Pascal appeared pale, even in the weak candlelight. Rob had his manic grin on again, which I was glad to see.

I said, "We're wasting our time here—"

Abruptly Danièle and Pascal's eyes sprang open in alarm. Rob's grin vanished.

Frowning, I turned back to the Painted Devil, and discovered he now held a matte-black pistol in his hand, pointed at me.

CHAPTER 17

PASCAL

Pascal could hear his heartbeat in his head, the way you could when nursing a really bad hangover, and he felt strangely light, as if he were floating. He would have run already, his legs wanted to, but the Painted Devil and the other two stood between him and the exit. His eyes darted around the room. There was nowhere else to flee to. They were trapped.

At least the pistol wasn't aimed at him. He had never seen one up close before, and it filled him with a sickening dread. One wrong move on his part, a jumpy finger on the Painted Devil's part, that's all it would take, and he would be lying on the ground, bleeding into the sand.

Pascal realized he was frozen with fear, and he had to work his throat to swallow. He licked his suddenly dry lips.

Maybe Will would attack the Painted Devil, he thought hopefully. He was the biggest one here. He should be the one to try that.

He would probably get shot first, but it might give the rest of them a chance to get away.

CHAPTER 18

"Whoa, man," I said, raising my hands. "What are you doing?" Although I was facing down a lunatic with a gun, I was surprised to find myself not so much afraid as calmly alert.

"Getting your attention," Ed Harris said.

"You have our attention. No need for guns."

"Who am I?" he demanded with bright malice. His blue eyes were chips of ice. His jaw was clenched tight, causing his right cheek to twitch. In fact, he was one tightly wound coil, everything about him screaming, "Deranged."

How had I not noticed this before? I wondered. But the answer was simple. I had been distracted by the silly uniforms, and cocky because I believed we had the strength advantage.

"The Painted Devil," I said.

"Then address me as such!"

I cleared my throat. "There's no need for guns...Painted Devil."

"Tell me what you are doing here."

"In the catacombs?" I kept my voice even. I didn't want him to interpret anything I said as insolence or sarcasm. Who knew what would set his trigger finger off? Prowling the catacombs dressed as a Nazi and carrying a pistol—the guy should be locked away in a mental asylum. I said, "I've never been here before. My friends wanted to show it to me. We're exploring."

"Address me properly!"

"Painted Devil," I said promptly, raising my hands higher. "We're exploring, Painted Devil."

He took a snarly breath, wiped the hand holding the flashlight across his mouth, looked at Danièle. "Is this true, *mon amour*?"

"*Oui, Diable Peint.*"

"You," he said to Pascal. "How often do you come here?"

"*Des fois, Diable Peint.*"

"You have heard of me too?"

"*Oui, Diable Peint.*"

"Then you should know how I detest Ravioli like you. You are *pigs*. You desecrate this area. *My home.*" He was scowling, his blue eyes dancing madly. "How would you like it if stupid ugly pigs came into your home and shit on your floors and painted on your walls?" He leveled the pistol at Pascal's head. "Answer me!"

Pascal's face melted into a plea. His mouth hung open, but he didn't say anything. Either he couldn't find his voice or didn't understand what the Devil was spewing.

I said, "We wouldn't like it, Painted Devil."

He swung the pistol back at me. "Of course you wouldn't. You would call the police. They would arrest the pigs." He wiped his hand across his mouth again. "Do you know what the police do to the pigs they find here?"

"They fine them," Danièle said softly.

"Yes, *mon amour*, they fine them. But these quarries are very large, they cannot find every pig, this is why I help them, why I help them help *me*. I fine each Ravioli I come across for their transgression."

"You want money, Painted Devil?" Rob said. "We got cash."

He scowled. "I don't want money. I don't *need* money. But I will take something else. Your batteries. All of them—right now." He waved the pistol between us. "Do not keep me waiting!"

"We won't be able to see," I said, adding belatedly, "Painted Devil."

He grinned that white smile. "Exactly."

Reluctantly—there was no other option with a pistol trained on you—we retrieved our helmets from where we had set them on the limestone bench and popped the head-lamp batteries free. Wormface collected them from each of us, sticking them in his pockets.

"Your bags," the Devil said. "Dump out your bags."

Cursing under my breath—I had been hoping these would be overlooked—I unzipped my backpack's main pocket and upended it in front of me. Wormface confiscated the brand new Energizers I had brought. He moved on to Danièle, Rob, and finally Pascal.

The Devil continued smiling; he was obviously enjoying this. "Well? Where are they? Give me your lighters too."

For a moment I considered telling the asshole that we didn't have any. But then how were the goddamn tealights burning? I glanced at the others—and remembered Pascal stuffing the map down his pants...and Danièle the lighter down hers. They must have heard of shit like this happening before.

At least we'll have one lighter to help us find our way out again.

I took the yellow Bic from my pocket and tossed it to Wormface.

"Who else?" the Devil asked.

"Only me," I said.

He nodded to Wormface, who searched us one by one. He gave the Devil a shrug. All clear.

The Devil nodded and focused on Danièle. She fidgeted, looking anywhere but at him.

"Look at me," he told her.

She did so hesitantly.

"You are very beautiful, *chérie*. It is a shame to cover up that beauty. Take off your clothes."

"You motherfucker!" Rob said, clenching his hands into

fists, his shoulders and neck muscles bunching into ropy knots.

I tensed more than I already was and calculated my chances of tackling the Devil successfully. But this thought came and went in a flash. It was too risky. He was a good ten feet away. He could put a bullet in me before I got halfway to him.

"Please try," the Devil hissed, brandishing the pistol between Rob and me. "Please. Someone. I am waiting."

"It is okay," Danièle said hollowly, to no one in particular. She stepped out of her waders, kicking them aside, then pulled her T-shirt off, revealing a flower-patterned bra. She dropped the tee on the ground and unbuttoned her jeans, shoving them down her thighs.

I met Rob's eyes over her head and read in them what he was thinking: *He can't take both of us out.* That probably wasn't true, but I was keyed up on adrenaline. I couldn't stand there and do nothing. I gritted my teeth and nodded imperceptibly.

"What is this?" the Devil exclaimed. He was referring to the hidden lighter outlined against the thin fabric of Danièle's panties. "Let me see—" Abruptly he cocked his head to one side, the way nutty people do when listening to nonexistent voices. But then I heard it too.

Music.

CHAPTER 19

I t was some sort of techno-pop, and it wasn't very far away. That was the thing with sound down here. It didn't travel. As we'd discovered with the Painted Devil and his cohorts, you didn't know anyone was there until they were almost upon you.

I glanced at Rob, wondering if we should charge, or wait to see what happened next.

The Devil acted first. He fired the pistol at the ground.

There was a loud report. I instinctively dove to one side, half expecting another shot to follow, this one accompanied by scorching pain.

There was none—only a brilliant red light burning a few feet away. Billows of smoke wafted from it, quickly filling the cavern.

A flare! He was holding a goddamn flare gun.

I stumbled away from the hissing, fiery flash, my dark-adjusted eyes temporarily blinded.

"Where'd he go?" Rob shouted from somewhere nearby.

"Don't know!" I replied. The heat was intense, the air acrid with a sulfur/tar stench. I covered my nose with my arm.

Danièle appeared beside me, carrying her clothes. "Will, this way!"

Head down, I followed her until we passed into the next room. Rob and Pascal bowled into us from behind, almost knocking me over.

"Where is he?" Rob demanded, spinning in a wild circle.

"Gone," I said. Spangles of light still danced before my eyes.

"Fuck!"

The music was loud and tinny now. Flashlight beams arced through the darkness twenty feet away. They zeroed in on us.

"*Qui est-ce?*" Pascal called, holding his arm in front of his face, squinting.

The voice that floated back was not one I wanted to hear.

▼

Dreadlocks and his two buddies approached us wearily. A cell phone dangled around Dreadlock's bullish neck by a lanyard. He tapped the screen. The music stopped.

Apparently the bad blood between us was forgotten, at least temporarily, as they seemed only interested in discovering what all the kafuffle was about. Pascal obliged their curiosity, talking excitedly and making elaborate gestures. I caught "Le Diable Peint" several times. The scuba guys hung onto every word, interrupting with questions or exclamations of disbelief. Then Pascal made a clapping noise and a vanishing gesture, apparently describing how the Devil had made his escape.

Dreadlocks looked at Danièle. She had pulled her clothes back on and was now stepping into her waders. He said, "*Tu vas bien?*"

She nodded. "*Ça va.*"

He turned to me. "You know what? I think, after this, you are *touriste* no more." He grinned broadly, proud of this generous proclamation. "You know what else? Because I punch your face, I feel bad, I give you gift."

I frowned suspiciously.

"What?" he said. "You no want gift?"

"Depends what it is."

"Batteries!" he announced, whacking me good-naturedly on the shoulder with a meaty paw. "We have many extras, and you have none."

▼

After much consulting and comparing of maps, Pascal and my new pal Dreadlocks determined that we were all going in the same direction and would thus travel together—so explained Danièle, my translator in all the goings-on.

As we refilled our backpacks and installed the gifted batteries in our headlamps, Danièle went on to tell me that there was a room with a Norman castle and gargoyles nearby, a room heaped with silk flowers, a room lined with paintings of film characters, and even a library—a small alcove littered with books cataphiles used based on the honor system. "I wanted to show you all of this, Will," she said. "But I do not think it is a good idea anymore with you-know-who around."

"Voldemort?"

"Do not be silly...Voldemort is English, not French."

"I don't think we have to worry about the Painted Devil," I said. "He only had the upper hand because he tricked us. And he's not going to trick us again."

"You do not know that for sure. We hurt his ego. We scared him away. He might want to get revenge somehow."

I didn't argue the point—I didn't care if we saw the feature rooms or not—and we rejoined the scuba guys and followed them to one of the Beach's exits, what turned out to be a narrow fissure where the floor angled upward and met the ceiling.

I wasn't claustrophobic, but an oily something coated my gut at the sight of it. "We're supposed to fit through there?" I said.

"We call it a *chatière*," Danièle said. "A cat hole."

That was an accurate description, I thought, as it didn't appear that anything larger than a domesticated feline could squeeze through it.

The scuba guys went first. They had introduced themselves to us by their catacombs monikers. The old guy was Zéro, the skinny kid was Chevre (which, according to Danièle, meant Goat), and Dreadlocks was Citerne (Tank), though I preferred "Dreadlocks" and continued to think of him as such.

Dreadlocks climbed the slope that rose to the ceiling, shoved the oxygen tanks and harness into the hole ahead of him, then crawled in after it. Zéro went next, then Goat.

"It is not so bad," Danièle told me as we ascended the gradient after them. "You put your arms in first, then you wiggle your hips to move." She shook her butt to demonstrate. "Just follow me."

When we reached the fissure, she slipped inside without hesitation, her willowy frame allowing ample leeway on either side of her body. I peered in after her, but could see little more than the soles of her boots kicking as she crawled forward.

"Let's go, nancy boy!" Rob said from behind and below me.

"Yeah, yeah," I said. I stuck my head and shoulders into the hole, decided to hell with that, then switched to a crab-walk, feet first.

"No, no, no," Pascal said. "That is not the proper way."

I scuttled into the narrow space quickly. My head was aching with faded adrenaline, and I didn't want to deal with any of Pascal's shit right then.

The walls and ceiling pressed tightly around me. I dug my heels into the ground and pulled myself forward, dragging my backpack behind me.

After about a minute of this, and struggling the entire way, I halted, contemplating whether to backtrack and start over again, headfirst, military-crawl style. But Rob had already entered behind me, blocking my exit. He cackled in that witchy way of his, as though he thought this cat hole was a trip, and said, "Get going, smurfdick!"

"I can't move fast on my back."

"Why didn't you listen to Rascal? Headfirst! This isn't a fucking waterslide."

I resumed pulling myself forward with my legs, but it

didn't get any easier. The shaft seemed to be narrowing, limiting my maneuverability.

My feet kicked rock. *A dead end?* I continued kicking, probing, and discovered the shaft had angled to the right.

My relief didn't last long, however, because laying supine wasn't ideal for turning laterally. I was like a straw caught in the elbow between two lengths of pipe. I would have to roll onto my side, so I could bend at the waist.

Problem was, the damn ceiling was now too low to do that.

"Boss," Rob said. "What's the holdup?"

"The shaft bends. I don't think I can get around it."

"Yeah you can. That big oaf did."

"He went headfirst. I can't twist the way I am. I think we have to reverse back out."

"No fucking way!"

"I don't have a choice!"

"I'm going to push you."

He began shoving my backpack.

"Stop it!" I said. "That's not helping."

"Then stop dicking around."

I attempted to roll onto my side, but it was difficult to generate torque without the use of my arms, one of which was extended past my head, the other pinned at my side. I crossed my ankles and bent my knees and corkscrewed my legs to the right. It took a couple of rocking motions, but I was finally able to flop onto my right side.

"You good?" Rob asked.

"Yeah…" I said, though I felt like a pretzel.

I began to inchworm around the bend, my upper shoulder scraping the ceiling. Everything was going well until the ceiling lowered even more. I slugged on, squeezing into the pinching shaft, telling myself the space had to open again. It didn't. Soon I could no longer move forward. I tried reversing, but couldn't do that either.

I was stuck.

"Dammit," I said softly.

"What's wrong?" Rob asked.

"I can't move."

"Come on."

"I'm stuck!"

"You're not—"

"I am!"

A pause. The silence was bleak. There was something inherently unnerving about being unable to move your body how you wanted to move it.

A commotion sounded as Rob shoved my backpack to one side. He saw me and said, "Fuck, bro, you gotta get flat on your stomach or back."

"I can't."

"You gotta twist."

"I'm all twisted up!" I snapped. "I shouldn't have kept going."

"You got in there, you can get out."

"Give me a sec."

"What are you doing?"

"Trying to think!"

"Danny!" Rob shouted.

"What...?" She sounded far away.

"Will's stuck!"

No reply.

"Danny!"

"Will?" she called. "Is this true?"

"Yeah!"

"I am coming back."

My helplessness infuriated me. I kicked and jerked. The rock securing me dug into my flesh like teeth.

"Hold on," Rob told me. "Danny will help you."

"What's she going to do?"

"She'll pull. I'll push."

"Will?" It was Danièle. She sounded closer—and also worried.

"What?"

"Do not move too much. Some of these *chatières* are not very stable."

Great, I thought. Exactly what I wanted to hear.

The panic that had been escalating inside me swelled to a suffocating force. Suddenly my lungs seemed too large for my chest. My breath clogged in my throat. I was on the verge of losing it and had to resist the impulse to thrash violently.

I closed my eyes. Almost immediately the darkness behind my lids gave way to a long-ago memory. It was spring. I was eight years old. Bulldozers had recently cleared a patch of forest behind our house in the suburbs of Olympia to make room for a new subdivision. Maxine and I were forbidden to play in the tangle of felled trees, but of course we did. What kids wouldn't? It was a gigantic fort full of nooks and crannies and passageways. We nicknamed it the Beaver Dam.

One afternoon Max and I had been fooling around on top of the dam and she lost her footing and dropped her Kewpie doll. It fell between a crosshatch of sticks and logs too small to climb through. She began bawling. She'd gotten the doll less than two weeks ago for her sixth birthday, and it was her prized possession. I told her it was okay, I'd get it, and so I climbed off the dam and made my way to the main entrance we always used, a convergence of felled trunks that formed a small passageway. I crawled inside and tunneled deeper and deeper, easing aside dead branches, worming under and over rotting logs, venturing farther than I ever had before.

I had just broken into a new cavity and could see the doll ahead of me when I struck something of structural importance and the dam collapsed on top of me.

Max heard me yelling and ran for help, while I remained trapped beneath hundreds of pounds of thicket, my face pressed into the mud. It was dark and damp. The only sounds were the croaking of a large bullfrog and my frightened sobs. I couldn't move any of my limbs, and it had taken my father, our neighbor Mr. Schorn, his two teenage sons, and Max more than an hour to dig me out safely.

"Will?" It was Danièle. "I can see your legs."

I opened my eyes.

Dark. Muddy. Stuck.

The panic flared dangerously.

"You are at the smallest point in the tunnel," she told me. "The ceiling is very low, but the ground dips also. You need to slip into the dip and come up again, like going under a fence. Do you understand?"

"I'm not on my stomach. I'm on my side."

"Can you roll onto your stomach?"

"No."

"What about your back?"

"No, Danièle, I'm…I'm wedged in here like Winnie the Pooh in his fucking honey hole. I can't move. At all."

"Will, I am trying to help—"

"What should I do?"

"You have to relax. When you are tense, your muscles flex, get bigger. You have to relax and breathe deeply."

"Now's not the time for fucking yoga!"

"Listen to me, Will. It is true. I will breathe with you. Ready?"

I had nothing to lose. "Yeah."

"Okay, breathe…"

I followed her lead for a good two minutes, inhaling and exhaling through my nose until I wasn't thinking of anything anymore…and amazingly I felt the tension seeping out of my fear-locked muscles, the fight or flight response to my situation ebbing.

"Do you feel relaxed, Will?" Danièle said, her voice pacifying, like a hypnotist's. "Whenever you are ready…"

I tried rolling onto my back—and did so successfully on the first attempt.

I began inching forward.

CHAPTER 20

Once I had gotten beyond the dip, the rest of the way along the shaft had been much easier. Standing full height in a proper-sized tunnel again, the rush of surviving a close scare buzzed through me. Danièle, however, didn't share my high. Instead, she gave me a furious lecture on how to follow instructions next time.

"You know what?" Dreadlocks said to me, butting in. "I make mistake. You are *touriste* still." Zéro and Goat chuckled obligingly.

Rob's head popped out of the hole I had just exited. Grinning, he drawled, "Heeeeeeeeere's Johnny!" then somersaulted onto the ground. Pascal came next, extracting himself silently, like a spider. They were both covered in the catacombs' ubiquitous chalky mud and resembled true spelunkers. In fact, we all did.

I said to Rob, "Remember what you told me this place reminds you of?"

"Vages?"

"Well, you're right, because it looked like that wall just gave birth to you."

"And you were almost stillborn, boss. What the fuck happened?"

"I—"

"Okay, enough with your disgusting sex talk," Danièle said, cutting me off. "We are falling behind."

Shrugging on her backpack, she started after the scuba guys.

▼

We went straight for a while, passing several branching corridors, made a right, went straight again, passed more corridors, turned left. This zigzagging continued on and on until everything began to look the same to me, and I conceded that I was hopelessly lost. This made me realize how much trust I had placed in Pascal. He was the only one in our foursome who had explored where we were going. If he was so inclined, he could totally screw us over. Lead us the wrong way, sneak off with his map, leave us to go crazy and rot. Of course, he had no reason to do this. He was friends with both Danièle and Rob. Still, the fact he *could* made me uneasy. Maybe I was just on edge because of the recent scares with the Devil and the tunnel, but my life was literally in his hands.

When the passage we were now traversing opened wide, I caught up to Danièle and said, "What's up, Froggy?"

She made a face. "Are you trying to tease me? Because it does not bother me when you call me that." She cocked an eye at me. "You know, I have been thinking of a cataphile name for you."

"Cool," I said. "Any good ones?"

"I cannot decide between two. The first is Macaroni."

I was nonplussed. "As in the pasta?"

"No, it has meaning. It is from that song."

I frowned. "'The Macarena?'"

"No, you know..." She began to hum.

"'Yankee Doodle?'"

"Yes!"

"Are you teasing me now?"

"No, why? Americans are called Yankees. That is the name of one of your baseball teams. It is not derogatory."

"I don't want to be called Yankee or Yankee Doodle or

Macaroni, thanks. What's the other nickname?"

"Honeybear."

"Even better."

"You made me think of it when you said you were stuck like Winnie the Pooh in his honey hole. I found that cute. I think it is a good nickname."

"I can't wait until Rob and Pascal start calling me it."

"Oh—you are right." She frowned. "Maybe it can be my private nickname for you?"

I shrugged. "If you want. But I'm going to think of a better one."

"You cannot give yourself a nickname. That is not how it works."

"Speaking of Pascal," I said, changing course, "I was wondering about something." The ceiling lowered. I ducked accordingly. "What if he gets lost later on? You know, when we get closer to the video camera? He's only been that far once, right? So what if he makes a wrong turn and gets totally lost? It wouldn't be that hard to do."

"He won't," Danièle said confidently. "He knows the way. He has marked it on his map. We are perfectly safe."

"What if he loses the map, or something happens to it? The Devil could have taken it back at the Beach."

"That is the Beach. We know the way out from there—"

"I mean, what if the Devil had jumped us later, deeper, and took the lighters and map then? Would you or Pascal have been able to find the way out?"

"The Painted Devil would not do that. He would only take our stuff at the Beach because it is a popular spot, and he knows someone would come along again and find us."

"Come on, Danièle, you don't know that. The guy's a lunatic." I paused, remembering something. "What did he mean by 'Raviolis?' When he was speaking to Pascal, he said he hated Raviolis like us."

"I do not know for sure, but I imagine that is what he calls all cataphiles because many eat boxed dumplings—and leave the boxes around."

"He was acting as if he owned the catacombs. He called it his home. Do you think he actually lives down here?"

She shook her head. "He meant his...I do not know the word. Like a gang has."

"Turf?"

"Yes, like that. If he lived here, he would not have a job. He would not have anything to eat. He would have taken our money."

She was right, I thought. Besides, the uniforms he and his cohorts wore weren't ragtag; they were museum quality, which meant they would have been expensive.

"So what do you think he does for work?" I asked.

"If he has money, maybe he is a doctor or something."

"A doctor?" I said, surprised.

"Why not? One cataphile I met told me he worked for the president's office."

"You said catahpiles don't speak of that stuff."

"As a general rule. But some people, they like to talk. They tell you everything about themselves."

"Do you tell people you're a florist?"

"I am not a *florist*, Will."

The hardness in her voice made me glance at her. Her features had tightened.

I said, "I didn't mean that you're a florist, like as a profession...forever... I just meant..."

"I have a degree from one of the most prestigious universities in the country. I could get an important office job anytime I want. But I have no desire at this point in my life. I thought you understood that."

"Yeah, I do."

"No you do not. You think I am some poor gypsy girl with no plans for the future."

"I—"

"Because I do have plans."

"I believe you."

"I hope so."

I did—she was a smart girl—and I also understood where she was coming from. I sometimes didn't like telling people I was a travel writer. People never took writers of any ilk seriously. You could have a weekly column in a posh magazine, or be a bestselling novelist, and to anyone you introduced yourself to as a writer, their first impression would be of a struggling, eccentric loner that needed a regular nine-to-five job to straighten them out.

"What about them?" I nodded ahead to the scuba guys, feeling as though I should say something to temper the awkwardness that had bubbled between Danièle and me. "Did they tell you what they do?"

"No, they did not. But Citerne mentioned he is an accomplished diver."

"Dreadlocks?"

"Yes, the one with dreadlocks."

"Accomplished douchebag's more like it. What's he expecting to find down here anyway? Sunken treasure?"

"I do not know, Will," she said. "But look. They have all stopped. Maybe we will find out."

▼

Dreadlocks pointed down a gaping black hallway to our left and announced that was where the well was. The floor was cobblestone, covered with a sheen of crystalline water, unlike the murky stuff we had passed through earlier. Pascal got all excited. Danièle explained to me that he had never been this way before. It was marked as a dead end on his map.

"How far is the well?" I asked.

"Only ten minutes," Pascal told me. He glanced at Rob and Danièle. "It is okay?"

"I'm game, boss," Rob said.

"Me too," Danièle added.

Pascal looked at me expectantly.

"Yeah, sure," I said. "Let's fill in that map of yours."

▼

The well was made from carved stone blocks and rose three feet from the ground. The mouth was circular, twice the circumference of a manhole. There was no graffiti here, no litter anywhere, indicating not many cataphiles had been this way before.

While Pascal lit some tealights, Dreadlocks changed into a drysuit. He strapped the twin cylinder rig onto his back, then pulled on short, stiff fins and a compact mask with an opaque skirt. Sucking on the regulator that dangled from the manifold outlet, he lowered himself into the well, a bulky primary light in one hand, a reel of nylon guideline in the other. Everyone gathered close, watching as he sank beneath the surface of the water, though there was little to see. The water was cloudy. The lights from our lamps shattered into emerald oblivion.

The ripples on the surface finally smoothed, then disappeared altogether. The guideline remained taut. I said, "How deep is he going?"

Danièle translated my question. Zéro mumbled something back.

"Probably between five and fifteen meters," she told me. "That is how deep the others wells they explored have been."

The wait was tense. One minute inched into two. I glanced at Zéro and Goat, who were staring intensely at the water. They didn't speak, but I knew what they were thinking.

This was taking longer than expected.

I caught Rob's eye. He stuck his tongue out the side of his mouth and drew a finger across his neck. Danièle jabbed him in the ribs with her elbow.

Zéro glared at them, annoyed.

Finally bubbles materialized on the surface of the water, at first just a few, then an eruption. Dreadlock's head appeared next, his red helmet glistening.

Zéro and Goat heaved him up onto the lip of the well.

Danièle gasped, and it took me a moment before I saw the skull clutched in Dreadlock's hand. He spat the regulator from his mouth and jabbered in French. Everyone reacted with exclamations and outbursts. A rapid-fire discussion ensued. Eventually Danièle acknowledged my nagging for clarification and said, "He says there is a complete skeleton at the bottom of the well."

I waited for more. When nothing was forthcoming I said, "So what? This is the catacombs. There are six million skeletons down here."

She shook her head. "You do not understand, Will. This one is new."

"New?" I frowned. "You mean, from a recently deceased person?"

"Yes. There were clothes on it. A T-shirt, blue jeans, rubber boots."

"Fuck off!"

"Pascal thinks it was a woman."

I looked at Pascal. He had taken the skull from Dreadlocks and was pointing to different parts of it.

"What, he's a forensic anthropologist?" I said dubiously.

"He is writing his dissertation on the catacombs. He has studied many bones from here."

Pascal passed the skull back to Dreadlocks. They were both nodding.

"What's he saying?" I asked.

"Citerne is going to replace the skull. Then he will return aboveground and tell the police the location of the well. The catacops can investigate what happened."

"What about us?" I said. "Shouldn't we go with him?"

"Go with him?" Danièle seemed surprised by the question. "No, Will. He does not need us. Have you forgotten—we have another woman to look for."

CHAPTER 21

THE SUNDAY TELEGRAPH,
OCTOBER 13, 2013

Mummified Man's Body Found in Paris Catacombs

A group of urban explorers made a shocking discovery last week when they entered an illegal section of the Paris catacombs: the mummified body of a London man who had gone missing in the maze of underground tunnels two years before.

The body has been identified as Stanley Dunn, a twenty-three-year-old man from Enfield, London. In 2011, after friends of Mr. Dunn reported him and two other men missing in the catacombs, police conducted a three-day search to no avail.

A police source said that Mr. Dunn's remains were discovered in the far western reaches of the catacombs, a remote area that is seldom explored because of the extensive deterioration of the tunnel system there. The body was fully clothed and curled in a fetal position. The two other men remain unaccounted for.

Investigators believe the nearly perfectly mummified remains are due to the cool, dry environment in which they were discovered. Dr. Stephen Murphy, with the Department of Forensic Medicine at Kingston University, explains: "Some parts of the catacombs of Paris are damp, some are dry. In the latter situation, the decomposition process is slowed down, while both drying-up and autolysis of tissues prevail."

An autopsy is scheduled to determine the exact cause of death.

Claude Provost, a former police officer with the special brigade that monitors the catacombs, told Agence France-Presse that during any given year his unit would discover multiple bodies not reported by the press, some mummified, some not. "They go in to commit suicide," he says. "Others—they simply get lost and never find their way out again."

CHAPTER 22

I had an overactive imagination, especially when it came to death, and as we plodded through the labyrinthine warrens on our way to God knew where next, my thoughts were fixated on the remains at the bottom of the well. What had happened to the person—or the woman, if you believed Pascal's conclusion? Had she been sitting on the lip of the well, fallen backward, struck their head, and sunk like a stone? Then again, that would have presupposed the fact she was by herself. And who explored these tunnels by themselves? Hadn't Danièle said the first or second rule of the catacombs was never to go anywhere on your own?

Perhaps the woman's fate was the result of something more sinister then. Did someone dump her body into the well to conceal a murder? If so, had she been killed aboveground and transported to her final resting spot? Or had she been a cataphile who had the bad luck of running into a meth head or morphine addict—or the Painted Devil?

This last possibility gave me pause. I didn't think the Devil was a cold-blooded murderer. He was carrying around a flare gun fashioned to look like a pistol after all. He was nothing but a joker, a cowardly bully. Yet at some point did he take his harrying too far and cause someone to have a heart attack and need to get rid of the evidence?

Danièle said Dreadlocks would report the remains to the police, and the catacops would investigate. But what would they learn? What *could* they learn? All they had were teeth and bones to work with. These were helpful when investigators had dental records to compare them with, or when there were relatives with comparable DNA. But the woman was a total unknown. I guess they could determine her height, age, and ethnicity, and run theses details against recent missing person reports. If they found a likely match, then they could check dental records and so forth. On the other hand, maybe the catacops or whoever came to investigate would get lucky and discover a driver's license in a pocket of the jeans, or some other form of identification...something so they could give the skeleton a name and offer closure to the next of kin who would have been wondering why their daughter or mother or wife had not come home one day.

"*Ciel!*" Pascal called out.

"Sky!" Danièle said.

Ahead of me Rob ducked. I did too. The ceiling dropped sharply, and we were forced to troll-walk again. I kept close to Rob, taking advantage of the backsplash of his headlamp.

The next while went past in a blur of hallways and junctions angling off into black infinity. Some were finished with neatly mortared stone and well-designed archways, others were low-ceilinged and half-collapsed and riddled with sinkholes. We hiked for miles and miles, twisting and ducking, climbing and crawling, jack-knifing our bodies in ways most people never did. We went through more cat holes as tight as sphincters and chambers as large as ballrooms. The entire time Pascal kept up his brisk pace, stopping only to consult his map or when Danièle wanted to point out interesting features in the tunnels: the millennia-old fossils of sea creatures embedded in the limestone; black streaks on the ceilings from the torches of seventeenth-century stonecutters; relics of the wooden braces the quarry inspectors had used to shore up weak spots that could lead to cave-ins.

At one point we came across a rocky cavity filled with the skins of dozens and dozens of dead cats. Pascal said it was the lair of a minotaur-like beast that fed upon felines. When Rob told him to go fuck himself, Danièle shined her light above us, illuminating a vertical shaft that vanished into darkness. She explained we were standing at the bottom of a well that connected with the surface. Rumor was, a nearby Chinese restaurant was responsible for the discarded skins.

Despite my back hurting from all the bending over and my feet squishing inside my wet shoes and the run-in with the Painted Devil and the close call in the first cat hole and the discovery of human remains, I found the catacombs were growing on me. There was something quietly comforting about them. Prehistoric man's evolution, after all, had occurred within the confined spaces of caves and underground tunnels and alcoves such as these. They were where our ancient ancestors built their fires and cooked their meals, sheltered from ice- and thunderstorms, created their first works of art, raised their families. They were, in a sense, home.

I became so absorbed in my Paleolithic recreation I wasn't aware we had stopped until I ran smack into Rob's back.

"Sorry," I said, straightening my helmet. I looked around. "What's going on?"

"We have reached the Bunker," Danièle said. "The one the Nazis used."

I spotted another cat hole in the wall. "And I guess that's the entrance?"

She nodded. "Yes. But you are getting good at them, no?"

Pascal crawled inside first. I went second. Wiggling forward army-style, I'd found, was much easier than humping along on your back. I tumbled out the exit ass-over-tits and pushed myself to my feet. Pascal and I stood in awkward silence for a moment. I didn't want to wait there with him until the others arrived, so I wandered off to explore.

The walls here were constructed from red brick. Black wires snaked along some of them, beginning and ending at rusted electrical boxes. Decrepit oil drums sat here or there, remnants of a long-ago time. Spray painted fluorescent arrows pointed in conflicting directions. Hand-painted signs read: "*Rauchen Veroten*" and "*Ruhe*." I was familiar with these words, I had seen them around Paris, and they meant "No Smoking" and "Quiet" respectively.

The Bunker was a mini-maze in itself, consisting of numerous small rooms often separated by rusty iron gates and iron doors with round handles that resembled steering wheels, the sort you might find on big walk-in bank vaults.

I stepped past one door and peered into the dark beyond. I couldn't see much besides rubble and some rubbish.

I was about to head back when I heard the others approaching.

"Over here!" I called.

Danièle, Rob, and Pascal arrived a few moments later.

I hooked my thumb at the door. "What the hell were these used for?"

"Guess the Germans wanted to keep the frogs out of their hideout," Rob said.

I shook my head. "There's only the one entrance. They were meant to keep people *in*."

"In?" Rob squeezed past me for a look. "Shit, you're right. But why would they need doors like this to hold some poor shmuck? A bit overboard, don't you think?"

I did, and another possibility came to mind, though I decided it was too outlandish to mention.

▼

Pascal led us to a small grotto complete with an iron door for a table and stone slabs for seats. Several empty beer cans had been left on the table. Danièle slit the belly of one with a Swiss Army knife. She peeled the tin back and placed a red candle inside the hollow, transforming the contraption into a lantern. If she had string, she could have strung it up by the pop tab.

"*Voilà!*" she said, clearly pleased with herself.

"Nice work, MacGyver," Rob said.

She cast him a sharp look. "I do not care what you call me, Rosbif. It does not bother me anymore."

"MacGyver!" he barked amusedly. "It's not an insult, Danny. It's a compliment. He's like James Bond."

She eyed him suspiciously.

"It's true," I said. "A compliment."

"Thank you then."

We unloaded the food we'd brought onto the table to share. Danièle had a package of French biscuits with chocolate centers. Rob had beef jerky and Twizzlers and other junk food. I contributed a bag of trail mix, three apples, and a couple hard-boiled eggs.

"Eggs, boss?" Rob said.

I shrugged. "I didn't have much in the kitchen."

"Here." He tossed me a demon beer.

"No, Will," Danièle said, slapping my hand away from the can. "Do not touch that hobo drink." She withdrew the cardboard cask of wine from her backpack. "This is a nice Merlot."

"And I'm the hobo?" Rob said. "You're drinking out of a box, Danny."

"I do not litter, and bottles are almost as heavy to carry empty as they are full."

She poured two plastic cups and passed me one.

"*À votre santé*," she said.

"*Santé!*" Rob said.

"Cheers," I said.

We tapped drinks. A dollop of wine sloshed over the rim of mine.

I turned, looking for Pascal. He was at the far end of the room. He began hammering some sort of spike into the wall.

"China's down, Rascal!" Rob said.

"That is for his hammock," Danièle explained. "You might be warm now, because you have been moving. But the floor is so cold to sleep on. You will freeze if you lay on it."

Rob harrumphed. "Fuck you very much for the heads up,

113

Danny. What are Will and me going to do?"

"Will can sleep in my hammock with me. Only you will freeze on the floor."

I nearly choked on the wine in my mouth. I glanced at Pascal again. Had he heard? He was hammering away, and it didn't appear so. Still—what was Danièle thinking? She was well aware that Pascal liked her. His disdain for me was written in flashing neon. Did she really believe we were going to be lying up together in a hammock?

Rob was shaking his head. I could tell that he was debating with himself whether to say something or not.

"So how long are we resting here for again?" I said quickly.

"One hour," Danièle said.

"I'm not really tired."

"Then drink your wine. It will make you sleepy. You need to rest."

Pascal finished setting up his hammock and joined the table, choosing a spot between Danièle and Rob. He produced a self-heating meal of meatballs and tomato sauce from his backpack and poured himself a glass of wine from the cask. He wouldn't look at anybody, and now I wasn't sure he hadn't overheard Danièle's proposed sleeping arrangement after all.

Rob played some music from his iPhone to kill the background silence. Then he and Danièle began speaking to Pascal in French, apparently trying to pry him out of his shell. I took the opportunity to dry my feet. I slipped off my Converse and was surprised to find steam rising from my socks. I peeled them off, wrung the water from the fabric, and lay them flat on a stone. It felt both odd and pleasant to be barefoot in the catacombs, to feel the chalky dirt between your toes.

When I returned my attention to the others, a Ziploc bag full of greenish-brown marijuana sat in the middle of the table. Danièle was rolling a heap of it into a large joint.

I frowned apprehensively. I'd only smoked pot twice since the boating accident on Lake Placid, and both times it made me paranoid and anxious.

Danièle perfected a tight cone, licked the glue, and sparked the thing up. She took two tokes, then handed it to Pascal. It went to Rob next, then me. I took a single drag and passed it on. I held the smoke in my mouth, then blew it out without inhaling.

The joint went around the circle three times more before Danièle stubbed it out on the ground. Everybody except me had become mellow and heavy lidded.

Pascal lit a cigarette. I lit one too.

"I love it," Rob said, a small, wistful smile on his face. "Smoking a J in the catas. Hell yeah."

"I have a funny story," Danièle announced, sitting ramrod straight as she always seemed to do when she told a story, her eyes cloudy but bright. "Pascal and I, we were in this same room years ago, when we first started exploring the catacombs. We were smoking weed, hanging out, when five other cataphiles arrived. They were all drunk. One was so drunk he could not continue with the others. He passed out on the ground here, and his friends left without him. He snored so loudly. Pascal and I decided we could not leave him, so we waited until he woke up. But it turned out he knew the catacombs well, and he could find his own way out."

An expectant silence hung in the air.

"That's the story?" Rob said finally. "Why the fuck's that funny?"

"Because…" Danièle twisted her lips, as if she were reevaluating the story in her head. She shrugged. "Maybe it is not supposed to be funny."

"Nuh-uh, you said it was a funny story."

"Shut your mouth, Rosbif."

He held up his hands. "I'm just saying it wasn't funny."

"*Mon Dieu!*" she exclaimed. "You are infuriating!"

"Rascal," Rob said, draining his beer. "You gotta have a funnier story than that?"

Pascal scratched an eyebrow, nodded, and began speaking in French.

"English, bro," Rob said. "How's Will going to understand?"

Pascal scowled. "We are four people. Three speak French. Why must we speak English?"

"Because *four* speak English."

Pascal mumbled something that sounded like a curse.

"It's fine," I said. "Talk French. I'm good."

Pascal flicked his plastic cup away and stood. Ignoring Rob and Danièle's protests, he snatched his flashlight and stalked out of the room.

"He can be emotional sometimes," Danièle told me quietly.

I said, "Should someone go get him."

"Yes, Rosbif, you should go find him."

"Me?" Rob chuffed. "Why me?"

"Because you made him angry."

"Bullshit. I just told him to speak English."

"It is dangerous for him to be by himself—especially high like he is."

"I'll go," I said, grinding my cigarette out in the dirt.

"Fuck that," Rob said. "He'll never let you find him."

He stood and left.

"About time," Danièle said, exhaling heavily. "Some quiet."

I said, "You understand why he doesn't like me, right?"

"Who? Pascal? Yes, I told you. Because he has a crush on me."

"Right. So do you think it was a good idea announcing that we're going to sleep together? I think that's what he's pissed about."

"But we are going to sleep together."

"No, we're not."

"The floor—"

"No, Danièle, no way."

She sighed dramatically. "I cannot help it if Pascal has a crush on me, Will. What am I supposed to do, never be with someone to make him happy?"

"You could be more discreet."

"You know, you are cute when you are embarrassed." She

plucked some more weed from the Ziploc bag and began to grind it between her fingers.

"I've had enough," I said.

"Do not be a party pooer."

"Pooper."

"Do not be that."

I didn't argue. I simply wouldn't inhale again.

She lit the joint with my lighter and took several quick puffs to get the ember burning. But instead of passing it to me, she flipped it around, stuck the lit end in her mouth, and beckoned me with her finger.

"Aw, no..."

She made a mmm-mmm noise.

I leaned close to her. Our lips touched. Her cheeks puffed out as she blew hard. The reverse-engineered joint shot a jet of smoke straight into my lungs. I jerked backward and commenced a coughing fit. My eyes watered, my throat burned. It took me twenty seconds to get myself under control.

"That is good?" Danièle said, offering the joint to me.

I shook my head: no to it being good, and no to any more.

She took a long drag, then put it out. "Come, Honeybear, I want to show you something."

"What?"

"Come."

She stood, pulled me to my feet, gathered the beer can lantern, then led me from room to room. My head was spinning, and I had to concentrate on walking properly. I'd gone from sober to stoner-high in a matter of seconds.

Danièle entered one of those rooms with the iron doors. She went to a wall, raised the lantern to eye-level, and carved something into the brick with her Swiss-Army knife.

I peered over her shoulder. It was a crudely drawn heart encircling W + D.

"Should be H plus SG," I said. "Our catacombs names."

She turned, wrapped her arm around my neck, and kissed me. In the back of my mind was a vague thought of Bridgette

and the cop fiancé, then another of Pascal appearing un-
announced.

Danièle dropped the lantern, though it continued to burn.
She fumbled with my belt buckle, tugging free the prong. I
shoved her tight jeans down her thighs, then her panties, then
entered her. She moaned.

"Shhh," I whispered into her ear.

I slipped my hands around her waist, down over her but-
tocks. *She's so thin, almost like a child.* I'd thought the same
thing when we had sex at her place on the weekend, though I
didn't remember thinking that until now.

I've always liked rounded girls, like Bridgette, with curves
to them. Someone so thin felt oddly delicate—and light.

I heaved Danièle off the ground with little effort, pressed
her against the wall.

"Oh Will," she said. "Yes, keep doing that."

I was moving back and forth, trying to find a rhythm,
though it was somewhat difficult while standing and supporting most of her weight.

"Yes, Will, yes." She was kissing my neck, running her hands
through my hair. "Oh Will, don't stop, yes, yes, yes...it feels
so good." She locked her ankles behind my back and gyrated
her hips, talking dirtier and dirtier, kissing, biting, even fucking snarling...and, man, I got into it, losing myself. She was so
wild, so free, so sensual. Bridgette had never been like this—

Fuck Bridgette, I thought. I'm with Danièle now, and Danièle
is nuts, *fun* nuts, I'm totally enjoying this, and if this is what
sex is like with her...well, damn...why had I been brushing her
off for so long...we could have been doing this every night...

"Oh fuck Will fuck yes harder Will fuck me fuck me."

I did what she wanted and drove her harder into the wall,
my hands cupping the bottom of her thighs, holding her as if
she weighed nothing, moving harder, faster, my face buried in
her hair, breathing in the flowery freshness of it, her body so
thin, so sexy, like a model's... "You ready?" I grunted, unable to
hold off any longer.

"Yes, Will, yes!" Her fingernails tore my skin like claws.

I swallowed a groan as my body thrust and convulsed and turned to mush.

Danièle shrieked.

"*Shhh!*" I told her.

She all but screamed.

I shut her up with a long, forceful kiss.

CHAPTER 23

PASCAL

Pascal had never removed his helmet in the grotto, so he still had the headlamp to see by. No one had called out to him. No one had tried to stop him. He was sure they were all whispering about him in hushed tones. And what were they saying? Nothing good, or they wouldn't be whispering.

He had half a mind to sneak back when they were sleeping, collect his backpack, and leave the lot of them. But he knew he wouldn't do that. He didn't want to return to where he found the video camera by himself. He wasn't scared. He was sensible. Someone did something to the woman, murdered her most likely. It would be reckless of him to return there by himself. That's the reason he didn't stick around to search for her, or her body, in the first place. He'd played the footage, heard her screams...and then he was out of there. Anybody in his position would have done the same.

He passed through several rooms until he spotted another makeshift table nestled behind a support column. This one had been created with bricks for legs and a large circular saw for the surface. Sitting cross-legged on the ground, he took a cellophane baggie from his jacket pocket, tapped out two powdery lines onto the table, thought one was rather small, and added a third. He rolled a ten euro note and snorted all of them. The cocaine burned the inside of his right nostril. He sniffed deeply, then sat there listening to the silence as the high kicked in.

He had first tried coke three years ago when a friend offered him a key at a party. It didn't do anything for him. He didn't know whether it was bad blow, or whether he didn't do enough, but he didn't try it again until last July. The girl he was casually seeing, Marlène, pressed up against him while they were at some bar, kissed him, and stuck a small baggie in his hand. He went to a stall in the restroom, placed his credit card on top of the toilet tank, and tapped a single line onto it. For the next hour he was flying, and all he could think about was when Marlène was going to give him the baggie again. He got in touch with her dealer a few days later, a yuppie from an affluent family, and had bought from him ever since.

Pascal recalled how excited he had been to get Danièle high. They always entered the catacombs at night and rarely left before dawn. It was sometimes hard to stay alert, and blow seemed to be a perfect remedy for that. But when he offered her some at a party at the Beach, she flipped out, asked him all these questions. Where did he get it? Who did he get it from? How often did he do it? Defensive, he told her someone gave it to him, and, no, he'd never tried it before. She accepted this, and he'd never mentioned it to her again.

Still—maybe he should give *her* a lecture about smoking so much fucking pot…

"Rascal?" It was Rob.

Pascal considered not answering, but he said, "Here."

"Where?" Closer.

"Here." He peered out from behind the column and saw the light from Rob's headlamp ten meters away.

A few moments later Rob stood before him, a can of beer in each hand. He plopped down across the table. "I think I get what you dig about this place," he said affably, handing a beer to Pascal and cracking open the other. "Peace, serenity. Awesome."

Pascal rolled the cool can from one palm to the other. "Did Danièle send you over here to check up on me?" he asked. "Because I don't need her or you or anyone checking up on me."

"I'm not checking up on you, boss. I—" He saw the baggie of coke. "You're doing that shit down here?"

"So?"

"I thought you were getting clean?"

He shrugged.

"I don't want to bust your balls—"

"Then don't, Rob!" he snapped. "You and Danièle. Fucking Danièle. How much pot does she smoke? You never say anything to her."

"Blow's different. It's addictive—'"

"Addictive! You're going to lecture me on addiction now? What number beer are you on? Five? Six? And those ones—twelve percent? That means you've had like twelve regular beers. And you're going to tell me about addiction?"

Rob's lips tightened. He looked away.

Pascal immediately regretted the outburst, and he was thinking of something to say, a way to patch things up, when Danièle cried out.

CHAPTER 24

ROB

Rob and Pascal jumped to their feet. Rob grabbed Pascal's bicep, preventing him from leaving, but Pascal tugged free. "Something happened!" he exclaimed.

Rob shook his head, watching Pascal. Understanding registered in his eyes, and they thundered over. He flinched backward, almost as if slapped.

Rob wanted to say something to him, but there was nothing to say.

Pascal left.

▼

Rob didn't go after him. What was the point? If Pascal went off on his own, he would want to be by himself. If he went after Will...well, Will could handle himself.

Rob slumped back to the ground and listened. Danny, thankfully, didn't make any more sex shrieks, nor was there any sound of a confrontation.

He shook his head. Danny needed a fucking frontal lobotomy. What the hell was she thinking? He got it. She didn't like Pascal romantically. Fine. It was perfectly within her right to see other people. And it was a tough situation. She and Pascal were friends; they got together on a regular basis. He was bound to see her with other guys. Nevertheless, did she have to be so insensitive to his feelings? All the touchy-touchy stuff with Will in the restaurant and the van was one thing—but having an orgasm loud enough to wake the dead?

Rob skidded a hand over his face and wondered if they should cancel the whole expedition. Maybe Pascal was gone already, heading off to find the woman on his own, and maybe that would be for the best.

He brought the beer can to his lips, hesitated, then set it back on the table.

How many *had* he had? Two at the Beach. Two where they had set up camp. This one. Five.

Was he soused? He had a buzz, but he felt more high than drunk.

Goddamn Pascal had sounded like the wife there for a bit. Dev was on his ass all the time about the drinking. It seemed they fought about it every day. Rob simply didn't get her. He'd been drinking ever since they met, it didn't bother her then, but all of a sudden it's some sort of problem? Fuck that. He'd never become a Mr. Hyde, never gone on a drunken rampage, never turned violent, never done any of that bad-drunk shit. So it wasn't him who'd changed. It was her. They would be fine if she wasn't always nagging and getting into moods.

And that last fight, before he'd left to meet Pascal and Danièle at La Cave—sweet Jesus, that had been bad. He knew the gloves were off as soon as Dev stepped through the front door. She'd been tight, withdrawn, you could see it in her walk, and she had gone immediately to the master bedroom to change. Rob stayed out of her way, in the kitchen, making macaroni and cheese for the girls. When she came out, she was wearing an old tee and joggers.

"Guess your work thing's no black tie event?" he kidded.

"I'm not going to the dinner," she stated, opening the fridge and snatching a bottle of chardonnay.

Rob stopped stirring the pasta. "Why the hell not?" Though he knew why, of course. She was making a point. She was pissed off he was going out—"abdicating his responsibilities" was the phrase she liked to toss around—and to make a point, she would stay in.

Rob said, "The babysitter's coming in thirty minutes."

She took a wine glass from the cupboard, filled it nearly to the rim. "Better call her and cancel."

He clenched his jaw. He should have done just that: called the sitter, cancelled, let Dev stay in and sulk—but her behavior was so petty it was begging to be rebuked. Yeah, she'd told him about her work dinner last week, and yeah Pascal had only invited him to the catacombs two days ago, so she had dibs on going out, but situations like this were the reason babysitters existed. How was hiring one abdicating his parenting responsibility, for Christ's sake? He had been home with the girls—and Dev—all weekend. "I'm not canceling," he told her. "You're going to your dinner—"

"No, I'm not."

"—and I'm going to the catas with Rascal and Danny."

"Where you will no doubt get drunk."

"Give it a break, Dev."

"We have two daughters, and you're abdicating—"

"Don't fucking start!"

"Don't worry. The situation is resolved. I will stay home with Bella and Mary. Go have fun in the catacombs and drink yourself retarded."

Rob flicked the wooden spoon he was using to stir the pasta against the stove's stainless steel backsplash. It bounced back at him and clattered to the floor. He kicked it into the next room.

"Very mature, Robert."

"Fuck you, Dev."

He made to leave the kitchen.

"I don't know anymore," Dev said.

He stopped, turned. "You don't know?"

"Nothing," she said quietly.

"You don't know?" he repeated.

"Go, Robert."

"Go fuck yourself, Dev."

"Yes, maybe I will. Why not? I do everything else myself."

He grabbed his jacket and backpack from the foyer, then left the flat, slamming the door behind him.

▼

Shoving these memories aside, Rob lifted the beer to his lips again and took a long swallow.

CHAPTER 25

Danièle and I made our way back to the grotto hand in hand. Rob and Pascal were still gone, for which I was grateful. I was sure they would have heard Danièle, and I would rather be asleep, or at least lying on the ground and pretending to be asleep, when they returned.

We set up her hammock, she climbed in it, then told me to join her.

"You're crazy," I said.

"You will be cold."

"Better than getting an ice pick in my back when I'm sleeping."

"If you change your mind…"

I chose a spot a respectable distance away from her, stretched out on the slab of stone, used my backpack as a pillow, and closed my eyes.

I was still ridiculously high. Colors and images and bizarre thoughts flashed behind my closed eyelids. I tossed and turned, listening for sounds of Rob and Pascal's return. There was nothing but vacuum silence.

Gradually my mind shifted to Danièle, and how I felt about having sex with her for a second time. The answer: not as bad as I would have thought. That wasn't very romantic. I could imagine how she would react had I voiced this. But it was true. Despite the bombshell Bridgette had dropped on me earlier this evening, I couldn't simply shut off my feelings for her, and I'd assumed having sex with Danièle again would be nothing more than rebound sex, cheap and guilt-ridden with no emotional attachment. Yet that wasn't the case. In fact, I felt strangely invigorated. This wasn't solely because the sex was good—it was because I felt suddenly closer to Danièle than before. It was as if a mental curtain had been drawn back, and I was seeing her for the first time, only now realizing how special she was.

I didn't think Danièle and I would ever get too serious—how could we if I was only in France for another two months—but we had the present, didn't we?

I opened my eyes, saw Danièle watching me in the candle-light.

"You okay?" she asked.

"Yeah."

"You sure you do not want to join me?"

"Yeah."

"You sure?"

"Yeah."

She smiled lazily, closed her eyes. I did the same.

I had no idea of the time. I considered checking my wrist-watch, but didn't. It didn't matter. Time didn't matter down here.

Still, it must have been late, and I must have been exhausted, because moments later I was asleep.

▼

I crept silently through the Bunker, though it wasn't the Bunker, more of a mile-long corridor. Everything was bathed in red light. The floor was shiny with blood the color of jelly and lumps of what might have been fecal matter. Those iron doors with the steering wheel handles were set into the brick walls on both sides of me at even intervals. Some were fitted with barred windows. Occasionally a door stood ajar, a bad overhead fluorescent flickering inside, revealing mutilated bodies strapped to gurneys, experimented on, tortured, dismembered.

Straight ahead, at the end of the passage, was a door larger than all the others. I was drawn to it, slowly, inexorably. Abruptly the dream reality hiccupped, and I stood before the door. I spun the wheel handle. This activated a bolt-lock system. Gears churned. The door swung inward on silent hinges.

I stepped into a dark room and moved forward cautiously. Shadows closed around me so I could barely see a few feet ahead.

A noise froze me to the spot.

"Come out," I heard myself say.

Nobody appeared.

"Who are you?"

No reply.

I pressed on. Two steps, three.

A gurney rolled from the margins of my vision. The wheels clattered on the stone floor. It stopped before me. A person lay on it, covered by a white sheet.

"Hello?" I said.

No reply.

I pulled away the sheet. My lungs shallowed up.

Maxine lay on her back, staring at me with liquid-black eyes. Her face and hands were bloated and as white as a slug's belly. Her long hair was wet, as if she had just exited the shower—except she was wearing the off-the-shoulder cream dress with the hanky hemline that she had died in. The fabric was soaked through and clung to her body, so I could see the outline of her small breasts, her nipples. She sat up, swung her legs to the floor. "Am I going to miss it?" she said.

"Miss what?" I asked.

"The wedding."

"We're not getting married anymore. Things didn't work out."

"Things didn't work out for me either."

"I'm sorry, Max."

"You left me."

"She was drowning."

"*I* was drowning—and I'm your *sister*, Will."

Bridgette and I had wanted a small wedding, fifty guests, mostly family, some close friends. At the rehearsal dinner Max, who was one of Bridgette's bridesmaids, toasted me. It had been touching and honest and peppered with wit. Later that evening, after the older folks had retired to their bedrooms, Bridgette and I had been in the main lodge with all the bridesmaids and groomsmen. There were eight of us in total. Everyone was drinking except for Bridgette and me. We didn't want to be hung over for the ceremony the following day.

Brian, one of my best friends since high school, suggested we take the boat out for a spin. We had rented a fully-restored 1950s mahogany Chris-Craft Capri for the weekend. I was chosen as the designated driver.

I said, "That guy shouldn't have been out there without lights."

Max was still sitting on the gurney, still dripping wet. It seemed the water was leaking from her pores. "And we shouldn't have had so many people in the boat," she said.

"That didn't cause the accident."

"Didn't it?"

It had been a tight fit with the seven of us in the Chris-Craft —Liz, Bridgette's maid of honor, had remained behind on the dock—and everyone was laughing and whooping. Then, out of nowhere, a fisherman in an aluminum bass boat appeared directly before us. I should have plowed straight over him. If I had, he likely would have been the sole fatality. But how do you do that? How do you run a man down like road kill? Anyway, it wasn't my choice to make. Instinct took over. I yanked the wheel to the right, and the Chris-Craft's port side slammed into the bass boat's bow at a forty-five degree angle. The sound of the impact had been unremarkable, like a giant plastic milk jug buckling, followed by another, smaller wooden thunk. I think this was the Chris-Craft's propeller taking off the top of the fisherman's skull.

"You're right," I told Max. "There were too many of us. We were too loud. I didn't hear him. Still, he shouldn't have been out there without any lights."

I hit the water facefirst. It felt as though I'd kissed concrete. I went under and didn't know up from down. When I finally burst through the surface, the Chris-Craft was upside down. The wooden hull side rose from the water a few yards away from me. The six-cylinder engine gurgled and sputtered.

Three bodies, the only bodies I could see, floated nearby. They began to sink almost immediately.

"I was closer to you, wasn't I?" Max said.

"I don't know." I shook my head. "You were there one second, then gone the next."

"But you chose to save her?"

This was what no one understood. I didn't *choose* anybody. I didn't weigh the pros and cons of whom to rescue, the way you might ponder different brands of the same product at the supermarket. There was no reasoning, no calculating happening inside my brain at that moment. Nothing but an overwhelming need to act, to do something, anything.

And then I was swimming to where Bridgette's body had been moments before. I dived. The water was black. I couldn't see. But my hand brushed her back. I slipped my arms around her body and kicked until we surfaced.

The aluminum boat drifted past the stern of the Chris-Craft. I swam to it, pulling Bridgette with me. I gripped the gunwale and yelled for help. Liz, who was still on the dock, heard me. She woke my parents. My father and Bridgette's father arrived in one of the lodge's boats. Bridgette's father gave Bridgette CPR, while my father and I dived for Max, but the lake was too deep.

Police divers recovered all six missing bodies—including the fisherman's—the following morning.

"What was I supposed to do?" I said. "Bridgette was unconscious. If I let go of her..."

"So you let me drown?"

"I'm sorry, Max."

"And how did she repay you?" Maxine said, staring at me with those black, haunting eyes. "She left you. I wouldn't have left you, Will. I'm your *sister*. I wouldn't have left you no matter what anybody said."

▼

I woke stiff and cold and disorientated, though the fog cleared quickly. I was beneath Paris, in the catacombs. Candles glowed softly. I tried to recall the dream I'd been having. The Bunker that wasn't the Bunker. The rooms with the bodies on the gurneys, peeled open like oranges, their insides exposed— rooms my sleeping mind had no doubt extrapolated from the real one with the bank-vault door, the one I'd outlandishly speculated (but didn't say out loud) to be a torture chamber where Nazis had performed hideous experiments on the French freedom fighters they'd caught in the catacombs. And Max—Jesus, Max, in the dress she'd worn on the night she'd died...

I sat up, shaking my right arm, working feeling back into it. Rob lay a few feet away from me, folded into a ball to keep warm, a string of drool stuck to his cheek.

Then—*shft*. The sound was loud in the empty silence. I snapped my head toward it and started.

Someone stood at the doorway.

CHAPTER 26

He was old, over sixty, and tall, maybe six feet. Wisps of spider web hair curled out from beneath a mud-caked green bandana. What I could see of his face in the poor candlelight was pointed and fierce, his complexion as dusky as damp earth. He wore an olive fatigue jacket over a black T-shirt, black jeans, and black Doc Martins, maybe steel-toed. No backpack, no waders, no helmet. No cataphile gear whatsoever.

"*Zeigen sie ihren ausweist!*" he barked in a commanding voice.

"Jesus," I said, stumbling to my feet.

Rob stirred. "Wha...?" He saw the guy and sprang into a crouch, then lost his balanced and toppled backward onto his butt. "Who the fuck...?"

Danièle and Pascal sat up in their hammocks, alarmed.

"*Zeigen sie ihren ausweist!*" the man repeated.

"And if we do not?" Danièle said loudly, now standing.

The man seemed momentarily surprised she understood German.

"What's he saying?" I asked.

"He wants to see our IDs."

"IDs...?" The guy couldn't be a catacop; he looked like a bum. Another prankster then—?

Was he in cahoots with the Painted Devil?

The man switched to heavily accented English. "Don't you

133

know it is illegal to be here?" he said sternly. He eyed Danièle's cask of wine, Rob's empty beer cans. "What are you drinking? Mind if I join you?" Before anyone could reply he plopped down at the table and withdrew a bottle from his jacket. "Vodka and vitamins," he announced, offering it to Rob. "Try —it is good for you."

Grinning, Rob accepted the bottle—stupidly, I thought— and took a belt. A moment later he cringed, wooted, and shook himself like a wet dog, all at the same time. "Motherfucker!" He passed the bottle back.

Danièle and Pascal began dismantling their hammocks. I figured they wanted to move on as soon as possible. I was fine with that plan. The old guy's BO smelled like onions left uncovered in the fridge.

I fetched my still-wet socks and shoes and pulled them on.

"My name is Zolan," the man said, sipping the vodka as if it were water. A shark-tooth necklace encircled his neck. It seemed to be missing as many teeth as he was. Black wool gloves covered his hands. The tips of the gloves' fingers and thumbs were cut off.

"I'm Roast Beef," Rob said. "That's Stork Girl, he's Chess, and he's…"

I was at a loss. "Macaroni," I said.

Rob gave me a look. Zolan passed him the bottle again, and he took another belt, longer than the first. His reaction was tempered this time.

"Do you know someone called the Painted Devil?" I asked.

Zolan fixed me with dark and feral eyes. "Le Diable Peint is a stupid shit."

I blinked in surprise. Rob hooted in delight. Danièle and Pascal paused their packing and watched us.

"How do you know him?" I asked.

"I have come across him many times. He thinks he owns these tunnels. He knows nothing."

"He speaks German, like you."

Zolan spat. "He *pretends* to be German to scare people. He is a fake."

I was about to remind Zolan that he'd tried to scare us too, but Rob said, "How long you been coming down here, boss?" He was clearly enjoying the old guy's company—that, and the free vodka.

"A long time," Zolan said simply. "Do you have anything to eat? I'm hungry."

"Danny," Rob said, "where're your cookies?"

"I have packed them already."

"Break them out. Zolan's hungry."

Danièle had been buckling her backpack closed. She re-opened the main pocket, searched through it, and withdrew the package of biscuits. She offered them to Zolan. He shoved one biscuit into his mouth, then another, crumbs spilling onto his chest.

"Okay, everyone ready?" Danièle said. "We must continue now."

"So soon?" Zolan said, appearing disappointed by our abrupt departure. "Where are you going?"

"We're looking for a woman," Rob told him, oblivious to the smoldering look Danièle shot him. "Rascal—Chess found her video camera about a week ago. Someone was chasing her. She dropped the camera and started screaming and—"

Danièle kicked him in the side. "Get your stuff, Rosbif. We are leaving."

"Ow, Danny, fuck." But Rob seemed to get the message. He got his stuff together and stood. "Guess we're off, boss. Thanks for the drink."

The rest of us said goodbye, and we were at the exit to the grotto when Zolan said, "Val-de-Grâce."

We stopped, turned.

"Excuse me?" Danièle said.

"The video camera," Zolan said, his back to us. "It was beneath Val-de-Grâce."

Pascal and Danièle exchanged glances.

Then Pascal spoke for the first time: "How do you know

that?"

"I met the woman you talk about," he said. "I saved her life."

CHAPTER 27

Zolan's revelation caused temporary pandemonium. Everyone began talking at once, raising voices, no one making an effort to mask their skepticism. Zolan grinned, as if he had expected this reaction. He withdrew a folded square from his jacket pocket, opened it, and spread a map onto the table. We went over to examine it. Pascal gasped audibly, obviously impressed. Indeed, it made Pascal's beloved map look barebones in comparison, and I guessed it must have detailed almost every nook and cranny beneath Paris. It was hand drawn in black ink. The torn, aged parchment had at some point been laminated, and the plastic was covered with burn marks and stains and additional annotations scribbled in permanent marker.

Zolan pointed with a chipped and dirty fingernail to a spot in the upper right corner. "Val-de-Grâce hospital is here." He indicated another spot several inches away. Had there been a legend, the distance likely would have measured a few hundred meters or so. "The woman was here, fifty meters deep, in the lowest level of the catacombs."

Pascal bent close to study the squiggle of lines.

"Is this correct, Pascal?" Danièle asked him. "Is he right? Is that where you found the video camera?"

Pascal nodded slowly, clearly devastated, and I actually felt sorry for the guy. This had been his show, his little *Goonies* adventure, he'd been convinced he was going to find that woman's body. Now it turned out it was all for naught.

"So what happened to the woman?" I asked Zolan.

"I guided her to the surface," he said simply.

"I mean, why'd she scream? How'd you save her life?"

"Ah." He nodded. "There had been a cave in. She was separated from her friends. She wandered for two days by herself. Then she stumbled upon a nest of rats."

"Rats?" Danièle said, surprised.

"Large ones. The size of cats. They sensed she was weak, they sensed a meal, and they attacked her. I heard her screaming. That is how I found her. I scared them off. She had many bites. Here, here, here." He touched different parts of his body. "But she was okay. She could walk."

"You never took her back to get her camera?" I said.

"She never mentioned a video camera to me." He shrugged. "Given what she had been through, and the condition she was in, I suspect it had been the last thing on her mind."

▼

Danièle and Pascal moved away from the rest of us to converse with themselves. When they returned, they explained that the expedition was over and we would return the way we had come. It was an anticlimactic outcome, surely, but with the woman safe on the surface, there was little reason for us to continue farther. So we kitted up, turned our headlamps on, said goodbye to Zolan for a second time, then backtracked through the maze of World War Two era rooms. I was the last one to enter the cat hole that led back to the tunnel system at large, and when I climbed out the other side I was surprised to find Danièle and Pascal speaking to Rob in hushed, conspiratorial tones. "What's going on?" I said, going over to them.

"He was lying," Danièle told me in a harsh whisper. Her eyes were wide, luminous, concerned.

"Who?" I said, confused. "Zolan?"

"He told us the woman was attacked by rats," she said. "But

there are no rats in the catacombs, Will. There is nothing for them to eat here. He made that up because he does not want us to know the real reason why the woman screamed."

"And why's that, Danny?" Rob asked.

"Because he killed her," Pascal stated.

I looked at him, then at Danièle. They both seemed serious —and frightened?

"You two are bat shit crazy!" Rob blurted.

"You are!" Danièle said. "You drank with him. Like he was your best friend. You drank with a killer!"

"He's not a killer," I said.

She whirled on me. "Why not?"

"He's just some bum."

"Bums do not kill people?"

"I've never heard of any killing people, no."

"He sees a woman, lost, alone. He knows he will never be caught…"

A chill touched my spine as I pictured Zolan straddling the Australian woman, his dirty hands locked around her throat, squeezing, cutting off the screams that nobody could hear.

"I don't think so," I said.

"Okay, Will," Danièle said. "Why did he lie about the rats?"

"We don't know he did."

"There are no rats in the catacombs! None! Pascal and I have never seen one. Not one."

"Maybe not here, maybe deeper—"

"No," Pascal said, shaking his head adamantly.

"Think about it," Rob said. "If that old fuck Zolan killed this woman, why tell us he met her at all? Why incriminate himself?"

"Because thanks to you, Rosbif," Danièle said, "he knew that we knew where she was, and that we were going looking for her. He did not want us to discover her body. That is why he told us he guided her to the surface—so we would not go looking for her anymore."

"Man oh man," Rob said, chuckling. "You buying this, Will?"

Danièle and Pascal glared at me. They had become openly hostile.

"No, not really," I said.

Danièle huffed and started away from us down the corridor.

"Hey—where you going?" I called after her. "I thought we were going back? That's the wrong way."

She stopped, turned. Her face beneath her red helmet was set in a mask of determination. "No, Will, that is only what we told Zolan. We are still going to look for the woman, and we are going to find her."

CHAPTER 28

Twenty minutes or so after setting out from the Bunker we arrived at a low crawl that looked no different than the dozens of others we had passed through. However, this one, Danièle explained, was special. It was the entrance to the tunnel system beneath Val-de-Grâce.

Pascal called a break to study his map, and Danièle went on to tell me that from here on in the passageways became increasingly dense and complicated, and if we weren't careful, we could easily become lost and wander aimlessly forever—which, apparently, was exactly what happened to one of the first ever cataphiles.

His name, Danièle said, was Philibert Aspairt. He was the doorkeeper of the Val-de-Grâce hospital. He entered the quarries via a staircase located in the hospital's court. No one knew why for sure. Some suspected he was hunting for treasure. Others believed he was searching for the cellars of the Carthusian convent, under the Jardin du Luxembourg, to steal bottles of their famous Chartreuse. Whatever the reason, he was never seen alive again. Eleven years later, however, his remains were discovered in one of the quarry galleries. He was identified by the hospital key ring hanging from his belt. "You can visit his grave," Danièle concluded. "He was buried where his remains were found, and a tombstone marks the spot. Many cataphiles made a pilgrimage there every year, where they light a candle to pay respect to his memory."

"Have you been to the grave?" I asked.

She nodded. "Several times."

"Are we going to pass it tonight?"

"Unfortunately, we are not going in that direction."

A moment later Pascal stuffed his map away, said, "*Vas-y*," and ventured into the small tunnel.

I gestured for Danièle to proceed next. "Ladies first," I said.

▼

I had no idea how long we walked for, but it felt like a very long time. This section of the catacombs was honeycombed not only with the traditional horizontal hallways, but shafts angling through the stone at zany angles. It was as if we were wandering an Escher drawing where the rules of physics no longer applied.

Moreover, the farther we went, the less graffitied and more desolate the tunnels became, so soon they all looked the same. Pascal had taken a piece of chalk from his backpack and was marking the walls with arrows, to make sure we could find our way out again. But getting hopelessly lost wasn't my only concern. The ceilings and chambers here were crumbling and in shockingly bad shape, raising the concern of a potential collapse and cave-in.

Despite all of this, however, I had faith in Pascal's navigating abilities to see us through safely. He threaded the maze with an uncanny confidence, seeming to rely as much on experience and features in the rock he recognized as he did on his trusty map. A few times, though, he made wrong turns, and we were forced to backtrack and try different routes.

It was hard to gauge how deep you were when you were underground, as there was no sky to reference. When I asked Danièle to guestimate our depth, she only shrugged and told me we were very deep.

Then, from ahead of us, Pascal issued an excited cry. We joined him a moment later at a dead end. He was already fussing over a jumble of stones and timber in one corner, moving them aside piece by piece. We joined the effort and soon cleared all the debris to reveal a symmetrical hole in the ground. A rusted foot ladder descended into bottomless blackness.

"Jesus, Rascal," Rob said, whistling softly. "You went down there alone?"

"Yes, of course," he said proudly.

"How much farther is it to the fucking video camera?"

"Not far. Just down the ladder, then a short walk." He grinned. "And there is a surprise on the way."

▼

Pascal went first, and I volunteered to go next. I sat at the rim of the hole so my legs dangled into the abyss. Then with Rob and Danièle supporting me, I attached myself to the iron foot ladder. The rungs were cool to the touch, and rust sloughed off beneath my grip. I started down. The shaft was only a little wider than the width of my shoulders, which meant I had to keep my elbows tucked awkwardly into my sides. I felt as snug as a cigar in a tube case, and I tried not to think what would happen if one of the rungs broke free.

I guessed I must have descended a good thirty feet before the shaft opened around me. From there it was another ten or so feet until I reached the ground. My legs, I found, were rubbery from the stress of the descent.

I glanced up and saw a distant light: Danièle or Rob.

Pascal stood nearby, watching me.

"What?" I said.

"So you and Danièle—you like her, yes?"

Shit, I thought. Really? "Like her?" I said, playing dumb.

"You fucked her in the Bunker?"

"Listen," I said, keeping my voice neutral. "I don't know what's gone on between you and her in the past. But to my knowledge she's single now. And what she and I do is none of your business. Okay?"

"She's using you, you know? She just broke up with her longtime boyfriend. She is lonely. You're convenient."

"Thanks for the tip. I'll keep that in mind."

He glowered at me a beat longer, then stalked off into the darkness.

I stared after him. Fucking guy! *You fucked her in the Bunker.* Who said shit like that?

I should have told him, Yeah, I did, and it was fan-fucking-tastic.

When Danièle reached me a minute later, I was still fuming over Pascal's gall to confront me like he did. "Wanna know what your buddy asked me?" I said.

She frowned. "What?"

"He asked me if I fucked you in the Bunker."

"He *asked* you? What did you say?"

"What does it matter what I said?"

"Did you tell him it was true?"

"I told him it was none of his business."

"What's none of my business?" Rob asked. He was coming out of the hole in the ceiling.

"How ugly you are," Danièle said.

Rob slid down the remaining distance, fireman-style. "Seriously, you talking about me?"

"No, Pascal," I said.

"He heard Will and me making love earlier—"

"All right, Danièle, enough," I said, cutting her off.

"Yeah, I heard you fuck bunnies too," Rob said. "I was with Rascal. Couldn't you have turned down the volume a bit, Danny?"

"It was impossible," she said. "Will was too good—"

"Jesus," I said, and started off in the direction my arch nemesis had gone. Danièle was crazy. She really was. Bragging about the sex we had to her brother-in-law?

I passed through a doorway into a cavernous chamber and came to an abrupt halt. Giant, soaring pillars, carved to resemble naked men and women, lined the four walls. The capitals supported a bas-relief frieze depicting more naked figures, these masked and dancing alongside winged, mythological creatures. Perched atop the cornice were dozens of ornamental gargoyles, their grotesque faces staring down at us.

"Holy Zeus!" Rob exclaimed from behind me. "What is this place?"

"*Merveilleux*," Danièle said softly, stopping at my side. "Pascal told me about this room, but I never imagined... He thinks it was built by King Charles the tenth."

"The *king*?" Rob said.

"When he was still the Comte d'Artois. He often held torch-lit parties—what he called *fêtes macabres*—in the catacombs."

"Bullshit!"

"It is well documented, Rosbif. He invited all the ladies in waiting from the court in Versailles. It is rumored he built several grand rooms in which to host these parties. This was likely one of them."

"Parties?" I said, studying the frieze. "More like orgies."

Danièle nodded. "You are probably right, Will. The nobility of the Old Regime were a depraved lot. They also loved novelty. The fact they could dance and make love directly above millions of human remains would have been a thrill for them."

"Directly above?" I said, surprised.

Danièle took my hand. "Yes, you must see this." She led me to the center of the room. A stone staircase, built into the floor, circled away into darkness. "Pascal?" she called.

"*Ici!*" His voice floated up from below.

"Come," she told me, grinning.

My heart was beating fast in my chest as we started down the steps. They spiraled around a center column before terminating in the middle of a small stone island. My breath hitched audibly. Spreading away from us, for as far as the light from our headlamps would allow, was a sea of moldering bones.

"*Bienvenue à L'Empire de la Mort,*" Danièle whispered.

CHAPTER 29

THE SUNDAY TELEGRAPH,
DECEMBER 13, 2013

The Mystery of the Missing Skulls

In July, 2011, three British men were reported missing in the Paris catacombs. Two years later, the mummified remains of one of those men was discovered in a remote area of the tunnels. Now, in a final twist to this story, the decomposed remains of the two other men have also been found—and each was missing his skull.

The remains of Roger Hiddleston (24) from Bexley, London, and Craig Formby (25) also from Bexley, were located by French urban explorers—known colloquially as cataphiles—roughly ten miles from the remains of fellow doomed adventurer, Stanley Dunn (23) of Enfield, London.

According to police, DNA tests confirmed the victims' identities. What authorities have not yet determined is why their skulls were missing.

Although the answer may never be known for certain, police captain Vincent Reno told French radio he believes the skulls were taken by cataphiles as souvenirs. People, he asserts, are fascinated with human bones. He points to the 1.7

kilometer catacombs museum open to the public at Place Denfert-Rochereau as an example, where every day security guards catch dozens of tourists attempting to smuggle bones out of the ossuary in their bags and purses.

"And, yes, I think some cataphiles wouldn't hesitate to take the skulls of those two London men, who were fully clothed and obviously explorers like themselves. Because they have become desensitized to death. They see so many bones, there is nothing special to them anymore, nothing sacred. A human skull is something that would make a good paperweight, or a candle base. If you ask me, they are sick, they don't belong down there, nobody does, and they need to face much greater prosecution by the law."

Currently, specially trained police officers conduct regular patrols of the catacombs and issue a court summons to anyone they catch. Offenders risk fines ranging from sixty to one hundred euros.

CHAPTER 30

It was a dizzying montage of death on display: rotten femurs and cracked craniums and broken pelvises and nude jawbones and empty eye sockets that seemed to stare jocularly up at you. They were all shapes and sizes, all once part of living, breathing people. Artisans and aristocrats, peasants and children, revolutionaries and soldiers—now anonymous, disarticulated, individually forgotten.

Bones in a mass grave.

"Oh man!" Rob said, coming up behind Danièle and me. "Look at this shit! What do you and Rascal do down here, Danny? Surf the mosh pit of humanity's dead?"

"I have never been to this ossuary before," she said. "I have been to the popular one, beneath Montparnasse, and some others. But they are not like this, not this big..."

Pascal, I noticed, was a dozen yards away, kneeling at the edge of the island, his back to us.

"*Qu'est-ce que c'est?*" Danièle called to him.

He mumbled something.

"What'd you find, bro?" Rob said.

Pascal got to his feet and came over to us. He passed what appeared to be a chunk of spine to Danièle and pointed to different lesions on it. "Malta fever," he said.

"Fever?" Rob said, shying away. "Better not be contagious."

"*Vous êtes stupides*," Pascal chided. "You cannot catch anything from a bone."

"How did that sucker catch it?"

"From an infected animal, probably their milk. I think he or she must have been a cheese maker."

Danièle passed the vertebrae to me. It was slightly spongy, like old wood, and covered in a layer of grime. I passed it on to Rob and thought of hand sanitizer.

Rob turned it over a few times, the way you examine something not particularly interesting, then gave it back to Pascal, who stuck it in his backpack.

I frowned. "You're taking it?"

"*Oui*. I need to study it more closely."

"You can't steal it."

"I am not *stealing* it," he said acidly, and for a moment I was bizarrely certain he was going to lunge at me. But the manic look in his eyes passed. "I will bring it back."

"So which way now?" Danièle said quickly, too quickly, and I suspected she'd seen the look in Pascal's eyes also. "Which way to the video camera?"

"*Vas-y*," Pascal grunted, starting off.

"Whoa, wait up, boss," Rob said. "I'm not walking over dead people."

"It is okay," Danièle told him.

"Okay? How would you like it, Danny, if a bunch of people went stomping around on your skeleton one hundred fifty years from now?"

"Whoever they once were, Rosbif, they are dead now. They do not mind if we step on them."

"I'm with Rob," I said. "It's, I don't know, disrespectful."

Danièle waved vaguely. "Does any of this look respectful to you, Will? These people have been dug up from their original resting ground, their skeletons broken apart to make them easier to transport, and dumped into these rooms like garbage. They have already suffered much more indignation than us walking on them would cause."

Apparently the discussion was over, because Pascal and Danièle set out across the bone field.

"Guess we don't have a choice, bro," Rob said, and followed.

I stepped where Rob stepped, to mitigate damage. Nevertheless, femurs cracked and splintered beneath my weight, and I wondered how deep the bones went. Five feet? Ten? More? I was having a hard time getting my head around the sheer number of dead. It made me feel not only mortal but insignificant. The ego liked to trick you into thinking you were the center of the universe, but in truth you were nothing but a dust mote in a never-ending shaft of dimming light. Really, I thought, how was my life, or Rob's, or Pascal's, or Danièle's any different, any more meaningful, than the lives of all the lost souls beneath our feet? Like us, each of them once had dreams, fears, beliefs, agendas, a sense of self-worth…and look at them now.

Bones in a mass grave.

This train of thought wasn't very cheerful, so I stopped with the introspection and concentrated on placing one foot carefully in front of the next. When we reached the far wall, we followed it left to a window that looked into another room filled with more bones. These were piled so high there were only a few feet between the uppermost ones and the ceiling. Pascal and Danièle climbed through the window eagerly, Rob and I less so. We crawled forward on our hands and knees, the carpet of brittle bones crunching beneath us, until we came to a crack in the ceiling.

I was the last to pull myself up and through it, relieved to discover that it opened into a regular stone hallway.

Everyone was several yards away, huddled close, discussing something of apparent importance. Danièle stepped aside as I approached, her eyes shining excitedly, and I was able to see what all the fuss was about.

On the floor at their feet, a bone-arrow pointed ahead into the darkness.

CHAPTER 31

"**T**hat was in the video!" I exclaimed, bending close to examine it.

"Yes," Danièle said. "These are the hallways where the woman shot the last of her footage."

Rob said, "Where she thought someone was following her..."

"Where *Zolan* was following her," Danièle stated.

Pascal spoke in French and started off.

"He says we must hurry," Danièle told me. "We are behind schedule. He has been late for class too many times before, and he cannot be late anymore."

I succumbed to my curiosity, tugged up the left sleeve of my pullover, and checked my wristwatch. It was 4:17 a.m. This surprised me not because it was almost dawn, but because I'd had no idea of the time whatsoever. For all I knew it could have been 1 a.m. or 8 a.m.

A short trek later we came to the first and only graffiti in this hallway. It was the painting of the stickman that the woman had paused to study in her video. The lines were quick, frantic, and there was little detail, not even a face. The arms and legs were spread wide, resembling someone making a snow angel.

"Spray paint," Rob observed, scraping the paint with a fingernail.

"Who do you think made it?" I asked.

"Probably whoever made the bone-arrows."

"Zolan," Danièle said again.

"Give the guy a break, Danny," Rob said.

"Why should I? He admitted he was here."

"I'm sure a lot of people have been here."

"Does it look like that to you? Where is the graffiti, the garbage? Where are the beer cans? There is nothing—nothing except some bone-arrows and *this*." She waved at the stickman.

Rob shrugged. "That doesn't mean anything. We're not going around spray painting the place, are we?"

Danièle folded her arms across her chest. "Why are you protecting him, Rosbif? Did his vodka poison your brain?"

"You frogs have to get over your prejudices and not judge people based on how they look."

She scowled. "I told you not to call us that."

"Yeah, yeah, it's not fair to amphibians, I forgot."

"*Vous êtes une pomme de terre avec le visage d'un cochon d'inde!*" Danièle fumed.

Pascal continued on. Rob, laughing, went with him.

"What did you say that was so funny?" I asked her.

She seemed put out. "It was not supposed to be a joke. It was an insult."

"What did you call him?"

"A potato with the face of a guinea pig. My mother used to say it to my father...before he left her."

"When you were seven," I said, recalling what she'd told me during one of our lessons.

"Yes..."

"Your mom never told you where he went?"

"She never talked about him. She erased him from her life. A couple years later, when I had the flu and was allowed to stay home from school, I went searching for the family photo albums. I found them in a box under her bed. There were no photos of my father."

"She threw them all out?"

"She cut him out of all of them. Actually, she did not cut *him* out. That would have left obvious gaps in the photos. Instead she cut everyone else out and pasted them back together again."

"So you don't know what your dad even looks like?"

"I have a vague memory, but that is all."

I contemplated what it would be like to grow up without a father. It seemed a pretty brutal thing for a kid to go through. "How's your mom now?" I asked.

"She is well. She has several boyfriends."

I raised an eyebrow. "Several?"

Danièle nodded. "She meets them on some online dating website. She is only forty-eight. And she is still pretty."

"Like you." The words were out of my mouth before I realized what I'd said.

Danièle's eyes sparkled. "You know, Will, that is the first time you have told me something like that."

"Really?"

"Yes. And you can tell me that I am pretty more often. I will not be offended."

I didn't say anything.

She sighed. "Why are you so mysterious?"

"Mysterious?" I shrugged lamely.

She tiptoed and kissed me on the lips, pressing her body against mine.

"Want to come over tonight?" she asked playfully.

"I think I'm going to need to catch up on my sleep."

"You can sleep all day. Even better—you can sleep at my place in the afternoon, then cook me dinner in the evening."

"Oh shit," I said.

Danièle frowned. "You have another excuse?"

"What do you mean 'another?'"

"Are you going to be hung over again?"

"No…but I already have dinner plans."

"With who?"

"My neighbor."

Danièle glared at me dangerously. "Are you dating her?"

"No!" I said. "She's like ninety. Her husband died a long time ago. She's lonely. She's always catching me in my hallway and giving me desserts and stuff. So earlier today—yesterday —I told her I was studying French cooking and wanted some feedback."

"You study French cooking? You have never told me this."

"I don't. I made it up so she wouldn't feel like she was intruding."

"How do I know you are not making up that this woman is ninety? Maybe she is twenty and beautiful?"

I hesitated. "Come then."

"You really want me to?"

"I'm sure Madame Gabin won't mind."

"Madame Gabin, hmm?" Danièle studied me. "Yes, okay. I think I will join you and this Madame Gabin for dinner. And, Will, she better be as old as you say she is, or you are dead meat."

▼

We caught up to Rob and Pascal at a T-junction. The woman in the video had gone left, so we went left also. A little ways on Pascal stopped and announced, "This is where I found the video camera. It was there, next to that puddle. See, I marked the wall." He pointed to a chalk asterisk.

Rob peered ahead into the dark. "Did you go any farther, boss?"

Pascal shook his head. I was tempted to make a scared barb, to get even with him for the ones he'd sent my way, but I didn't because I didn't blame the guy for turning tail. Watching that video down here, alone, right where whatever happened had happened...I wouldn't have stuck around either. I asked, "How much time on the video passed from the point she dropped the camera to when she screamed?"

"Forty-one seconds," Danièle told me. "Which means her

body should be right up ahead somewhere."

CHAPTER 32

I t wasn't. We searched for more than twenty minutes, checking every crumbling and bone-riddled room we passed, continuing along the hallway for much farther than should have been necessary. When we stopped for a rest, I said, "Looks like Zolan was telling the truth. He found her and showed her back to the surface."

"I still cannot believe his story about the rats," Danièle said, shaking her head. "I am sure he was trying to persuade us not to come down here. Why would he do that if he had nothing to hide?"

Pascal took off, mumbling something in French.

"He needs to drop a deuce," Rob translated for me, flopping down on the ground. "You have to go?"

I didn't, and neither did Danièle. We sat as well.

"He seems upset," I said. I fumbled in my pocket for my pack of Marlboro Lights and lit one up.

Danièle nodded. "He really wanted to find the body."

"It was his MacGuffin," Rob said.

"His what?" Danièle said.

"Movie talk," I said. "The object of a quest."

"Ah, yes." She nodded again. "The body would have been his McMuffin."

"MacGuffin," I said.

"Right. McMuffin," she repeated, smiling, and I realized she was having me on.

Rob noticed the flirting too. "You guys want a room or something? There are plenty down here."

I exhaled a stream of smoke and decided I was in a good mood. Part of the reason for this was the fact the expedition was coming to a close. As much as the catacombs had grown on me, I was filthy and wet and tired and more than ready to leave. Also, I was looking forward to the dinner with Madame Gabin and Danièle later this evening. I had no idea what I was going to cook, but I figured I could find some French recipe on the internet. And afterward...well, Danièle would stay over, wouldn't she? That seemed like a big step for me: having a woman sleep in my bed. True, I'd already slept in her bed, but her sleeping in my bed, that felt significant, intimate, like a relationship. "Hey, Rob," I said. "You got any of those beers left?"

"Hell yeah." He unzipped his backpack, took two out, and lobbed me one.

We cracked the tabs and foam spurted festively.

"You know," Rob said, "this has been surprisingly fun. Thanks for the invite, Danny."

"I did not invite you," she told him sternly. "Pascal did."

"But you okayed it."

She shrugged. "Yes, well...I like sharing the catacombs with people. I guess I am happy you had a good time."

"Wow," I said. "Are you two having a moment? Is this a breakthrough?"

"She says shit about me all the time," Rob said, "but it's just for show. She loves me."

"I do not!" Danièle said.

"A little bit."

"Not even a little bit."

"Bullshit, Danny. If I wanted a sister sandwich, you'd be all over it like a fat kid on a McMuffin."

"MacGuffin," she said, and produced one of the joints she had rolled back at the Bunker. She sparked it, then passed it to me.

I was about to decline, but decided what the hell. We deserved a small celebration. "So where's the other exit Pascal knows about?" I asked, inhaling. The smoke burned the lining of my throat, tickled my lungs. I held it there, then exhaled.

Danièle said, "It is back past that crack in the floor."

"Past it? You mean we don't have to crawl over the bones again?"

"No."

"Thank God. You know how many bones we broke? Rob, you were like a bull in a china shop. You must have smashed five or six skulls."

"And you didn't?"

"Skulls? No, none. I avoided touching them."

"Hey," Danièle said, a bit spacey. "Beef comes from a cow, right? And a bull is a male cow, right? So is it not funny that I call Rob 'Rosbif,' and you call him a bull?"

Rob shook his head. "I hate to be the one to break this to you, Danny, but you're just not funny. You try too hard."

"I am too," she protested, waving at the smoke in front of her face.

"Nope, you're not. When God was giving out shit, you got the looks, and you got a pretty good brain, but I think you forgot to pick up your sense of humor on the way down to Earth."

"Maybe you do not think so, but other people do. Will, am I funny?"

"Of course he's going to say you are. You two are shagging."

I glanced down the passageway, to check that Pascal wasn't within earshot. The corridor was empty.

"Anyway, Danny," Rob went on, "regarding your sense of humor problem—"

"I do not have a problem."

"How about this: whenever you tell a joke, just say 'joke' afterward, so we know it's a joke."

"You are a smart guy—joke."

Pin-dropping silence.

Then Rob exploded in laughter, cackling so hard I thought he might choke. It was contagious and I got going too until my eyes started to water.

"See," Danièle said proudly. "I *am* funny."

CHAPTER 33

PASCAL

P ascal could hear them laughing. Having one big party. Without him.

Mumbling a curse, he took the roll of toilet paper from his backpack and wiped his ass. He stood, pulled his boxer briefs and pants up, then his waders. He turned and kicked dirt over the small latrine he had dug with the forked end of his hammer. Some cataphiles were not so considerate. They came to the catacombs only to drink and smoke and party, and they left the place a mess. They were slobs—the Painted Devil had been right about that much at least—and they were getting worse year by year. Some of the old-timers Pascal had met, veterans who'd been visiting the catacombs for decades, told him it was a different world pre-nineties. Back then, they said, it was a closer-knit community. They would still have parties, but they weren't the trashy type that Danièle liked. Mostly they would cook, they would bring cooking pots and food, and they would have cooking contests.

Then the internet came along and changed everything, made it so much easier to find a guide, someone with a map. Now you had the idiots who took pictures and posted them all over social media and left their garbage behind and shit every-where—all of which cheapened the experience, killed the feeling that you were exploring a forbidden place.

Really, in the main network beneath the 14th arrondissement, there was nothing sacred anymore. If you wanted a real adventure, you had to press farther, deeper, go where no one had been before.

Pascal stomped the ground flat and was about to return to the others when he heard a noise. Some sort of cluck. It wasn't very loud, but when you were used to hearing nothing, you heard everything.

It came from the far end of the room.

"Rob?" he said. His headlamp revealed nothing but support pillars and, beyond them, shadowed walls.

Rob didn't answer.

Pascal thought of the video footage, heard in his head the woman's manic screams.

"Rob?" he repeated.

Nothing.

He was still holding the hammer, which gave him some confidence. He unclipped the MagLite from his belt with his free hand and swept the powerful beam across the room.

Nobody.

He started forward, slowly, peaking around each pillar he passed.

At the far end of the room a door led to a connecting chamber.

He hesitated, considered turning back.

Another cluck. Almost like the sound you make when you click your tongue against the roof of your mouth.

Pascal froze. Everything inside him froze.

Who was making that sound?

What was?

Get out of there! Go! Now!

He whirled to leave.

And screamed.

CHAPTER 34

O nce I got my giggling fit under control, Danièle offered me the spliff. I shook my head. I was already higher than I wanted to be. Rob finished it off while I lit another smoke. I was chain smoking and didn't care.

"Cool how Rascal knew what that *fromager* died from based on his bones," Rob said. He was lying on his side in that recumbent position he favored. His eyes were heavily lidded, and his usual in-your-face energy had been replaced with lazy meditation. "Weak way to go, no doubt, but better than the fate of some of the other sad fucks in that grave, I guess."

"Have you ever wondered what the worst way to die is?" Danièle said. She was slumped against the wall so low her knees poked up in front of her face.

"Getting lost in an underground maze," I kidded.

"No, getting torn in half," Danièle said. "They used to do that, you know. You bend two young trees close together, tie a hand and a foot to each one, then release the trees."

Rob said, "Have either of you two ever seen anyone die?"

Danièle shook her head. "But I have seen a body. I was very young. My sister and I—"

"Dev was with you?" Rob said, surprised.

"Yes. Devan is Rob's wife, Will."

I opened my mouth, to tell her I'd gathered as much, but articulation seemed too difficult right then. I nodded.

Danièle continued: "We were playing in this construction

site in our neighborhood. The developer had dug holes for the basements of two dozen houses. Sometimes there were long pieces of wood descending into the pits, so the workers could climb in and out. Dev and I were looking for puddles to splash in because it had just rained, and we found a boy lying facedown in one of the excavated basements. He lived three blocks away from us. I had seen him at school, but I did not know him personally. He hit his head on a cinder block, but that is not how he died. He died from drowning in two inches of rainwater."

Rob frowned. "Dev never told me this."

"We were so young. Maybe she forgot."

I shifted uncomfortably, thinking of a different topic to move onto, when Rob said, "There was this guy in my high school, he was a year or two older, his name was Claude Linder. He was a rich kid, his parents had their own twin propeller plane, which he was learning to fly. One day I was at the field where I played soccer twice a week. We were in the middle of the match when this plane comes swooping over us, smoking and too low and shit. It turned out Claude had hit some geese and they fucked up the engine. The refs stopped the game, and the coaches and parents called everyone to the sidelines. The plane banked, then came back. Claude touched it down safely, used the field as a fucking runway, but the field wasn't long enough, and he smashed through the chain-link fence at the far end."

"But he was okay?" Danièle said.

"No, Danny, the guy died. Why do you think I'm telling this? When he went through the fence, the propeller knocked one of the metal fence posts back through the windshield. It impaled Claude right here." Rob tapped his chest above the heart. "When the first of the soccer moms and dads got there to help, he was still alive, but pinned to the seat. He died before the cops and firefighters could cut him free."

"That is awful," Danièle said, and squirmed. "He was just stuck there?"

"Saw him up close and personal. Wish I hadn't. I had nightmares for months after that." Then, to me: "What about you, boss?"

"What about me?"

"You gotta know somebody who's croaked."

I shook my head, wondering if he could tell I was lying—

A scream erupted from farther down the tunnel.

We started, then leapt to our feet. My head spun from the pot.

"That was Pascal!" Danièle exclaimed.

"Fucker's just horsing around," Rob said.

"I do not think so." She cupped her mouth with her hands and called Pascal's name. When he didn't reply, she called it again, and again.

I didn't like this one bit.

"Rascal!" Rob shouted, angry. "Stop screwing around!"

Silence.

"Come on," Danièle said to us, then started in the direction the scream had come from.

She and Rob continued to call Pascal's name, while I tried to clear the fog from my thoughts and figure out what the hell was going on. Had Pascal tripped and cracked his head open, like that kid Danny told us about? Was he lying facedown in a puddle of water, dead? Had he fallen down a well?

No—that scream had not been one of pain; it had been fear, fear and surprise, as if all six million catacomb dead had risen from their graves before his eyes.

So was Rob right then? Was this all a joke? Was Pascal hiding somewhere, readying himself to jump out from the dark and yell, "Gotcha!?"

Twenty meters onward a room opened to the right. We stuck our heads inside, glanced around. It was large and filled with a number of support pillars.

A lot of places to hide.

"Rascal!" Rob shouted. "Seriously, bro! This ain't cool!"

"He never plays these games," Danièle said, her concern reflected clearly in her face.

"Are you guys having me on?" I said. "Because I'm pretty fucked right now, and it's not funny—"

"We're not fucking with you," Rob said, stone-faced. "Rascal's fucking with *us*. There!" He pointed to the corner. "See the dirt?"

We went closer to examine it. There was a faint odor in the air.

"Knew it!" Rob said, and he half chuckled. "Rascal! Get your ass out here! We know you're here! We can smell your shit!"

No answer.

"Is that a door?" I said, nodding across the room.

"Yes, you are right," Danièle said. "He must be through there."

We approached quietly, apprehensively. I don't know why we bothered with the stealth, but it felt like the right way to proceed.

This new chamber, it turned out, was smaller than the last one. There were no pillars to hide behind, and we could see it was empty.

"Where the fuck is he?" Rob said, frowning.

"Wait—what is that?" Danièle pointed to a dark shadow in the lower portion of one wall.

We went closer and discovered a cat hole.

The three of us crouched before the crevice, peered inside. It was a couple feet high and appeared manmade, perhaps carved with a pickaxe or some other crude tool. It stretched away into blackness.

"Rascal?" Rob called, though not as loudly or confidently as before. "We're not coming in after you."

No answer.

"Oh God," Danièle whispered suddenly, grabbing my wrist so tightly I winced. "Look! There! Look!"

I looked. I had been so focused on the hole I hadn't paid attention to the rock surrounding it.

"Is that...?" I started.

"Blood," Rob finished.

▼

"Maybe he tripped and hit his head and got disorientated?" I said.

"And crawled into a fucking hole?" Rob said skeptically.

"Then what happened to him?" Danièle demanded.

I bent close to examine the blood. "It's fresh, and it looks like a handprint." I turned, scanning the ground. "There—there's more blood. And there." We followed a string of small black splotches back to the entrance to the room.

"He must have hit his head here—"

"He didn't hit his fucking head, Danny!" Rob said. "Someone surprised him, knocked him out cold, and dragged him off."

"*Zolan,*" she hissed. "It has to be. He followed us down here."

"There was no woman, no body," I reminded her. "Why would he follow us? Why would he attack Pascal?"

"Because he is crazy."

"What about the Painted Devil? He was pissed we scared him off. He lost face. This could be his revenge.'"

"But how did he get past us?" Rob said. "Whoever attacked Pascal was ahead of us."

"Zolan knew we were going to the spot where the video camera was," Danièle said. "Maybe he knew a different way to get here."

"And arrived here ahead of us and waited?"

"Maybe..."

"Whatever," I said, frustrated. "Guessing's not helping any. We have to do something."

Rob nodded. "We gotta go get Rascal—now. He's injured."

I looked at the cat hole. "You want to go in there?"

"We have to. We can't just leave."

"Yes," Danièle said, swallowing. "We have to go after him."

"What if it's a trap?" I said.

"We don't have a fucking choice!" Rob said.

He was right, I knew. We couldn't abandon Pascal. Nor could we stand here discussing our options. His condition could be critical.

We returned to the wall. Rob dropped to his knees and peered inside the hole. It was large enough to enter with his backpack on. He glanced up at us, as if for confirmation that we were really doing this, then crawled inside and disappeared.

CHAPTER 35

ROB

This was insane, Rob thought as he snaked forward deeper into the tunnel. Total fucking insanity. Had someone really attacked Pascal?

He still wanted to believe it was all some elaborate joke, but Pascal wasn't the practical joker type.

So who had gotten him?

What had gotten him?

Rob almost laughed at that, but didn't, because scientists were discovering new species all the time. Just last week he read about this team of zoologists and filmmakers that descended into a never-before-explored caldera in Papa New Guinea and documented all this nature-gone-wrong kind of shit, like frogs with fangs and kangaroos that lived in trees and woolly rats that grew as large as dogs.

So what if something even more crazy—something with lobster-claw horns, or a tail that could shoot spikes, or three heads and translucent skin—lived down here? What if—

Rob stopped and sniffed. God, what was that smell? It had come from nowhere.

"Ugh," Danièle muttered a moment later. "What *is* that?"

"Don't know," Rob said, peering ahead. The shaft continued straight for another ten feet before turning sharply to the left. "It's coming from ahead though—"

The sentence died on his lips. A steel fist squeezed the air from his lungs.

"Back up, Danny," he managed in little more than a breathless croak. "Back up right now."

CHAPTER 36

Fear ballooned inside me when Rob began speaking in the soft, scared-stiff way of someone who'd just realized they were standing in the middle of a viper pit.

"What is it?" Danièle demanded. "What can you see?"

"Back...the fuck...up." Then Rob's voice rose several octaves. "Oh no... *Oh shit oh shit—go back!*"

Danièle started kicking me in the face as she attempted to reverse directions.

"What is it?" I shouted. "What's happening?"

"Go, Will!" she shrieked. "Go!"

Rob began yelling now. Low grunts tinged with higher notes of hysteria. Then he screamed—in pain.

Danièle landed a heavy heel against my nose. Stars exploded across my vision. I tasted dirt and coppery blood.

"Will, go!" she wailed.

I elbowed my way backward, battling a frenzied terror. *What the fuck was happening—?*

Something cold gripped my ankle. I tried to snap my head around to see what it was, but the shaft was too restrictive to do even that. A second something latched onto my other ankle.

Hands.

They tugged. I kicked wildly, freeing myself.

"Someone's behind me!" I shouted. "Go forward!"

"It got Rob!" Danièle screeched feverishly. "He is gone! It

took him! It just took him!"

I still couldn't see past her, but I didn't doubt that someone had indeed taken Rob; he was no longer yelling. Even so,
forward was better than backward for me. I placed my hands
squarely on Danièle's rear and shoved.

"Go!"

With a soulful moan she lurched forward—just as the pair
of hands grabbed my ankles again. Sharp nails—*claws?*—dug
into my flesh.

I kicked and twisted and freed myself again and was right
behind Danièle, urging her to move faster in a voice I scarcely
recognized as my own, tearing the skin from my elbows in my
manic flight.

Danièle jackknifed around a corner and put distance between us. I kept waiting for those terrible hands to clamp onto
me once more, to drag me backward into the dark, but they
never did.

Then, from a little ways ahead, Danièle cried out—and vanished.

▼

I shot out of the shaft a few seconds after her, momentarily
airborne, dropping several feet to the hard ground. I sprang to
my feet and whirled toward the hole, peering inside. Nothing.

Then Danièle was beside me.

"Where is it?" she said. Her tone was oddly nonchalant, as
if she was trying to be conversational, only she was screaming
too. "It must have come back out this way. It had Rob, it..." She
buried her face in her hands.

I examined the room we were in. It was made of stone and
resembled all the others we had come across, though there
were no bones here. An open doorway led to another room,
and a doorway there to yet another room still.

"Who took Rob?" I asked her quietly. "Did you see him?"

"He...it..." She bit her lip to stop it from quivering. "It..."

"What do you mean 'it?' Jesus, Danièle, who did you see? The Painted Devil?"

"Its face…it was all… It was a monster."

A ball of dread punched me in the chest. Then I got ahold of my imagination. "It wasn't a fucking monster, Danièle! Who was it? The Painted Devil? Was it the Painted Devil?"

She shook he head and began to sob.

"Shhh, shhh, shhh," I told her, pulling her hands away from her face so I could look her in the eyes. "You have to be quiet. Danièle? You have to be quiet."

She nodded but continued to sob.

"Danièle!" I said, shaking her. "They could be coming back."

Her breath hitched. Her body went rigid.

She looked at me, pleading. "It took Rob. Where is he?"

"I don't know—"

An unholy caterwauling exploded from the shaft, and for a moment I was numbed with superstitious terror.

"It is coming," Danièle said monotonously. She no longer sounded afraid; she sounded accepting, which was somehow worse.

Run or fight? I thought. What had Danièle seen? A flesh-and-blood monster? There were no such things. She had to be confused. She was in shock. She was short-circuiting.

Run or fight?

I flicked off my helmet's headlamp. Danièle stared at me blankly.

"Turn yours off too," I told her quietly. "We're easy targets with them on."

She shook her head, looked like she was going to flee.

"There's nowhere to go," I said. "We have to take these guys out one by one. You stand on that side of the hole. I'm going to be right here, on this side. When whoever comes out of it, we attack him." She started to shake her head again. I added steel and urgency to my voice: "Turn off your fucking headlamp, Danièle. *Now*."

For a moment I was sure she would refuse. But she reached

up, fumbled with the battery box at the back of her helmet, and flipped the toggle.

We were plunged into blackness.

▼

My breathing seemed extra loud in the nothingness, and I tried to quiet it. There was no other noise. The seconds dragged. The air seemed thick and greasy.

Then I heard faint, careful movement inside the hole. *Someone coming*. Yet there was still no light. Had the person turned off his headlamp, expecting an ambush? Had I broken it when I kicked him?

The sound became louder, stopping, starting, stopping, starting.

Sniffing us out, I thought, and hated myself for thinking that.

My heart was pounding, adrenaline was burning through my veins like gasoline, but I was ready. I was going to take this motherfucker out, I was going to knock him up for answers, find out what was going on, where Pascal and Rob had gone—

I swallowed, gaging. That cloying stench was back, come from nowhere. It was almost a physical presence.

From the darkness nearby Danièle made a retching sound.

No, quiet, don't—

She retched again.

A howl erupted from the hole, savage and close.

Danièle snapped on her headlamp. For a moment I was blinded by the light. Then I saw her staring at me, her eyes wide as saucers, as if she were seeing a ghost.

"Will!" she said with the woodsaw rasp of a crow, pointing a shaking finger at me.

No—*behind me*, I realized.

I started to turn, but something heavy cracked into the back of my helmet, knocking it off and sending me to the ground.

Head throbbing, I rolled over and caught a glimpse of a mutant face and a swinging bone a moment before everything exploded in excruciating pain and searing whiteness.

CHAPTER 37

DANIÈLE

Danièle couldn't breathe, couldn't make a sound, couldn't think. The thing came for her, grinning hideously.

She ran.

CHAPTER 38

I saw her from across the room. Her blonde hair was pinned up in a ballerina-like bun on her head, accentuating her slender neck. I couldn't tell the color of her eyes, the room was too dark, but they were large and expressive, her lashes long. Her nose was small, not much more than a comma. Her lips were painted bright red, and she was smiling—a quirky smile. It gave her face depth and personality.

She wore an effervescent green dress, strapless, revealing delicate shoulders and toned biceps. It tapered down her sides and clung to her curvy hips and ended above her knees.

I must have been watching her for only a few seconds when she glanced over at me. Maybe she felt my eyes on her, maybe it was coincidental. I looked away and went to get another drink. I mingled with some friends on the way, but the entire time I was thinking about the girl in the green dress. She had to be with Delta Kappa Delta; it was the only sorority we'd invited to the party tonight. But if she was, why hadn't I seen her before? Rush had been in September, and we'd had several events with DKD since then.

I moved on to the kitchen. A few girls were crowded around the two-gallon Rubbermaid cooler filled with Kool-Aid and vodka. Some more of my friends were hanging out by the keg. I joined them, filled my red plastic cup with beer, and bantered a bit. Duane Davis, the chapter's treasurer, was complaining about how DKD were becoming the ugly sorority, and

I wasn't sure the DKD girls at the Rubbermaid cooler couldn't hear him.

I returned to the room where I had seen the girl in the green dress. She was no longer there. I went to the basement and wandered the busy rooms. She wasn't there either. On the porch outside, I described her to my friends smoking cigarettes and asked if they had seen her. No one had.

I was pissed off. I should have gone straight over and talked to her. Why had I decided to get a drink?

As a last resort I stepped over the police tape strung from newel post to newel post across the bottom of the staircase and climbed the steps. I didn't believe she would be on the second floor. It was off limits to anyone who didn't live in the townhouse.

I heard voices down the hall, coming from the last room on the left. I knocked and opened the door. Five of my friends sat on chairs arranged in a circle around a low glass table, which was littered with baggies of blow and rolled bills and credit cards. I asked them if they had seen the girl in the green dress. They hadn't.

Halfway back down the hall, the bathroom door opened and there she was. I was so surprised all I could manage was, "Oh."

"Hi," she said, smiling. "Sorry. I know. I'm not supposed to be up here. But the bathroom downstairs was occupied."

"Yeah, no problem," I said. "I was actually looking for you."

"For me?"

"I saw you in the living room. I wanted to talk."

"Am I in trouble?"

"No, I mean, just talk, talk."

"Well, I like to talk talk."

I cleared my throat. "I haven't seen you around before."

"I'm not with the sorority. My friend Suzy—Suzy Taylor? —she invited me. I'm not into the whole Greek thing. I don't mean that there's anything wrong with it. You're a Pike?"

I nodded.

"How is it? Frat life?"

"Nothing special really."

"I've never been in a frat house before."

"This isn't a frat house, not officially. We rent it."

"But you guys live here?"

"Some of us do. My room's right down there."

"Can I see it?"

"Yeah, sure."

I unlocked the door to my room with my key and followed her inside. The room was pretty bland. Some oak furniture that came with it. A life-size cardboard cutout of Mr. Bean I'd stolen from a fast-food chain during my initiation. Curling posters of AC/DC and Led Zepplin and other old school rock bands that I'd picked up at the poster sale on campus. A purple lava lamp I'd been meaning to toss out.

My laptop sat on my messy desk, the screensaver displaying a slideshow of scantily-clad women. I went to it and closed the lid.

"By the way," I said, offering my hand, "I'm Will."

"I'm Bridgette," she said, squeezing.

"I like that name."

"My parents were big bridge fans."

"Huh?"

"Bridgette," she said. "It's a two-player bridge game. It also means 'exalted one.' Yes, I checked. I was bummed out when I learned I was named after a card game. What's in there?" She indicated the door to the closet.

"Nothing," I said.

"Can I see?"

"There's nothing in there."

"Why won't you let me see?" Her voice had turned petulant, and it wasn't Bridgette anymore. It was Danièle. She was naked.

"There's nothing in there."

"Why are you never honest with me, Will?"

"I am."

"I want to see."

I had no idea what was in the closet, only that it was something that made me uneasy.

"No," I told her.

"Will, stop it." She pushed past me.

I seized her by the upper arms. "Danièle, don't."

"Don't what?"

"Just don't."

She shook free and yanked the closet door open. Relief flooded me. There was nothing inside but my clothes neatly arranged on their hangers.

"See?" I said.

But she wasn't listening. She stepped into the closet, slipped between the clothes, and disappeared.

"Danièle!" I shoved the clothes aside. She was gone. "Danièle! Come back!"

Her voice was different, scared. It came from beyond the wall.

"Will, where am I?"

I banged the plaster. "Danièle!"

"Will, help!"

"Danièle, come back!"

"I cannot!"

"Come back!"

"Will, look behind you—"

▼

I was strapped to a gurney of some sort. My eyes were open, but I couldn't see. It wasn't too dark; it was too bright. Then, gradually, the ceiling resolved into detail: chiseled stone affixed with a series of fluorescent lights. I turned my head to the right. Chipped wooden counters and cupboards, painted white. The cupboard doors featured glass windows through which I could see a variety of bottles and beakers like those found in a science classroom.

I tried to move. My arms were secured in leather cuffs.

From behind me a metal table on wheels rattled into my field of view. The surface was neatly lined with a dozen crude tools that would look equally at home in a dentist's office or a fifteen-century torture chamber.

I jerked at the restraints. They held firm.

The person pushing the table appeared. It was Maxine. Her hair was wet and plastered to her skull, her cream dress soaked through.

After a brief glance at me, she turned her attention to the tools before her. "They did this to me too, Will," she said.

"Did what?"

"An autopsy. You'd think they'd know what killed me. I'd been at the bottom of the lake all night. But they still had to open me up and look inside. The good thing about being dead is that nothing hurts."

"I'm not dead!"

Max picked up a pair of scissors and cut open my shirt. She exchanged the scissors for a scalpel.

"Max! Stop it!"

She made a Y-shaped incision into my flesh, extending from my armpits to the bottom of my sternum, then down to my lower abdomen.

Blood pooled out from it, black and thick as syrup.

"Look, Max! I'm bleeding. I'm not dead."

She frowned. "They told me you were."

"Who?"

"Them."

"I need to get out of here."

"You can't."

The restraints, however, had vanished, and I was able to sit up. My head and bladder throbbed dully. I pressed a hand to my stomach to prevent my guts from spilling out.

"Where am I, Max? Where are my friends?"

"You shouldn't have come down here."

"Where, Max?"

"You shouldn't have come down here."

"Stop saying that."

"You shouldn't have come down here."

"Stop it, Max!" I was suddenly incensed at her. Not for her I-told-you-so advice. But for dying on me. For leaving me. For blaming me for her death.

"You shouldn't—"

I leapt at her, squeezing her throat. She plunged the scalpel into my left ear. I screamed and fell to the floor, where I rocked back and forth, back and forth, rocking, rocking, rocking...

▼

I jerked awake. I was curled in a fetal position, perspiring, short of breath. Relief flooded me as I realized I had been dreaming. Then everything else came crashing back in a whirlwind of images—the tunnel, Rob yelling, the mutant swinging the bone—and for a bewildered moment I thought this all must be a dream too. But when the all-encompassing blackness didn't relent—in fact, it only became more oppressive—I understood it was real.

I tried to sit up. My hands, I discovered, were cuffed behind my back, and I toppled to my side. The abrupt movement shot a lightning bolt of pain through the left side of my skull where I had been struck by the bone. The throbbing escalated, an alternating current of fire and ice. I squeezed my eyes shut. My mouth gaped open against the cold dirt floor. Moaning, waiting for the excruciating pain to subside, I became aware of my protesting bladder. It felt as if it might burst.

I shoved myself to my knees, wobbling but keeping my balance, then to my feet. I swayed but didn't fall.

My bladder.

Fuck. Oh fuck.

I couldn't hold out any longer. Hot urine splashed down my inner thighs and calves. The first second was orgasmic, the relief so great. I pissed myself for what must have been a full minute.

"Ugh," I grunted when I'd finished, partly in disgust, but mostly because of the pain still stampeding inside my head like a herd of elephants.

I stumbled forward, not knowing where I was going in the dark, only wanting to get clear of the acrid puddle pooled around me.

I took one step, then another—then metal clacked and the cuffs dug into the skin around my wrists.

I was not only bound; I was anchored to something, like a dog leashed to a pole.

The primal alarm of imprisonment thudded in my chest, and I jerked my arms in frustration. The cuffs bit deeper.

"Fuck," I said.

I glanced about me.

Blackness.

I blinked.

Blackness.

"Fuck," I said.

Where was Danièle? Where was Rob? Pascal? Was I alone? Or were they right next to me?

"Danièle?"

No answer.

"Rob?"

No reply.

"Fuck," I said.

I squashed the fear running wild inside me and tried to figure out what the hell was going on. I closed my eyes to concentrate, though this changed nothing, the blackness was the same, it was simple habit, and visualized my attacker. A flash of white skin. Two piggish air holes for a nose. A permanently grinning set of gums and teeth for a mouth.

Had this...abomination...been real? Or had it been a person wearing a mask? The Painted Devil? I kept coming back to him, but for good reason. He was a showman—a sick, reckless showman who had a proclivity for theater and got a thrill out of terrorizing cataphiles. So was it a stretch to conclude he swapped the SS uniform for a Halloween mask, knocked us all unconscious, and tied us up as prisoners?

No, maybe not. *Except what I saw wasn't a mask.*

I was reasonably sure of that. I might have only seen the face for a moment, but it had been a heated moment, and my mind had been exceptionally clear, my perception sharp.

And then there was that nauseating stench. The only time I had ever smelled something so foul had been when, as a kid, I'd discovered our family cat in the back of the our little-used garage, where it had gone to die, and where it had been half consumed by a blanket of squiggling white maggots. And although it was conceivable the Painted Devil might swap costumes, it was absurd to suggest he would go so far as to alter his scent.

Which meant whoever had attacked me was indeed gruesomely deformed. But who had disfigured him, and why? And what did he want with us? And how had he snuck up on me? There was no way he could have seen Danièle and me in the blackness. Not even with a pair of night vision goggles; there wasn't a sliver of ambient light in the catacombs.

Moreover, it wasn't *him*; it was *them*. Because there had been at least two of them, one behind us, in the cat hole, and one in front of us—

From the darkness, nearby, came a sob.

CHAPTER 39

DANIÈLE

Danièle realized someone—or something—shared the
dark with her. She heard movement, scuffling, maybe
ten feet away, maybe twenty, it was impossible to as-
certain for certain. Then a moan followed.

It was Will.

Nevertheless, she didn't call out to him. Her body was in
too much pain, her throat too sore. Besides, what would talking to him accomplish? He was a prisoner, like her. Like Rob
and Pascal, if they shared this room also. He couldn't free any
of them. He couldn't do anything.

None of them could.

She heard a harsh patter, and it took her a moment to realize he was peeing. She didn't need to urinate or defecate, but
when the urge came, she knew she would have no choice but
to soil herself. Then she would have to sit there and sleep there
in her own filth, with no light and no food and no water.

Tears welled in her eyes. Her lower lip quivered. She bit
down hard on it, drawing blood.

Will began to move again. Danièle wondered what was running through his head. Had he seen the thing that had struck
him? Even if he hadn't, he knew that something had attacked
them in the cat hole, knew that it had gotten Rob. Knew it had
hunted them like prey.

So why wasn't he screaming like she had when she came around, screaming in despair and terror at the unjustness of this incarceration, screaming until his throat went raw and he couldn't scream anymore?

He called her name. His voice was thick, urgent.

Danièle opened her mouth, closed it.

She was too tired, too injured, too depleted.

She drifted into semi-consciousness, floating, spinning, forgetting. Then a single thought: Dev. *Dev knows about the video camera, the lost woman, the expedition! So when Rob doesn't return home today, and she can't get ahold of me or Pascal, she'll conclude that something happened to us. She'll contact the police.*

And they would...do nothing.

Danièle's hope nosedived.

Like she'd told Will earlier, it wasn't the police's job to hunt down cataphiles who got themselves lost in the catacombs; it was their job to hand out fines and meet quotas. Yes, they would visit the Beach and Room Z and some of the other popular areas, they would question the cataphiles they caught. But that would be all. There would be no extensive manhunt.

If only they knew the truth! she thought. *That...that what? What were those things that had attacked us and brought us here? Zombies?*

This sounded so farcical, so bad-TV-movie, but the thing Danièle had seen had no nose or lips, as if they had rotted off its face, and after it had knocked Will out, it had chased her, caught her, pinned her against the wall, rubbed its hands over her face, sniffed her, licked her, as if it was possessed of an urge, not sexual in nature, it hadn't been interested in her body, not right then, but of something more primal than sex, a hunger, as if it wanted to tear her apart and consume her then and there.

But it didn't. It held back. It reigned in its impulse, which indicated control. Were zombies capable of self-control? And then it threw her to the ground and beat her unconscious instead.

But why?

Sea turtles.

Sea turtles?

Giant sea turtles. They could survive for months without food or water. Sailors used to store them in the ship's hold during long voyages.

A fresh food source.

Danièle opened her mouth to scream again, but all that came out was a miserable sob.

CHAPTER 40

"Danièle?" I whispered hoarsely. "Danièle? It's me, Will."

Another wrenching sob, then another. They sounded as if they were being torn from her body by a barbed fist.

"Danièle? Are you okay?" I moved toward her until my chain snapped taut. I grunted. The pain in my head flared. "Danièle?"

"Yes..."

Her voice was soft, cracked, barely there.

"Come toward me."

No reply.

"Danièle?"

"Can't."

"You can't move?"

"Can't."

My heart was pounding.

What was wrong with her?

How badly was she hurt?

I said, "Are you bleeding?"

"No."

"What did they do to you?"

No reply.

I wanted to hold her, touch her, help her. I yanked at my restraints in frustration.

I said, "We have to get out of here."

No reply.

"We're *going* to get out of here."

I wondered how long we had been here. Hours? Or days? I didn't feel hungry. I was thirsty though. God, I wished I hadn't thought of that. My tongue suddenly felt twice its normal size. I moved it around inside my mouth, which was dry and sticky.

"Will...?"

"Yeah?"

"So...scared."

"We'll be okay."

"What...they do to us?"

"Don't think about that."

"I think..."

"It's going to be okay."

"I think...they eat us."

The fear inside me hardened to ice as I stared into the blackness.

Now it was my turn to fall silent.

▼

I followed the length of the chain attached to my manacles and discovered it was attached to an iron ring bolted into the wall at a corner of the room. I worked at the ring, trying to pry it free from the rock, until my fingernails bled and I gave up.

I fanned away from the corner, feeling with my feet for a stone or something I could potentially use as a hammer. I came across nothing but hard-packed mud.

I slumped to my butt, trying to ignore the wet denim sucking against my legs and the itchy sensation it caused.

If I could somehow surprise one of our captors, I thought, I might find something on him I could use to free myself. But how would I accomplish this? Play dead when he approached?

Kick him in the face when he stooped to examine me? Could I perform this cleanly, without an alarm being raised?

I wanted to tell myself that this was all a big mistake, that we would soon be released, but that was bullshit. The iron ring installed in the wall and the handy chains and manacles suggested our captors had kidnapped others before. They had an agenda.

So what was that? To use us as slave labor? To play out sick torture fantasies on us? Or, as Danièle suggested, to fucking eat us?

I shoved myself to my feet decisively, breathed deeply. I wasn't going to go down that path. I wasn't going to give in to despair.

I started to pace. I wanted to channel my frustration and fear onto Danièle and Pascal; I wanted to blame them for the predicament we were in. But that wouldn't be fair. They'd had no idea what awaited us down here.

No, the only person I could blame was myself. I had accepted Danièle's invitation to search for the lost woman. Nobody put a gun to my head.

And now I was going to pay for that stupidity.

No, not just me, I realized. Everybody close to me. My parents especially—for when their emails and phone calls to me went unanswered, they would suspect something was amiss and get the French authorities to investigate. When I didn't turn up in a hospital somewhere, or a jail cell, or wherever else...they would conclude what? The last person I had spoken to had been Bridgette. She had told me she had gotten married and was pregnant...

Shit, I didn't want them to think that.

Not fucking suicide.

Would they be able to cope with the loss of both Maxine and me? My father probably. He was like my grandfather had been, as hard as the knocks life threw at him. If you didn't know better, you would have said he had been none the different after Max died—but I did know better. I saw the chinks in his armor. The weariness that crept into his voice. The cynicism not so much in his eyes but in the crow's feet around them. The stoop in his walk that had never been there before. Yeah, the chinks were there, but I think he still could hold it together even if something happened to me too. My mother, no way. There was little left to hold together anyway. At my wedding reception she had been a healthy fifty-two-year-old woman with full chestnut hair and glowing skin and an easy smile. At the airport when I left for London, her hair was gray with streaks of white, she was twenty pounds underweight, and worst of all, the light inside her had been switched off. She never went back to her job at the library, and I wasn't sure what she did around the house all day. I had a horrible picture of her sitting on the settee on the front porch for hours on end, a book open in her lap, staring at the page but not seeing the words.

I jerked at my restraints for the hundredth time. The cuffs seared my already abraded skin. I jerked again and again, grunting each time.

"Will...?" It was Danièle, groggy, still out of it.

I kept yanking at the restraints. Slimy blood lubricated my wrists.

"Will?" Panicked now. "What are you doing? Stop it."

I wasn't listening. I tugged and tugged, unable to control myself. Danièle was shouting at me, though she seemed distant, unimportant.

Then abruptly, jarringly, a noise cut through my bubbling madness.

A rooster crow.

CHAPTER 41

DANIÈLE

Danièle thought she must be dreaming, or hallucinating. A rooster in the catacombs? But then it cock-a-doodle-dooed again.

She tried pushing herself to her knees and failed. Her right arm was useless, maybe fractured. She had raised it to protect her head when the zombie-man had rained blows down on her with his bone-weapon.

She moved her left arm under her chest and propped herself onto her elbow. Rotating onto her hip, she was able to sit up.

The movement, however, caused dagger-sharp pain to lance through her skull. She remained still, praying for the agony to subside.

Then: "Danièle! Look!" It was Will.

Look? she thought. Look where? It was permanent night, black everywhere…only it wasn't, not anymore. From an indeterminable distance away, a faint light appeared.

Someone was coming.

CHAPTER 42

I t was a girl, or a woman, I couldn't tell from this distance. She wore charcoal tights and a too-big sweater that went nearly to her knees. Her hair was long, dark, flowing around her head. In her left hand she held a candle with a small flame.

She stopped at the entrance to our room, and in the fluttering light I could see the surroundings for the first time—

"Rob!" Danièle cried huskily. "Pascal!"

To the left of the girl, in the corner, lay Rob. He was on his stomach, unmoving. His hands were cuffed behind his back, a chain snaking from the manacles to an iron ring in the wall. To the right, in the adjacent corner, lay Pascal, unconscious and bound as well.

I glanced in Danièle's direction. The light didn't reach this side of the room, and I could see little but her silhouette against an almost equally black background. She seemed to be propped up with one arm while the other one dangled lamely.

I returned my attention to the girl.

Was there something wrong with her face? Or was that the play of shadows?

"*Comment allez-vous?*" Danièle said. "*Est-ce que vous parlez français?*"

The girl didn't speak.

"*Quel âge avez-vous? Pouvez-vous m'aider… S'il vous plaît?*"

No reply.

"Do you speak English?" I tried, though I couldn't fathom why she would.

Nothing.

"Why are we here?" I said. "What's going to happen to us?"

She turned to leave.

"Wait!"

Danièle and I yelled after her to stop, to come back, but then she was gone from sight and the blackness returned and we were blind once more.

CHAPTER 43

DANIÈLE

Hours passed. Maybe two, maybe five, Danièle couldn't tell. However many, it felt like an eternity. She and Will said little to one another. Occasionally they would call Rob's name, or Pascal's. There was never an answer. She tried not to think about them. She and Will were lucky in the sense that they had both regained consciousness, but what if Rob and Pascal never did?

What if they were dead?

No—Danièle would not let herself believe this. They couldn't be dead. Rob was married to her sister. He had two little girls waiting at home for him. Pascal was only twenty-five. He was too young to be dead. They both were.

This was a stupid way of thinking, of course, because death didn't care if you were young or if you had kids, it didn't care if you were wealthy or poor, it didn't care if you were pretty or disfigured, a king or a queen—it would strike you down when it wanted to strike you down and there was nothing you could do about it.

So had it come for Rob and Pascal then? Was this their time, premature as it may be? Was this her and Will's time as well? Were they going to become those people who friends and acquaintances commented upon with a shake of their head and something banal like, "I can't believe they died…it's so tragic."

Danièle didn't want to think about any of this; she wanted to sink into sleep so the worrying and the pain and the fear would all disappear. But as much as she tried, her mind wouldn't rest, wouldn't shut off, and now it moved on to the girl who had visited them. She couldn't imagine where the girl came from, or why she was here in this godforsaken place, wherever this was, because she wasn't like the zombie-man. Danièle didn't mean her face—she hadn't seen it clearly enough to know whether it had rotted off too—she meant the girl's manner, because while the zombie-man had been feral, vile, a base animal, she had been, well, just a girl.

Could she be a prisoner too then, only one who was allowed to roam freely? Yet if that were the case, wouldn't she attempt to flee? And if she made the trouble to visit this chamber, to reveal herself, why not speak? Did she not understand French or English? Surely, though, she could have attempted to communicate in some other manner?

So many unknowns! Danièle's head felt ready to explode. But as she continued to play over the "ifs" and "whats" and "whys," turning them this way and that, looking for new possibilities, she uncovered a positive thought among the overwhelming negatives: whatever the girl's role in all this, the fact the zombie-man hadn't torn her apart and consumed her flesh confirmed what Danièle had suspected earlier: the zombie-man, or however many of them existed, weren't completely mindless, they had some measure of self-restraint.

As small a relief as this seemed to be, it was a relief nonetheless, and Danièle held onto it as though it were a lifeline, afraid to let go.

CHAPTER 44

T he man who had attacked me must be the girl's father, I thought. He had been maimed in a horrible accident —a fire, an explosion, perhaps exposure to acid—or he had leprosy or another flesh-eating disease. Either way, his life was ruined. He couldn't go out in public without people pointing and staring and viewing him as a monster. So he took his daughter, who loved him unconditionally, and fled to the catacombs. But over time he grew lonely. He wanted adult companionship. So he returned to the surface and recruited others with hideous deformities to join him underground, so that now there was a flourishing community of Quasimodos...

I touched my head against my knees.

A cult then? A satanic cult that practiced self-mutilation and sacrificed unwary cataphiles to their dark god? Druggies who had a bad acid trip and thought their faces were trying to eat themselves so they cut them off—?

Whoa, I thought. Whoa, whoa, whoa. Could *I* be under the influence of drugs? Had Rob or Danièle or even Pascal slipped me something, and I was currently riding out the mindfuck of all mindfucks? For a moment I hoped against hope that this was true, but I knew it wasn't. I might not understand what was happening right now, but there was no doubt it was happening, no belief that it was a dream or hallucination; it was all too real. The memories, the smells, the lucidity of my thoughts—and the pain, that was real, there was no denying it, and drugs might make you see things, and hear things, and hell, maybe even smell things, but they didn't make you feel as if you've been run over by a Mac truck.

"Will, there!" Danièle said abruptly, snapping me out of my musings. I blinked dazedly. It was the first time she had spoken in ages.

After a moment of disorientation I saw the light. It grew in brightness. Yet this time its arrival was accompanied by sounds as well. Snorts, hollers. Words? If so, I had never heard the language before.

I struggled to my feet. I heard Danièle doing the same.

"What should we do?" she hissed.

"Let me do the talking."

"Talking? What are you going to say? They are animals! They do not understand!" She was near hysterics.

The torchbearer appeared first, followed by eleven others, seven males and four females. An eclectic mix of clothing that spanned several decades covered their pale, cadaver-like bodies: button-down shirts, bell-bottom pants, a houndstooth jacket, cotton dresses. All of them had piggish holes for noses and lipless, skeletal grins, and all were barefoot. Because of their deformities it was hard to gauge their ages, but they ranged from young adult to ancient. Each carried a long off-white bone.

The torchbearer stopped where the girl had stopped earlier, though his torch was much brighter than the girl's candle, and the light clearly exposed Danièle and me. The mob fell silent. Ignoring Danièle, the torchbearer came over to stand directly before me.

My blood went gravestone cold as I stared into his eyes—reptilian eyes—for the whites were yellow, the pupils the size of dimes, eclipsing the irises. His teeth, partially black with decay, stood in stark contrast to the delicate pink of his exposed gums. The cavities in the center of his face were lopsided, the left larger than the right, exposing lumpy red tissue within.

His freakish eyes held mine, and it was only with effort that I didn't look away. He made sniffing noises through the holes in his face. I tried not to gag on his stench.

Without warning he swung his bone. It struck the side of my left knee. I dropped, landing hard on my side. I pulled my knees to my chest in expectation of another blow, but he turned away from me and shook his weapon in the air and howled. The mob responded in a cacophony of celebration. Then he leveled the bone at Pascal and barked what might have been an order.

Two males went to Pascal and heaved him to his feet. His limbs dangled lifelessly. His head was lolling from left to right.

The torchbearer crossed the room and slapped Pascal hard across the face. He peeled Pascal's eyelids open with his thumb. Then he stepped back, lifted Pascal's shirt, and thrust the flaming end of the torch into his stomach.

Pascal's head snapped back and his mouth went wide in a silent shriek.

CHAPTER 45

PASCAL

The pain! It started in Pascal's gut and blazed outward. His eyes bulged, but he couldn't see anything. He gasped for breath, felt hands on him, holding him upright. He looked ahead and saw a flaming ball of fire and smelled singed hair and burned flesh. Then, next to the fire, a blurry face—the thing he'd bumped into when he'd turned around, the thing that had...what? He didn't know. He couldn't remember anything after turning around.

Pascal realized his arms were pinned behind his back. His wrists were being handcuffed. No—being *released*, it turned out, because a moment later his arms flopped free. The thing before him shoved the scrolled end of a femur at his chest. It said something, though he couldn't understand what. Everything was happening in a fog, a dream state. It shoved the bone at him again and again until he took it.

His vision began to focus, and beyond the thing he noticed a number of other grotesque horrors. And beyond them, standing in the shadows, Will.

Pascal screamed his name.

CHAPTER 46

DANIÈLE

D anièle couldn't bear to watch, but she couldn't turn away either. The zombie-man with the torch, the leader as far as she could tell, handed Pascal a bone, then accepted another bone from a female, then the mob formed a loose circle around Pascal and him.

They were going to fight.

Pascal realized this too. He stopped shouting for Will to help him and backed away from the leader and begged to be left alone.

The leader roared and attacked with his bone. Pascal, usually nimble and athletic, stumbled awkwardly out of the way, tripped, and fell to his rear.

The leader pressed the attack and swung the bone in a downward arc. Pascal raised his bone horizontally in both hands, deflecting the blow. He scrambled to his feet and attempted to flee. Those gathered in the circle spun him around and shoved him back into the fray.

Before Pascal could regain his coordination, the leader slammed the bone across his back, knocking him to his knees. Choking on tears, Pascal tried to crawl away. The leader reared up behind him and raised his bone in the air.

"Pascal!" Danièle cried.

He spotted her for the first time. A myriad of emotions

shimmered across his eyes in that brief moment. Fear, confusion, anger, anguish. And worst of all, what she would never be able to forget—heartbreak, of the kind when you know you will never see someone you love again.

The knobby end of the leader's bone struck Pascal on the top of the skull with a sharp, liquid crack. His face went slack. He fell flat to his chest.

Danièle bent over and vomited.

CHAPTER 47

Jesus Christ, there was nothing left of Pascal's head. There was nothing left of his head. That fucking torchbearer had bashed it over and over again until it dissolved into a messy puddle of gunk. Nevertheless, I didn't have long to reflect on this, because the torchbearer—Jaundice, I thought of him as after seeing those yellow eyes—pointed the bloody, brain-speckled femur at me and barked an order. An elderly male moved behind me, sprung the shackles from around my wrists, and pushed me into the circle.

Jaundice kicked Pascal's bone-weapon toward me with his bare foot. I didn't want to pick it up. If I did, I would be accepting his challenge. Then again, if I didn't, he would likely kill me anyway.

I retrieved the femur and choked it like a baseball bat. I considered using it to bash my way through the circle and make a run for it. But I had no headlamp, no flashlight, no torch. I wouldn't make it twenty feet in the blackness before I was caught again.

Still, what chance of survival did I have if I held my ground and fought? I was bigger and stronger than Jaundice, but he seemed to be experienced at this bone fighting or whatever it was. The blows he landed against Pascal had been swift and sure. Also, even if I defeated him, what then? There were another eleven of them. No way I could take them all out.

Jaundice approached me warily, his bloodied femur in one

hand, the torch in the other. The flame spit and licked. The ring of spectators were shaking their bones in the air and hooting and hollering like a troop of monkeys. This was obviously prime entertainment for them.

Jaundice roared and lunged, feigning with the femur while jabbing the torch at me. I dodged right, felt the heat of the whooshing flame on my face, and chopped Jaundice's extended forearm with my bone. He barked and dropped the torch. I was already swinging the bone again, this time at his head, but he parried, countered, and whacked me in the side.

I swung wildly. He jumped backward. He swung just as wildly. I jumped backward.

Then someone shoved me from behind. I stumbled forward. Instinct told me to veer right to avoid crashing into Jaundice. That's what Pascal did—and got the bone across his back that knocked him to his knees. So instead I careened straight into Jaundice. He swung his bone, but I had closed the distance between us too quickly, and there was no power behind the blow. The femur bounced off my shoulder. I threw my arms around him and dragged him to the ground, landing on top of him.

I released the bone-weapon, and with my left hand I grabbed Jaundice around the throat, pressing down with all of my weight, trying to crush his windpipe. With my other hand I formed a fist and hammered him in the face again and again and again. I was yelling and crazed and trying to smash his skull open like he had done to Pascal.

I would have done this too had I not been pulled off him. I struggled against the hands grappling me, but there were too many. Nails raked my flesh as they dragged me away and pinned me to the ground.

Then, amazingly, Jaundice rose to his feet. Blood painted most of his face red, and his mouth hung open and askew with several teeth now missing. He probed his unhinged jaw tentatively, tried pushing it closed. It fell dumbly open again.

He issued a strangled wail, picked up his bone-weapon, and

lurched over to stand above me. His yellow eyes blazed.

I bucked and squirmed and got a leg free. I kicked one of the fuckers holding me, a female, in the face, and another in the ear. But as soon as they fell away, others replaced them and secured my leg again.

Jaundice placed a foot on my chest, and even though his mouth hung open in an obtuse oval, I was sure he was smiling.

He raised the femur.

CHAPTER 48

ZOLAN

When Zolan had first begun trolling the red light districts of Paris, he'd known nothing about how they operated. The first night he strolled into a brothel that seemed fair enough. He bought a cocktail for the girl he was sitting with, a friendly twenty-five year old from Cambodia, and told her he wanted to hire her services. When she told him four hundred for everything, he knew he was in a tourist scam and said no thanks. Before he could leave, however, a gorilla of a bouncer handed him the bill: four hundred fifty euros for a beer and a cocktail. He asked the hooker if her offer was still good, which it was. So four hundred fifty for two drinks, or fifty bucks less for two drinks and a fuck—it wasn't a hard decision.

Zolan was no longer so naïve. Now he knew the red light districts in and out. He knew every corner of every boulevard, every speakeasy brothel, what they charged, who worked where, and who worked on the side.

Last night he had been with Sonia, a pretty Czech girl with the face of a sixteen year old and the body of a lingerie model. She was from a top shelf brothel hidden in plain sight in the middle of Pigalle. She'd been slutty and fearless with soft hands and a willing tongue, just how he liked them.

He'd been thinking about Sonia and the hall of fame fuck all the way back from the surface, but stopped as soon as he entered the Great Hall.

Something had happened in his absence.

Usually Odo would be lying on his piss-stained mattress, staring at nothing in that stupid way of his. Franz would be fussing over his Hot Wheels collection, organizing the cars into neat piles only to reorganize them into different ones. If Hanns and Jörg and Karl weren't out patrolling the tunnels, they would be lurking here somewhere, pissing the hell out of all the others. In contrast, only Nora was present, wandering aimlessly at the far end of the room, picking at the scabs on her breasts. Zolan didn't bother asking her where everyone else was; she had the mental aptitude of a two year old.

Then, distantly, he heard shouting. It came from the Dungeon.

Fucking Hanns, he thought immediately. Had to be Hanns. He was always acting up, causing mischief. The other day he hid several of Franz's Hot Wheels. The two of them nearly killed each other in the ensuing fight, and it took hours to get everyone to settle down again.

So what had he done this time?

As Zolan moved through the tunnel system, the shouting crystalized, and there was a frenzied mania to it the likes of which he had never heard.

What the fuck was going on?

When he arrived at the entrance to the Dungeon, Zolan saw everything at once. That cataphile he had run into earlier—Macaroni—pinned to the ground by Jörg and Karl and all the others. The quiet cataphile, Chess, lying a few feet away, his head a pulpy mess. Beyond them, the beautiful cataphile, Stork Girl, screaming hysterically. Zolan didn't immediately see the chatty cataphile, Roast Beef, but he didn't have time to wonder about this because Hanns, standing tall above Macaroni, raised his bone in the air.

"*Hanns!*" Zolan commanded. "*Halt!*"

Hanns spun around, his eyes wide with surprise.

"*Tut das nicht!*" Zolan said. "*Schlecht!*"

Hanns threw his head back and howled in fury. He glared at Macaroni, then at Zolan, then at Macaroni again, and Zolan knew he wasn't going to obey him.

He rushed forward as Hanns swung the bone. Macaroni jerked his head at the last moment, and the blow careened off his skull. Zolan shoved Hanns clear before he could attempt a second blow, shouting at him to leave the room, disbanding the crowd. He glanced again at Chess's lifeless body, then turned his attention to Stork Girl. Her face was streaked with tears, and she held a knuckled fist to her mouth. She seemed too emotional to speak, so Zolan said in French, "I warned you not to go searching for that video camera."

Her eyes rolled to the whites, and she fainted.

CHAPTER 49

DANIÈLE

T he room could have been mistaken for a prince's study —a very perverse prince—for despite the abundance of crimson drapery and silk pillows and turn-of-the-century furnishings and aged tomes scattered about, the walls were constructed—no, decorated—with bones. Tibias and femurs and humeri and others were affixed to every inch of available space, the geometrical handiwork punctuated here and there by staring skulls. The macabre display was lit by red candles burning in a half dozen different wrought-iron candelabras.

Danièle knew she must have fainted earlier, because when she'd opened her eyes a minute ago, she had been in this seat, Zolan crouched before her, patting her cheek.

Zolan the bum.

Zolan the drunk.

Zolan, Zolan, Zolan.

How could he possibly be behind all this—whatever *this* was?

A swath of fabric moved to her right, and Zolan emerged from a connecting room. He was dressed exactly as he had been in the Bunker, with the green bandana, olive fatigue jacket, and black T-shirt. He offered her the glass of water he had gone to fetch and sat nonchalantly on one corner of the adjacent desk, smiling hesitantly at her.

"Drink," he said in French. "It will make you feel better, and we have a lot to talk about."

Danièle didn't want to accept the water. She didn't want anything from Zolan, but her throat was parched, and she couldn't resist.

Her wrists, she realized belatedly, were no longer manacled behind her back. They were wrapped in white cotton gauze, tinged red with blood from the abrasions beneath. Smears of petroleum jelly covered the nicks and cuts on her hands. Her right arm was sore to move, the skin bruised purple along the forearm, but she no longer believed it was fractured.

She took the glass and sipped. The water was divine! She gulped the rest back and wiped her mouth with her hand.

"Would you like more?" Zolan asked her.

Danièle set the glass on the desk and shook her head.

"I want to begin with an apology," he said. "Your friend, I'm sorry about what happened."

Pascal! Poor Pascal. She wanted to feel anger, but she only felt empty—empty and frightened and hopelessly confused. "He is dead," she stated monotonously.

"If I were here earlier, it would not have happened—"

"Where is Will?"

"Macaroni?"

Tears sprung to Danièle's eyes. Had she only recently nicknamed him that? How could their fortunes have changed so dramatically in such a short amount of time? "Yes...him," she managed. "Where is he? Is he alive—?"

"He is fine. He is resting."

Relief washed through her. "And Rob?"

"Roast Beef, yes. He is resting also."

"You keep saying 'resting.'" She frowned. "What do you mean by that?"

"They are breathing fine."

"But they are unconscious?"

"Yes."

"They need medical attention."

"They'll come around."

"You are not a doctor!"

"I know you're upset... What's your name—your real name?"

Danièle considered not telling Zolan, but that would accomplish nothing. Her best chance of getting out of here alive, getting Will and Rob out alive too, was through cooperation, throwing herself at his mercy.

"Danièle," she muttered. "My name is Danièle." Hearing her voice so weak, so subservient, plunged her into despair. Her entire body began shaking.

"It's okay," Zolan told her. "You're okay now. Your friends are okay—"

"Pascal is dead!" she said shrilly, and buried her face in her hands. She squeezed her eyes shut and succumbed to wracking sobs.

Gradually, however, the tightness in her chest lessened, and she got her breathing under control. She rubbed the tears from her cheek and saw that Zolan had lit a cigarette. Smoke swirled around his head in a bluish membrane. He was studying her in a way she didn't like.

"Are you German?" she asked him.

"I am a French citizen," he said.

"You spoke German to those..."

"My parents were German," he said, nodding. "They taught the language to me. It is the only language my brothers and sisters understand."

It took a moment for Danièle to clue in to his meaning. "Those *things* are your *siblings*?"

"Some, yes. Others are nieces and nephews. Others still, grandnephews and grandnieces."

She shook her head and thought she might burst into sobs again. Instead she blurted, "What happened to them? Their lips and noses—did you do that?"

"Of course I didn't."

"Then who…?"

"My father," Zolan said, shifting his weight on the desk as if to get comfortable.

"Your father?"

Zolan nodded. "He was a Waffen-SS Sturmbannführer in World War Two. He served as a senior intelligence officer in Paris, helped that lunatic Alois Brunner ship one hundred forty thousand Jews to the gas chambers, and had a hand in the execution of thirty SAS prisoners of war captured during Operation…Bulbasket, I believe they called it." He tapped ash from the cigarette into the silver ashtray next to him. "Needless to say, after the Allied Forces liberated Paris, he had a high price on his head. Instead of trying to flee the city, as many SS personnel did, he and a handful of others went underground —literally. They gathered their families and whatever supplies they could carry, and they fled into the catacombs. The men surfaced every few nights to pilfer more supplies. Back then there were hundreds of different ways to enter—and exit —the catacombs. They could pop up in any part of the city they wanted and be gone again before anyone knew they were there."

Zolan took a final drag of the cigarette and stubbed it out in the ashtray. "Initially they planned to remain hidden for a few months," he said. "By then, they thought, the Allies would be out of France, people would begin rebuilding their lives and the city, and fugitive Germans would be all but forgotten about. This, of course, was not the case, and by the time the Nuremberg Trials finished, they had been underground for roughly two years. Everyone but my father wanted to take a chance on escaping to Syria, or South America. When he realized he couldn't convince the others to stay, he slit their throats while they slept, my mother's too, sparing only the children, who he raised alongside myself. It was a precautionary measure. He had feared they would be captured and give up the location of the hideout."

Danièle was listening to all this with a mixture of rapt attention and relief—the latter because the fact Zolan was sharing such information with her meant he likely wasn't going to kill her. What was the point in educating only to execute?

"So you are telling me," she said, with gathering composure, "that these people who attacked us, who killed Pascal, they are the descendants of Nazi war criminals?"

Zolan nodded.

"But surely your father could have left with the children at some point?"

"I agree. If he had wanted to."

"Why would he not want to?"

"Because he had already begun to lose his mind. He didn't tell me this, naturally. I was still a child then. But he kept a daily journal, which I have read many times. After the massacre, his entries devolved into a stream of consciousness. He would switch from topic to topic erratically, chronicle his day in one paragraph, go on a religious or political rant in the next. Soon the entries were nothing but illegible scribbles. Living underground in constant fear of discovery, isolated from society, lacking intellectual companionship, never seeing the sun…" Zolan shrugged. "I am not surprised he went crazy. I'm not surprised any of them went crazy."

"Except you."

"Except me."

"Why?"

"Where did you grow up, Danièle?"

She blinked. "Me? Halle. In Saxony-Anhalt, Germany."

"Did you have a good childhood?"

"Yes," she lied.

"I did too," he said. "Are you surprised by that? Life in the catacombs, you see, was the only life the other children and myself knew. We had none of the baggage my father had. No friends or family to miss. No memories of the atrocities he had committed. No fears of capture and execution. In contrast we played games. We explored the tunnels. We had the weekly Franco-Belgium magazines like *Spirou* and *Tintin* that my father brought back from his supply runs.

"For a child, it was acceptable. But the mind grows; the world becomes smaller. Despite being indoctrinated to the dangers of leaving the safety of the catacombs, my siblings and I—or my adopted siblings, I should say—began talking in secret about visiting the streets above us. Nevertheless, before we acted on this, I lost my nerve and confessed our plans to my father. He beat my two brothers and two sisters to within inches of their lives. Then, in our former playroom, what we began to refer to as the Dungeon, he installed four chains, one in each corner—"

"The same chains...?" she said.

"Yes—the same ones that held you and your friends. My brothers and sisters remained imprisoned there for what might have been months. I took care of them the best I could, though my oldest brother, Albert, became sick and passed away. This convinced my father to release them, though to make sure they never tried to escape again, he performed his fait accompli."

"He cut off their noses and lips."

"Turning them into monsters that would never be accepted by society." Zolan shook his head. "They had no medicine for the pain. They couldn't eat or drink properly. They moaned all day and all night. They were regressing before my eyes, losing their humanity. The guilt born from the fact that I had caused this had been too much to bear—it had all been too much—and I had to leave or I would go crazy myself. So that's what I did. I left."

"And...?" she said.

"And what?"

"What happened next?"

He shrugged. "Life happened."

CHAPTER 50

ZOLAN

It had taken Zolan several days to find a way out of the catacombs on his own, but he eventually discovered a drainage culvert that led to a blinding white light. He had never forgotten taking those first steps into that light and being overwhelmed with unfamiliar sensations: the breeze on his face, the heat of the afternoon summer sun on his pale skin, the smell of grasses and wildflowers, the sound of birds and crickets chirping. He must have stared at the sky, the sun, the drifting clouds, for a full hour without moving.

And then there was the city of Paris itself! He had seen pictures of it in the weekly magazines, but they couldn't compare to the real thing. The people, the restaurants, the churches, the traffic, the *size* of the city, the *speed* of it.

Zolan didn't have to worry about revealing his German heritage, because nobody wanted anything to do with a barefoot, wild-eyed gypsy wandering the streets in cartographic anarchy.

For the first week he survived by rooting through garbage bins for scraps of food and sleeping in parks at nighttime. Then early one morning he was apprehended by a shopkeeper when he attempted to steal a freshly baked baguette. When he refused to answer any of the shopkeeper's questions, the man summoned the police. Because he still refused to speak, and he possessed no identification, he was sent to a Catholic orphanage run by a congregation of women known as the Grey Sisters.

Zolan didn't know how old he was then—his father had never celebrated any of his or his siblings' birthdays—but based on the fact he had been born sometime around the end of the war, he guessed he was twelve or thirteen. The other boys at the orphanage were always complaining that there was never enough food, or there was no hot water, but he was in luxury. He had a soft bed of his own (where he hid any extra food he scavenged during the days), he had donated clothes (who cared if they didn't fit), and he had a small wooden bowl in which to "do his duties" (which was a lot easier than digging a hole). Everyone believed he was deaf and dumb and left him alone. He was fine with that. He quietly learned French and English, he devoured whatever books he could get ahold of, and he made friends with a dog that came by every now and then. He was happy.

When Zolan was thought to be sixteen, he was considered a man and sent into the world. That was in 1960. He got a job shining shoes, he got heavy into alcohol, and he killed a man. It had been an accident. He'd only wanted the man's wallet, but the dumb fuck had refused to hand it over and tried to run. Zolan left Paris and traveled much of France: hitchhiking, sneaking onto trains without a ticket, sometimes simply walking on foot. He stayed in Emmaüs shelters, psychiatric institutions, detox centers. Occasionally he found odd jobs as a mason or metal worker. He spent whatever money he made on booze and tranquilizers.

Five years later his past caught up with him. He was back in Paris, and after a late night bar fight he was arrested and charged with assault. While he was in police custody awaiting arraignment, an off-duty inspector thought he fit the description of the suspect who had stabbed to death an up-an-coming politician in 1961, and sure enough his fingerprints matched those collected at the scene of the crime. He was found guilty of first-degree murder, sentenced to eighteen years in prison, and released on parole after ten. He'd been free less than two months when he killed a prostitute. He didn't remember doing it. But housekeeping in a shitty motel found him passed out on the bed with a dead hooker. This time he was given a life sentence and released after twenty-one years. It was 1997, and he was fifty-three years old.

Zolan found work stocking shelves at a Carrefour, kept on the right side of the law, began his love affair with the red light districts, and led a fairly uneventful life for the next two years. That's when he began thinking about the catacombs again, and finding his way back to where he had grown up. He didn't believe his father or siblings would be alive. But he hoped he might find out what happened to them. Get closure of some sort—the type of thing you began caring about more and more the older you get.

So trusting a jumble of research and rumors, he made his way to a specific tunnel underground and followed it to its source: the basement of the Ministry of Telecommunications. He wedged himself between horizontal bars blocking the passage and ascended a staircase to the security office on the building's ground floor. A logbook indicated the guards were off patrolling. He took a spare key ring and combed the building until he discovered what he had come for at the bottom of a desk drawer: maps of the ministry's citywide network of tunnels. He stole a copy of each map, returned the key ring to the security office, and left through the ministry's grand front door onto an empty avenue de Ségur.

Even with the maps, however, which Zolan transcribed into one grand map (and had been improving upon ever since), it took him three years until he found his way home.

And what was waiting for him there.

▼

Zolan refilled Danièle's glass of water, which was somewhat awkward because he had the mother of all erections. It had started ten minutes before when she had been sobbing and bent over in such a way he could see down the throat of her shirt to her cleavage. He'd considered fucking her then and there—who was to stop him?—but he didn't, and he was glad he didn't. Because he was enjoying this interaction, this power trip, even more. She feared him, which meant she respected him. She knew he was her only hope of returning to the surface. She would do anything he wanted her to do. So why take something when he could have it given freely?

Zolan's erection became harder still while Danièle sipped the water and waited obediently for him to proceed.

"After I found my way out of the catacombs as a child, I didn't return to them for nearly half a century," he told her, retaking his seat on the edge of the desk, adjusting himself discreetly. "And when I did, and I made my way back here…how do I explain? It was hard to comprehend what had transpired in my absence. My father was still alive. He was roughly eighty years old then, and if you saw him on the streets of Paris, you would have thought he was mad as a hatter. And he was. But he was still functioning—and providing. Over the decades he had continued to make trips to the surface to gather food and supplies for not only my brother and two sisters but for the four generations that followed through inbreeding.

"This had become his kingdom of sorts—though he was a king of fools, because he gave up any effort to educate or civilize his children or their children or their grandchildren. He knew what would happen if he did. They would leave him for the world above. He would be alone. And being a king of fools was better than being a king of none, I suppose."

Danièle said, "But you said they understood German?"

Zolan nodded. "I should qualify that. They understand words. Pronouns and verbs mostly. 'Me want' or 'you go'—stuff any three or four year old picks up. That's about as far as most of them have matured intellectually."

"How could they live like that?"

"Because they didn't know any better, Danièle. They didn't —and still don't—understand anything is missing from their lives."

"So what do they do day after day?"

Zolan shrugged. "What our ancestors did for millions of years. They obey instinct. They eat, they shit, they fight, they sleep, and they fuck—oh, do they like to fuck. They're like rabbits. Had they been raised in more sanitary conditions there would be twice as many of them."

"And they kill," Danièle said.

"To them, you and your friends were intruders."

"Why not kill us on sight then? Why chain us up and fight us?"

"For sport," he said simply.

"Sport?"

"Entertainment."

"But you just said they are animals—"

"I never said they're animals."

"You said—"

"They function on instinct. But they still have emotions, for emotions are merely the awareness of instincts. They cry, they laugh, they get bored. They have their needs and wants, just like you or I."

"Which include killing innocent people?"

Zolan shrugged again. "We are all savages at heart, Danièle. We are inherently a violent species. We commit wars, genocide, murder. That is why every society is built upon the foundation of law and punishment. We cannot trust ourselves. We need to be kept in line."

"Did they do the same to you as they did to us when you arrived?"

"Imprison me? No—I was the first outsider they ever encountered, and they were too surprised to do anything of the sort before my father recognized me. He was dying then, and he believed my return was a preordained event. I was the son who had returned to inherit his kingdom. I remained for a week, then came back every few days after that, bringing supplies—proper supplies. My father had scrounged from alleyways and trash bins whereas I brought groceries from the supermarket. I was quickly embraced by everyone here. When my father died, I took over."

"And this is what you want?" Danièle said, gesturing vaguely.

"What is wrong with this?" Zolan replied with a faint smile. "Here, I am free—categorically free." He stood decisively. "Now, I imagine you are exhausted. You need to rest. I will take you to your room."

"My room?" She frowned. "But—I thought you would let me go? I will not tell—"

"And what of your friends? You'd leave them behind?"

"No... But, I mean, when they come to, you will let us go?"

"When they come around, we will talk. We will come to some sort of arrangement."

Her frown deepened. "What kind of an 'arrangement?'"

"I don't know," Zolan said, and that was the truth, for he only knew that none of them would leave the underground alive. He went to the door, opened it. "Are you coming?"

Danièle stood hesitantly. "In this room—are you going to chain me up again?"

"Don't be ridiculous," he told her. "You are my guest. You are free to do as you wish."

CHAPTER 51

A ball of searing light was trapped inside my skull and wanted out. That's what it felt like when I opened my eyes. I remained still and prayed for the pain to subside. It didn't, but the white stars cleared from my vision, and I was relieved to find I wasn't in total darkness. A soft yellow glow came from my right. I turned my head. A half-melted candle and—

I started.

Seated on the ground next to the candle was the girl who had visited Danièle and me before. She held a large green book in her hands. Over the top of it emerald eyes studied me attentively. They were utterly captivating.

For a moment I hoped against hope that this nightmare might be at its end, that the girl's face would be whole and beautiful, but even as these thoughts flashed through my mind she lowered the book, revealing her cruel disfigurements.

I focused on her eyes. "Elle…" I mumbled.

The girl—she couldn't have been any older than thirteen or fourteen—set aside the book. She put a finger to her ghastly mouth, indicating that I not speak, then picked up a glass of water. She held it to my lips, using both hands to tilt it. The water was cool. It trickled over my tongue, down my throat. I wanted to take the glass in my hands so I could drink faster, but I found my arms were once more secured behind my back.

The water filled my mouth, poured over my cracked lips,

spilled onto my chest. When there was no more, I looked at the girl, wanting to thank her, but my eyes were pulled to her mutilations. She noticed and tilted her face to the side, almost as if she was ashamed, or bashful.

"My friend?" I said. "Danièle? Where...?"

"Your friend is sleeping," she told me.

I stared. "You speak English?"

Her cheeks dimpled, as if she was smiling. She nodded.

"How...why?" I said.

"I don't understand."

"Who taught you?"

"I taught myself."

I must be dreaming, I thought. This couldn't be real. I was not lying here conversing in English with this hideous thing that spoke like a ventriloquist without moving her lips because she had no lips. "Who are you?" I asked.

"My name is Katja."

"Do you live here...in the catacombs?"

"I should go," she said abruptly, and pushed herself to her knees. "I'm not supposed to speak to you."

"Why? Who told you that?"

"My father. But I cannot—"

"Who's your father?"

She became visibly anxious. "I must go."

"Wait!"

She paused in a half crouch.

"I'm sorry," I said. "Don't go. Please. I...I just want some company."

She watched me for a moment, then retook her seat on the ground. She didn't say anything, and neither did I. I was trying to get my head around this madness. She could speak English. So could they all? No, I doubted that. The others had been different. This girl...she didn't smell like them or act like them. In fact, she seemed downright civilized.

So what the hell was she doing living with them?

I decided to treat her as I would a regular person.

"My name's Will," I said.

"It's a pleasure to meet you, Will."

Like out of a phrasebook. "Katja's a nice name."

"Thank you."

"I won't tell your father that you were here."

She appeared anxious again.

"I promise," I reassured her. "I promise. I just want to talk though. I don't know what's happening."

"You are safe here."

Safe? Maybe she was mad after all. "My friend is dead."

Her face fell. "I know that. I'm sorry. I should have tried to stop them. But Hanns, he does what he wants. He doesn't listen to me."

"Is Hanns your father?"

"He is my uncle."

"He's the one who killed my friend?"

She nodded.

Hanns. I recalled his yellow eyes. They had been filled with a lunatic hate for me. "I hurt him," I said. "I don't think he likes me. I don't think I'm safe."

"No, you are safe now. My father is back. He won't let anything happen to you or your friends."

"You said my friend is sleeping?"

She nodded.

"She is okay?"

Another nod.

"What about my other friend?"

"He is there," she said, and pointed into the darkness where I had last seen Rob.

"Is he breathing?" I asked.

"Of course."

I swallowed. "Why are we chained up, Katja?"

"So you don't leave."

"We won't try to leave."

"You might."

"Is your father like you? Does he speak English?"

"He speaks English and French and German," she said proudly.

I recalled that harsh back-of-the-throat language I'd heard before Jaundice—Hanns—knocked my lights out with the bone.

German.

The Painted Devil?

"What does your father look like?" I asked.

"Like you."

I blinked. "Like me?"

She touched my nose, my lips. The gestures were oddly intimate.

"I understand," I said. "But what does he *look* like."

"Like you."

I swallowed my frustration. "Does he control your uncle and the others?"

"Everyone listens to him, yes."

"You mentioned he was away before. Where did he go? To the surface?"

Her eyes brightened. She leaned closer, conspiratorially. "Have you been to the surface?"

I wasn't sure I heard her right. "Have I been?"

"Have you seen it?"

"That's where I'm from, Katja. I live there."

She seemed stunned by my response. Her brow knit. "You are not telling me the truth."

"Yes, I am. I live there. My friends too—"

"You're a liar! No one lives on the surface."

"Yes—"

"No!" She snapped to her feet.

"I can show you, I can take you—"

"You're a liar! My father told me you would try to lie to me. That is why I am not supposed to talk to you."

"I'm not lying, Katja. Your father is lying to you—"

"Stop it!"

She scooped up her candle and dashed toward the exit.

"Katja!" I shouted desperately. "Don't go! Come back!"
She didn't.

▼

I lay awake in the dark for a long while. I didn't bother to test my restraints. I didn't have the strength to. Instead I focused on the questions buzzing around inside my head. Why were Katja and Hanns and everyone in her so-called family carved up like they were? Why was Katja so different than the rest of them? Who was her father, and why had he told her nobody lived on the surface? Where did she think I came from if not the surface? Why did the mention of her father instill such fear in her? Why had she come to see me if she was forbidden to do so? Why had Danièle been moved to a different room while Rob and I remained here? Was Danièle really okay? Was Rob really still in this room? Was I really safe for the time being? *Was any of this really fucking happening?*

I took a deep breath. It came out shaky. I took another and another until I was breathing evenly. I rolled onto my side to relieve pressure from my burning shoulders. This proved extremely uncomfortable, so I returned to the supine position. I closed my eyes, opened them, closed them, opened them. I felt as if I were floating. I felt as if I were in eternity. I closed my eyes and imagined I was in deep space, floating, as light as a feather, floating through space, floating with no worries, floating, no up, no down, no direction whatsoever, floating and floating and floating...

▼

I was inside my bedroom closet in the fraternity house. Danièle was with me. We were hiding, but from what I didn't know. Neither of us spoke, and the silence dragged on. Then I heard movement. It was Danièle. She was moving closer to me. I wanted to tell her to stop making so much noise, but my mouth wouldn't work. She placed her hand on the top of my thigh. She left it there for several long seconds before moving it onto my crotch. I became aroused. This embarrassed me because I wasn't sure Danièle knew where her hand was. It was dark. Maybe she thought her hand was on my knee, or on my hip. If she realized I was turned on, she would likely think I was a depraved pervert. This wasn't the time or the place for sex. We were in danger, we should be focused on survival—

Her fingers worked the button of my jeans. They were strong, dexterous, efficient. They pulled down the zipper. They gripped my erection and moved up and down, slowly at first, experimentally, then faster and with more friction, faster until my heartbeat raced, faster still, faster until I groaned—and that sound shattered the dream, because it hadn't come from the dream.

I opened my eyes and discovered Katja bent over me, her fist pumping quickly.

I cried out and jerked away from her. She yelped herself and fell backward onto her rear.

"What the fuck?" I blurted, my breathing coming in gasps.

"I'm sorry," she said. "I thought—" She seemed about to flee.

"Wait, it's okay," I said, keeping the revulsion from my voice. "I was just surprised, that's all." I wiggled myself to my elbows, then rocked forward, so I was sitting upright. My shirt draped my genitals. "I'm glad you came back," I added just as genially as if we'd bumped into each other in the park.

"I thought you would like that," she said. Her teeth were white in the candlelight, in contrast to the bubblegum pink of her gums. She wore the same too-large Icelandic wool sweater and charcoal tights.

"I did. I do." I cleared my throat. "I—I was just surprised. I was dreaming."

"Do you want me to finish?"

"No, not now. Maybe later." *Maybe later?* "Where did you go earlier?"

"I returned to my room."

"Did you go to sleep?"

"I tried to, but I couldn't."

"What time is it? Do you have time here?"

"Of course we do." She pulled up her sleeve, revealing a yellow Timex wristwatch. "It is four thirty in the morning."

"That's a nice watch."

"My father gave it to me," she said happily. "Do you have time where you're from?" She folded her legs beneath her, planted her elbows on her knees, and cupped her chin in her hands. A sweet farm girl from a Norman Rockwell painting—on Halloween night.

"Yeah, I do," I told her. "What time does everyone here wake up?"

"Whenever they want to."

"You have a rooster? I heard it...yesterday?"

"His name is Colin. Have you read *The Secret Garden*?"

"No... Have you?"

"Yes! It is one of my favorite books. There's a girl in it, her name is Mary, who has to go live with her uncle Archibald Craven at his home called Misselthwaite Manor. When she's there, she hears someone crying in the middle of the night. It turns out this is her cousin Colin. He has some problem with his spine that causes him a lot of pain and to cry out. When I read this, I thought of the rooster, which always makes noise in the early morning. That's why I named him Colin. We also have six hens. We had seven, but one died last week."

"I...okay." I couldn't think of anything to say. This was too bizarre. "So you eat eggs for breakfast?"

"Sometimes. Do you?"

"Sometimes. Katja?"

"Yes?"

"What's going to happen when your father wakes up?"

"What do you mean?"

"Is he going to want to speak to me?"

"I imagine so. But remember, you can't tell him I visited you. You promised."

"I know. I won't say anything. Do you know what he will

want to speak to me about?"

"Where you came from, probably."

"Where—where did I come from?"

Her brow knitted. "I do not think you are well. I think you need to rest."

I licked my lips. "Katja, I think I lost my memory when your uncle hit me in the head. I...I can't seem to remember anything before I arrived here. I'm really confused."

She issued a high-pitched sound, and I realized it was laughter. "That is why you thought you lived on the surface!" She clapped her hands.

"Yes...so...can I ask you some questions? They might sound strange, but they will help with my memory."

"What would you like to know?"

"What year is it?"

"I'm not sure exactly."

"Can you guess?"

"Twenty ten? Twenty fifteen?" She shrugged.

"Why do you live underground?"

"For the same reason you do."

"Why is that?"

She gave me a skeptical look. "You really don't know?"

"I told you, my memory..."

"Paris was destroyed in the war."

"What war?"

"World War Two, by nuclear bombs. No one can live there. Acid rain falls from the sky, and the air is filled with radiation that is invisible, but it can kill you in minutes."

"But it doesn't kill your father? You said he goes to the surface."

"He has a special suit."

I nodded. A special suit. Why the fuck not. But at least it was all starting to come together—well, some of it. "Haven't you ever wanted to see the surface for yourself?"

"The suit is too big for me. But my father promised me he will find a way to take me one day."

"Katja, what would you think if I told you Paris wasn't destroyed in World War Two by nuclear bombs, there is no acid rain or radiation, and there are in fact several million people living there right now?"

Her eyes sparkled with amusement. "I would think you really need to rest."

▼

"You said you read *The Secret Garden*," I said. "What other books have you read?"

"Oh, too many to count. I have a bookcase full of them."

"What kind of books?"

"Mostly novels. But I have a lot of language books too. My father says learning languages is one of the best ways to pass the time and keep your mind sharp."

"Were any of these books published after 1945?"

"1945?"

"After Paris was destroyed."

"Of course not. That would be impossible."

"But have you checked?"

"How would I check?"

"Inside each book there is a publication date on one of the first few pages."

"Really? I have never seen those. But, no, none of my books would have been published after 1945. Like I said, that would be impossible."

I eyed her wristwatch, thinking of telling her it was less than ten years old. But there was no date stamped on it. To her, that was simply what watches were like pre-1945.

I ground my jaw in frustration. How did you convince someone, without any physical proof, that an entire alternate history existed?

I said, "How did World War Two end?"

"The United States developed the nuclear bomb and dropped a lot of them on Paris."

"Why would they do that? The French were on the Americans' side."

"But the Germans were in Paris and they wouldn't leave. It was the only option."

"So what about the rest of the world?"

"What do you mean?"

"The entire world wasn't destroyed, right?"

"I don't know."

"You don't know?"

"How could I? I can't go check."

"You father could with his suit."

She shook her head. "It only protects him for a short time. He wouldn't be able to leave Paris."

I wasn't getting anywhere with this line of reasoning. The worldview fed to her presumably by her father was a simple one, but the logic was sound. My only option, it seemed, was to tell her the blunt truth. Only how would she react to this? Accuse me of lying again and run off? I couldn't afford that. I needed her. She was, I believed, my only chance of escape. She painted her father to be a just man who would keep me safe, but just men didn't live underground with murderers and disfigure and brainwash their children.

I said, "Katja, can I tell you a secret?"

She leaned forward. "Yes?"

"Do you promise me you won't call me a liar?"

She knitted her brow suspiciously. "I don't know..."

"I promised you that I wouldn't tell your father we're speaking. You can at least promise me you won't call me a liar."

"Well, okay, I guess."

"Not all of Paris was destroyed in the war. Most of it was," I added quickly. "And you can't visit it without a suit because of the acid rain and radiation. You're right about that. I remember all of this now. But I also remember there is *another* part of Paris where the radiation isn't bad and you can see the sun and you don't even need a suit. Not many people know about it.

Your father probably doesn't know either. But my friends and I found it. We've seen it."

She stared at me for a long moment, the way a child might when trying to figure out whether you're pulling his or her leg or not. And that's what Katja was, wasn't she? A child. She might have the body of a young teenager, but she was intellectually stunted. Everything she knew came from the books she'd read, or word of mouth from her father. It was all taken on blind faith. Nothing was grounded in gritty experience.

Slowly, she began shaking her head. I was losing her, I realized, if I'd ever hooked her to begin with. "Katja—"

"You're a liar!"

"Katja, you promised you wouldn't—"

She backed away from me. "Liar!"

"Look at my skin! It's not like yours. It's dark. That's from the sun."

She hesitated.

"Katja, I'm telling you the truth! And I can take you to the surface. I can show you it without a suit."

"Stop it!"

"Please, Katja. If you free me, I'll take you, I'll show you—"

"You're tricking me!" she yelled. "You just want to escape! You're a liar, and I hate you!"

She fled, sobbing, into the blackness.

CHAPTER 52

KATJA

She should have listened to her father, Katja decided as she slowed to a walk. She should never have visited Will.

Originally she had only wanted to see what he and his friends looked like. She had not planned on speaking to any of them (and in this way she wouldn't really be disobeying her father's orders, would she?). Even when they spoke to her —the woman in French, Will in English—she had not replied. She had wanted to, because Will had fascinated her. With his dark hair and dark eyes, and his nose and mouth, he was how she imagined Prince Caspian to be in *The Voyage of the Dawn Trader*. Also, after that first encounter, feelings—strange, warm feelings she'd never experienced before—came to life inside her. She had not been able to stop thinking about him, and she'd even imagined she would marry him and become Queen of the Catacombs, just as Ramandu's daughter married Caspian and became Queen of Narnia.

So eventually, inevitably, she had gone back to see him again, and even when he lied to her, she had gone back yet again. And she had touched him. That memory shot a shiver of pleasure through her body, made her inner thighs go tingly, though this was quickly followed by a cloud of dejection. Because why had he wanted her to stop? Her uncles touched their penises all the time, and it always made them happy. Had she done something wrong then? Had she hurt him?

Katja reached her room and rubbed the drying tears from her cheeks. A tarpaulin with "Building Site, No Access" stenciled across the front of it covered the doorway. Her father had installed it there so she could have more privacy. Sometimes her uncles not only touched their own penises, but they wanted her to touch them too. She never felt an urge to do this like she had with Will, however, and during these occasions she would take refuge in her room, where they knew they were not allowed. Before the tarpaulin was in place, they would remain in the doorway and tell her to watch while they played with themselves. Now they left her alone for the most part—except for Hanns. He would simply push the tarpaulin aside. All she could do was turn her back to him and cover her ears with her hands and wait until he left again.

Inside the room Katja considered going to her bed and lying down, but she still wasn't tired. Instead she went to her bookcase. She set the candle on a shelf and plucked free one of her favorite books: *Anne of Green Gables*. It was the longest book she'd ever read, and she was always proud to feel its weight in her hands. She opened the cover. The first two pages displayed the table of contents, while the first chapter, "Mrs. Rachel Lynde Is Surprised," began on the third page.

Where was the publication date Will mentioned?

Katja returned the novel to its spot on the shelf and plucked free her next favorite story: *The Wonderful Wizard of Oz*. A quick look revealed no publication date. She checked a third novel—*The Lion, The Witch and the Wardrobe*—and frowned.

The second page, it seemed, had been torn out. A sliver of it, the edge jagged, poked out from the glue.

Feeling suddenly sick with something she didn't like, she opened two dozen other books—*The Tale of Peter Rabbit, The Wind in the Willows, Winnie the Pooh, The Velveteen Rabbit, Peter Pan*, more—and they all had pages torn out. She had never noticed this before because you really had to look closely to tell.

Had these missing pages contained the publication dates that Will had mentioned? Who had torn them free? Her father? But why? Because the books had been printed after 1945? But that would mean Paris wasn't destroyed—or at least some city somewhere wasn't destroyed. Why would her father not want her to know this?

Then she recalled what Will had said: *Katja, what would you think if I told you Paris wasn't destroyed in World War Two by nuclear bombs, there is no acid rain or radiation, and there are in fact several million people living there right now?*

Katja went cold all over. She didn't want to think about this anymore. But she couldn't stop herself either.

Paris had been destroyed. It was filled with radiation and acid rain.

It had to be.

But what if it wasn't?

She was tempted to go and wake her father right then, he would have an answer to why the publication pages were missing, he had answers to everything, but she didn't go and wake him, because that feeling she didn't like was still inside her, it was oily and nauseating and she didn't like it one bit, and it took her a long time to attach a name to what it was: betrayal.

▼

Katja studied the poster on her wall. Her father had given it to her several years before. It showed Paris in ruin. All the buildings were destroyed and covered in snow, and the Eiffel Tower was broken in half. Along the top of it were the words: "The Day After Tomorrow." Her father said that's what people called the day the United States dropped the bombs on Paris. She never understood why it would be called The Day After Tomorrow. Didn't that mean it happened in the future? Anyway, she never questioned him—and she never questioned why the bottom section of the poster had been torn free.

▼

Katja stood outside the door to her father's quarters and listened. She didn't hear him moving about inside, but that didn't mean he was sleeping. He could be sitting at his desk, reading. Still, she had to take a chance. She felt as if she were falling apart inside, and she needed to know who to believe, what to believe. She needed to know the truth.

She pushed open the door and let out the breath she'd been holding. The study was unoccupied. A number of candles burned softly, so she set hers aside. She didn't like this room because of the bones that covered the walls. Her father told her that her grandfather was responsible for this. She didn't remember her grandfather, but she'd always secretly hated him. According to her father, just after she was born, her grandfather tried to take their family to the surface without suits. Everybody became sick and returned underground, but the damage was done. They turned crazy and their noses and lips fell off. Only her father was unaffected because he had been smart enough to remain in the catacombs. And since she was so young, he was able to reverse the craziness inside her and raise her like a regular little girl.

He's done everything for me, she thought, fighting tears. *He wouldn't lie to me. I shouldn't be here.*

Katja crept forward. Books were scattered everywhere. She wasn't allowed to read them because they were for Adults Only. Some appeared really old, while others seemed much newer. She chose a newer one with a scary cover. It was thick and called *The Stand*. On the fourth page she read: First Anchor Books Mass-Market Edition, June 2011. And below that: Copyright © 1978, 1990 by Stephen King. There were other years on the page as well, but her eyes glossed over them. The print was too small, and her head was spinning.

The book fell from her hands and hit the floor with a

heavy thud. This snapped her from her stupor. Heart racing, she glanced toward the connecting bedroom. When her father didn't emerge, she pivoted, intent on leaving. That's when she spotted an orange bag peeking out from behind her father's desk. She had never seen it before—it was so bright and new—and she was sure it belonged to Will or one of his friends. She was also sure she needed to see what was inside it.

She approached silently, stepping as lightly as she could, careful not to bump anything. The stone floor was cool under her bare feet.

She rounded her father's desk and discovered four bags in total, all different colors. She knelt before the orange one and unzipped the main pocket. She cringed at the sound the zipper made, but there was nothing she could do to quiet it. She pulled out a red sweatshirt. Beneath this was a black can. She turned it so she could read the label: Bière du Démon. She had never seen this particular beer before, but she had seen several other kinds. Her father drank them often. Like the books in this room, they were for Adults Only. The only other item in the bag was a scrunched piece of white paper. She unfolded it and discovered a list of some sort. She recognized a few of the words—bread, cereal, milk—but not others. Schweppes? Nivea? And what were those numbers on the right?

Katja stuck this in her tights and unzipped the bag's smaller pocket. There was a blue wallet inside, what people used to use to hold their money. She opened it and gasped. There were several bills inside. She had never seen actual money before, and she reached for one—

"Katja, what are you doing?"

Her lungs locked in her chest. She dropped the wallet back into the pocket and yanked the zipper closed and stood just as her father stormed around the desk.

"What in God's name are you doing?" he shouted.

Katja shrank away from him. He had never hit her before like he hit her aunts and uncles, but she was sure he was going to hit her right then.

"I couldn't sleep!" she blurted.

"You know you're not allowed in here when I'm not up."

"I know! I'm sorry! I'm scared!"

Through the tears that blurred her vision, she saw his face change. The hard lines softened. "What are you scared of?"

"The visitors! I had a nightmare of them attacking us. That's why I couldn't sleep. So I came here, and I saw these bags."

"Did you open all of them?"

"Only that one."

Her father picked up the orange bag, took the beer out. "This is all that was in it?"

"And this." She handed him the red sweatshirt.

"Did you go through the other bags?"

"No, I promise."

He tossed the bag aside and held out a hand for her. She took it. He pulled her to her feet and kissed her on the cheek. "I'm sorry I yelled at you, my mouse," he said with a sigh. "But you know better than to come in here when I'm not up. We have rules for a reason. Without rules there would be no order, and without order, there would be chaos."

"I'm sorry, Papa. I won't do it again."

"Good. And you have no need to fear the visitors. They're chained up in the Dungeon. They can't go anywhere I don't want them to."

Katja wanted to ask him where the woman had gone, because only Will and the other man were in the Dungeon, but that would give away that she had visited them. Instead she asked, "What's going to happen to them?"

"Once I speak to them, and make sure they are not a threat to our way of life here, I will return them to where they came from, just as I have done with all the previous visitors."

If her father had told Katja this a few hours ago, she would have believed him wholeheartedly. She still wanted to, but she couldn't.

She couldn't believe him about anything anymore.

"Now," he said, stifling a yawn with his knuckles, "it is still some time until Colin crows. You can sleep in my bed with me if you wish."

"No, I feel better now. I will return to my room."

She started for the door.

"Katja?"

She paused. "Yes?"

"I love you. I would never let anybody harm you."

"I know, Papa," she said, fighting a fresh onslaught of tears. "I know."

CHAPTER 53

DANIÈLE

Danièle's "room" was furnished with nothing but a hammock, a plastic table meant for a four year old, a candle melted onto a ceramic plate, and a book of matches. She had waited a couple minutes after Zolan escorted her there, to make certain he was gone, then she stuck her head out the door. The hallway was lit with torches set in wall sconces, and some twenty meters to the right (the hallway ended abruptly to the left) she made out two zombie-men. One stood with his back against the wall, tapping a bone-weapon against his forehead. The other paced back and forth. At every about-turn he would touch a wall with a finger or toe ritualistically.

Apparently she wasn't free to do as she wished after all.

Of course she wasn't, she thought. How could she have allowed herself to believe this?

Danièle summoned her nerve and walked toward the zombie-men. She wanted to test her boundaries, but she also needed to find someplace to relieve her bladder and bowels.

The pacing zombie stopped. His left index finger remained pressed to the wall, as if he were ringing a doorbell. He stared at her, though she couldn't read anything in his hellish face. The one tapping his head with the bone stared too, then licked the end of the bone with his tongue. Danièle didn't know if this was sexual innuendo or an unconscious act, but it made her want to turn around and return to her room.

She didn't. She kept her back straight, her chin high. She was sure Zolan would have warned them not to touch her. But the question was: would they obey him? Zombies did whatever they wanted, didn't they?

Zombie #1 with the wall fetish didn't move to let her pass, and she was forced to stop directly before him. He stank. She couldn't remember ever smelling something so vile. There was the feces and urine and body odor, but there was something else mixed with all this, a peaty rottenness she associated with bogs. She guessed he was anywhere between forty and sixty. He was mostly bald, with greasy tufts of white hair sprouting above his ears. He had the normal disfigurements (God, was she already beginning to think no nose or lips as "normal?"), and his albino-white skin was etched with burst capillaries and scabs and smeared with mud. He wore a torn Rolling Stones T-shirt and frayed track pants soiled in the groin and knees. The body beneath the clothes seemed lean and hard.

She stepped right, to go around him. He matched her step. She went left; he went left. Zombie #2 issued a wobbly bellow that she assumed to be a laugh. Zombie #1 joined him, laughing in her face.

His breath was so foul she acted without thinking, shoving him aside so she could get past and get fresh air. When she realized what she'd done, she expected him to grab a fistful of her hair and drag her back to her room like cavemen did in the Sunday morning comics. He didn't, and she kept walking, staring straight ahead as she passed Zombie #2.

Danièle didn't know if they were following her, she couldn't hear them if they were, but she didn't check. She didn't want to show uncertainty, which would be interpreted as weakness. She went straight until a secondary hallway broke off from the one she followed. This led to Zolan's study, she knew from memory. As she glanced down it, she saw in her peripheral vision that the two zombie-men had indeed followed her. They hovered about ten yards back.

She resumed walking and came to another intersecting corridor, this one unlit. She paused at it. *Make a dash into the darkness?* No. She wouldn't get far. The zombies would catch her. They would tell Zolan she attempted to escape. Whatever privileges she had been afforded would likely be withdrawn. She needed to be patient, wait for a better opportunity.

She continued straight and after several minutes arrived at what seemed to be a kitchen of sorts. It was a large room with a high ceiling and a central fire pit, the embers within the circle of rocks glowing hotly. The air smelled of smoke and stale produce. Lining the walls were homemade shelves that overflowed with boxes and containers. On the ground sat a basket of potatoes, and another of mushrooms. On a crudely constructed table were an assortment of pots and pans, plates and bowls. And scattered everywhere: junk. Broken chairs, slabs of wood, sheets of rusted metal, a stack of flattened cardboard boxes.

She entered the room reverently, as you would enter somewhere you were not supposed to be—and sensed movement from the shadows. A zombie-woman sat among a pile of trash. She watched Danièle but didn't say anything. She held her gnarled hands tightly against her sunken chest. Her head was cocked to one side. Through a gap where several teeth had once been, her tongue protruded like a worm, liver red, running back and forth over her gums. She cackled, almost as if she were trying to speak. She repeated the cackle at intervals, cricket-like. From ahead, through an arched doorway, a loud, terrible groan responded.

Danièle recoiled a step, then dashed back past the zombie-men, all the way to her room.

▼

The rest of the day passed with excruciating slowness.

A zombie-woman—a different one than the decrepit thing that had made those cricket noises—brought Danièle breakfast a little after the rooster cock-a-doodle-dooed again: eggs scrambled with mushrooms and a cup of black tea. Danièle was hesitant to eat the eggs, but her hunger proved too great. Afterward she used the plate and spoon to dig a hole in the corner of the room to serve as a latrine. She had no toilet paper and felt disgustingly dirty after she did her business, but what could she do?

Sometimes the zombie-men in the hallway made loud noises, which she assumed passed for communication, but for the most part they were quiet, and when she checked on them, sedentary. They simply sat and stared, the way old people in nursing homes sat and stared at the same spot on the wall.

Danièle wanted to stay awake, stay alert, but her eyelids turned impossibly heavy, and she dozed off in the hammock. She woke later to Zolan standing in the entrance to the room.

"What time is it?" she asked, completely disorientated.

"Time?" He seemed amused, as if he was about to ask her if she had somewhere to be. Instead he said, "It is time to eat. Come."

"I am not hungry."

"You haven't eaten anything but eggs today."

"I am not hungry."

The simian smile remained on Zolan's face. "Come anyway," he said, though he was no longer asking.

Danièle got up and followed him. The two zombie-men were gone.

"You said I would be free to do as I wished," she said.

"You haven't been?"

"Two of your nephews or grandnephews sat outside my room all day."

"Jörg and Karl, yes. They were there for your protection. Only a fraction of these hallways are lighted. I did not want you to get lost."

"I would not have gotten lost."

242

"Maybe not. But you might have run into some of my other family members who aren't as…civilized…as Jörg and Karl."

Danièle recalled the groan from the room beyond the kitchen. She said, "Are we going to discuss the 'arrangement' for my friends and myself now?"

Zolan shook his head. "Unfortunately your friends have yet to regain consciousness."

This was the news she'd feared. "What if they are in comas? What if—"

"As I told you—"

"They need help!" She stopped on the spot. "I want to see them."

"That's not a good idea right now."

"Why not?"

"They need their rest."

"Are they dead?" Her voice cracked on "dead."

"Of course not."

"I want to see them," she repeated stubbornly.

"They are being cared for, and they will recover. You must be patient. That is all I am willing to say on the matter."

Zolan began to walk. Frustrated, feeling helpless, Danièle fell into step behind him. They didn't speak. The only sound was their footsteps and the spitting of the torches.

Zolan turned right at the corridor that led to his quarters.

Danièle stopped again. "Are we not going to the kitchen?"

"Our food will be brought to us."

She hesitated. She didn't want to be alone with him in his study again—or bedroom, for that matter. Almost immediately, however, she realized how foolish that concern was. If he wanted to do something to her, he would do it, regardless of where they were. Those zombie-things wouldn't interfere. In fact, they would likely join in.

They continued on. Zolan's quarters were located at the end of the corridor. He pushed open the door, and they entered. He saw her glance at the tomes scattered everywhere and said, "I'm a voracious reader, and the catacombs is as good a place as anywhere for such a pastime."

Danièle sat in the chair she had sat in earlier, while he took the one across the desk. She said, "What else do you do here?"

"In the catacombs?" He shrugged. "What you do: I explore. It has turned into an obsession of sorts for me. Also, I enjoy meeting the variety of cataphiles who now occupy the tunnels. It is nice to have fresh conversation sometimes."

For the first time Danièle wondered whether Zolan had a job or not. Did he climb out of the catacombs in the early hours of dawn and get on the Metro like everyone else? Did he bring clean clothes in a backpack and change in a train station restroom? Surely he didn't work at anything that required a suit and a tie. A construction worker perhaps? Or a McDonald's employee, the guy who flipped the burgers? This line of thinking led her to her job at the florist shop. Flo, the owner, likely had a meltdown when she discovered Danièle had never arrived for her shift. Flowers not watered, orders not taken, deliveries not made. Nevertheless, this was nothing more than a fleeting thought. Danièle was a prisoner in the catacombs, and Pascal was dead—

No, stop it. She had not allowed herself to think about Pascal since he died, and she wouldn't until she was free of this place. Then she would grieve. Now she had to deal with the madman Zolan—who was not only insane but also delusional. Because did he really think he had her fooled? Did he really think she believed he was going to let them all go? He would have to know they would head straight to the police, and the police would arrest him and his entire zombie family.

So why not kill us and be done with the problem then? she wondered. *Why is he stringing us along—or at least stringing me along? What's his plan?*

He obviously wanted something, and Danièle could guess what. She saw how he looked at her. Lustful. She was aware of this even back at the Bunker. Yet if he wanted to fuck her, why not do it? Why this charade that she was a guest? Was he trying to romance her? Did he think she would fall in love with him and live down here with him?

Yes, he really is crazy—as crazy as the rest of them.

Zolan took a bottle of vodka and two glasses from his desk. He filled one halfway to the rim, nodded to the other. "Will you join me?"

"No thank you," she said stiffly.

He fussed with something on the ground—she couldn't see past the desk—then held up her cask of wine. He raised an eyebrow.

"No thank you," she repeated.

"I know what you want then." He fussed again, and a moment later he produced her Ziploc baggie of marijuana. He saw the reaction on her face and smiled. "We all have our vices, don't we?" He tossed the baggie on the table in front of her.

Danièle stared at it. No way was she going to get high with Zolan...but, God, a few tokes would be nice. Just two, maybe three, just enough to calm her nerves a little.

"Please, indulge," he said. "It is not for me."

Zolan shot a second cigarette from his pack and lit up. The smell of the burning tobacco, and the fact he wasn't getting high too, decided it for her. She opened the baggie, withdrew the papers and a clump of pot, and crumbled the pot between her fingers. When she finished rolling the joint, Zolan passed her a brass Zippo. She accepted it guiltily, like a crack addict accepting the needle that had just killed her friend.

She lit the joint and inhaled deeply.

Zolan sipped his vodka and said, "Tell me something about yourself, Danièle."

She hated it when he used her name, it presumed a disturbing and artificial familiarity, but she didn't say anything. She held the smoke in her lungs for as long as she could, then exhaled. The act was Zen-like. The tension in her neck and shoulders seemed to leave her body with the smoke. "Something?" she said, opening her eyes.

"The past. A story." Zolan slid her the ashtray.

Danièle took another long drag. "A story?" She exhaled

again. She should put the joint out. Two tokes was enough. She only needed a small high, a medicinal high.

She tapped the ash from the end of it into the ashtray, but she didn't put it out. "I do not have any stories."

"Everyone has a story."

She took a third drag. She was already quite high. Her lack of nourishment and sleep likely had to do with this. Yet she knew she was going to smoke the joint until there was nothing left of it. She wanted to get fucked. She wanted oblivion.

Zolan was waiting patiently for her to tell him a story. A story! Who was this guy? Did he think he was her friend? She would kill him if she could—she would too, wouldn't she? She would commit murder?

Yes, if she had to. If it meant escaping here.

What about right now?

After all, it was just the two of them. There were no zombie-things outside. If she killed him, she could take a candle and flee into one of those dark tunnels. They would have to lead somewhere. She couldn't rescue Will and Rob, not by herself, but if she could find a way to the surface, she could return with help.

My God, she thought, she could do this—couldn't she? Yes! She had to. And look at him. The swine. The lust was all over his face. She could tell him a story, get him believing she was cooperating with him, she was accepting him, let him make an advance, and then, bam, she would kill him.

But with what?

Danièle stubbed the joint out in the ashtray—she would need her wits about her after all—and said, "When I was six years old, my father picked me up from school on a Monday afternoon. This was strange because it was always my mother who picked me up. He took me to the cinema to watch *The Last Unicorn*. It was a child's movie, but it scared me so badly we had to leave early. Afterward we got ice cream, then we returned home." She swallowed. She never talked about this. Even now, even in the predicament she was in, the memories were like razor blades inside her heart, and with each breath, with each word, they cut a little deeper. "My father led me to the basement. My mother was there. She was tied up in a chair, which had toppled onto its side, so her face was pressed against the floor. My older sister was tied up in a chair too. They both had gags in their mouths, stifling their screams. My father told me to sit in a third chair, though he didn't tie me up. I guess he didn't think I was a threat. Or maybe he was going to kill me first. I don't know. He explained to my sister and I that he had been fired from his job the week before, and that he would not be able to provide for us any longer. He told us that our mother no longer loved him. She had no faith in him. She thought he was a failure. He told us she wanted to leave him and take us with her. He told us he couldn't let that happen. He told us he had a better solution, one in which we would remain together, forever. He walked past us and retrieved a carving knife from where he had stashed it atop the old oil furnace. At that same moment our doorbell rang. This gave me courage and I jumped from the chair and ran. My father chased me up the stairs. He caught me in the foyer before I could reach the front door handle. He covered my mouth with his hand. I bit him. He let go and I screamed. My father had not locked the door—I guess that was not something you bothered to do when you were planning on murdering your family and yourself—and it burst open. My neighbor, Monsieur Rochefort, appeared with his daughter, my best friend. He drove us to Guides every Monday evening. My father attacked him with the knife, but Monsieur Rochefort was able to wrestle the knife away and subdue him while his daughter and I ran next door and got her mother to call the police. My father was charged with three counts of attempted murder and hanged himself while awaiting trial. We moved to France the following year."

An uncomfortable silence stretched between them. Zolan finished his vodka. Then he got up and came around the desk, came up behind her. He placed his hands on her shoulders and massaged her back with strong thumbs. "It seems, Danièle," he said, "that you and I have something in common."

Danièle never took her eyes off the vodka bottle on his desk. "And what is that?"

"Both our fathers are rotting in hell."

CHAPTER 54

Someone was calling my name, it came from the edges of the darkness, I heard it and knew I was asleep, knew I needed to wake up, but the darkness was too thick, too black, and I couldn't claw through it, and I wondered if maybe my injuries had caught up to me after all, and I wasn't asleep but unconscious, in a coma, and this terrified me because maybe I would remain in such a state forever, aware of the darkness, and the voices that called to me from the margins, but unable to do anything to reach those voices or a higher awareness, fated to live like a snail in the void—

I opened my eyes and found myself in a new darkness. But that was okay. Because this was real, I was awake, I wasn't brain dead—

"Will! Wake up, bro! Wake the fuck up!"

I rolled onto my side. The chains clinked. Everything from my shoulders down was pins and needles. "Rob?" I groaned.

"Will!" he barked, his voice hoarse, nasally. "Where the fuck are we?"

"The cata..." My throat was parched again. "Catacombs."

"I know that! But what *happened*? Some fucking guy attacked me. Drove a bone into my face. Broke my fucking nose. And now I'm chained up. What the hell? *What the fuck's going on?*"

So I told him.

▼

Katja spent the day reminiscing, scrutinizing, doubting, despairing. So many lies! Lies she had believed unconditionally. Lies like that photograph she had found in her father's study, the photograph he insisted was of her grandfather and grandmother before the war, even though her "grandfather" appeared identical to him, and her "grandmother" didn't appear to be much older than her. Lies like when he drank too much beer and mumbled in a stupor of a living, breathing Paris, mumbles he would dismiss the next day as "dream words." Lies like his explanation that their food came from a warehouse that hadn't been destroyed by the nuclear bombs —food that somehow remained fresh after all that time even when some of the bread and fruit and vegetables in their kitchen went moldy after only a few days.

A dozen other lies, two dozen, all so clear now, all leaving her feeling shaken and scared and thrilled and most of all angry.

What had she been denied all these years?

▼

Rob was full of questions while I explained to him what had transpired over the last day or so, but he went quiet when I finished. His silence lasted for several minutes. Then I heard a couple sharp intakes of breath and louder exhales, shuddering, gritty—a man trying to keep his emotions in check. It was the most depressing and lonely sound I had ever heard. "You know the last thing I said to the wife?" he said finally in a gruff voice. "I told her..." He began to chuckle. "Told her to go fuck herself."

"You tell everyone to go fuck themselves."

"This was different. I meant it. She knew I meant it. I think it was the end."

"The end?"

"The end! The marriage. The fucking end. I think it was over."

I didn't say anything.

"We'd stopped talking a while ago," he went on. "Meaningful talking. Now we're like bitter old fucks on TV sitcoms, only it's not funny. We don't talk about the news at breakfast, don't talk about our days, she tells me I'm making a mess while I'm cooking, and I tell her to get out of the fucking kitchen if it bothers her so much. You wanna guess why we're still together?"

"Your girls?"

"Yeah, my girls. They're the world to me. Bella's five, Mary's three. Bella's just started kindergarten. It's turned her into a diva. She's suddenly decided she doesn't like vegetables and only wants pasta and butter and cheese—for every meal, every day. She also thinks she's too old for naps. I'm good with that because by bedtime she's so tired she zonks off immediately. It's amazing how fast they grow up. I know people always say that, but it blows my mind. Mary can barely draw a circle and still has imaginary friends, while Bella can jump rope, skate, walk on a balance beam..."

"You're going to see them again, Rob—"

"Pascal's dead!" he snapped. "Danièle's gone! You think we're walking out of here? You and me—we're next. Dead. I'm not seeing my girls again. They're going to grow up with some knob jockey stepdad and forget what I ever fucking looked like."

CHAPTER 55

ROB

Rob flopped onto his back and rapped the back of his head on the hard-packed floor, overwhelmed with memories and emotions. He plucked a good memory, a pleasant one, out of the whirlwind. His wedding day—when everything in his life had been working, when everything had been right. Dev, so beautiful in her dress, stunning, unreal, entering the chapel, walking down the aisle slowly the way all brides do, her father beside her, proud to the point of bursting, Dev stopping at the altar, eyes so bright, filled with excitement for what their future together held. Later, searching for an apartment, one with a spare room that they could convert to a nursery, Dev stumbling out of the bathroom, her pants and knickers down around her ankles, shrieking that she was pregnant. Her water breaking during an episode of *Friends*, rushing her to the hospital, seeing Bella for the first time, a tiny dusky blue thing covered in ropes of blood and vernix, watching her take her first breath, her color turning to a rosy pink. Her first birthday, the flat filled with foil balloons; her second birthday, the flat filled with other toddlers. A couple weeks after that, having dinner in a nice restaurant, Dev saying she was pregnant again, celebrating with a bottle of wine, chatting like they were the only two in the place, in love...

Rob rapped the back of his head on the ground again,

harder.

Into the darkness he said, "You're right, boss. We're going to get out of here. I'm going to see my girls again. We're…" He squeezed his eyes tight. "Who's Max?"

Will sounded startled. "How do you know that name?"

"You were mumbling it in your sleep."

"What did I say?"

"Don't know. Just heard Max a bunch of times."

A long pause. "She was my younger sister."

"Was?"

"I killed her."

Rob pushed himself to his elbows, staring, unseeing. "You *what*?"

"I crashed a boat." Another pause. "Six people died. I could have saved Max, I saw her in the water, floating there, but I chose to save my girlfriend instead."

"You chose?"

"I always told myself it wasn't a choice, I acted on instinct, but that's only what I wanted to believe."

"Did the girlfriend make it?"

"Survive? Yeah."

"So—you split up?"

"Yeah."

"Shit, I mean… Did you do time?"

"I wasn't drinking, if that's what you mean. The guy I hit wasn't following maritime safety rules. He was under oars, didn't need navigation lights, but he should have had a flashlight or a lantern."

"So it was an accident."

"An accident…yeah. I chose my girlfriend's life over my sister's. I let my sister drown. An accident."

"That's not what I meant…"

Will didn't reply. Seconds slipped away, then minutes. The comfort that speaking had provided quickly faded, and the misery inside Rob returned. He summoned the faces of Dev and the girls, praying for a miracle.

CHAPTER 56

"Hey! Will! Wake up!" Rob hissed. "Someone's coming!"

"Huh?" I opened my eyes and winced against the pain pulsing through my head and body.

"Someone's coming."

I sat up and saw the faint glow of an approaching light. I was instantly alert. "If it's Katja," I said hoarsely, "let me do the talking, I think I can get through to her—"

"Tell her that if she lets us go we'll—"

"I know! Now quiet!"

He fell silent. We waited.

The light filled the entrance to the room, yellow at first, then a warmer orange. A silhouette appeared. "Will!" Katja exclaimed in a hushed whisper, then she charged across the room. For a moment I thought her intention was to attack me. Instead she collapsed next to me and gripped my arm tightly. "You were right!" she sobbed. "My father lied to me. He lied to me about everything. Paris wasn't destroyed, was it? Tell me this is true."

"Yes—it's true," I said, baffled.

"I knew it! I checked my books, but there were no publication pages like you said. My father ripped them out. But there was a book in his study that still had the publication page. It said 2011. It was printed *after* the war. And I looked inside one of your bags and found a wallet. There was *money* in it. And why would you have money if there were nowhere to spend it? Am I right?"

"Yes, you're right. I—we—use money every day."

"And I found this too! What is it?"

She withdrew a slip of paper from an incongruous pink purse dangling from her shoulder. She held it in front of my face. The words were too small to read in the candlelight, but it was recognizable enough. "That's a receipt, Katja. That's what you get when you purchase something, so you have a record of it."

"A receipt."

"Yes—see, those are the purchased items on the left, and those are the prices they cost on the right."

"I knew it! I knew it was something like that. Please, Will, I want to see the surface! Please take me. You have to take me there."

"I'll take you, Katja, I promise you, I'll take you right now if you release me."

"Will you let me live with you? I won't know anyone else or anywhere to go..."

"I, yeah, sure, you can live with me. You can stay as long as you want."

"And we can have a picnic outside, on grass? And you can take me shopping for a dress and help me make friends my age?"

"I'll do whatever you want. But you have to get these cuffs off me first."

"That's why I brought this." She pulled a hammer from the purse triumphantly—Pascal's hammer, I realized. "Will it work?"

"Yes!" I extended my arms behind my back, pressed my palms flat on the dirt, and splayed my wrists apart so the chain links connecting them went taut. "Can you hit the chain without hitting my hands?"

"I think so."

"Okay, do it."

She moved behind me. I tensed. Then—whack. The hammer struck the chain...with about as much force as you might slap at a pesky fly.

I said, "You're going to have to hit it harder than that, Katja. As hard as you can."

"I don't want to hit your hands."

"You won't. Try again."

This time the hammer struck the chain with more conviction.

"Did it break?"

"No—nothing happened."

"Keeping hitting it."

She struck the chain five times, each time harder than the last, but with no success.

I said, "You need to find a rock, Katja, to put under the chain."

"Okay." She searched the room for what seemed like an eternity before exclaiming, "Found one!" She returned to me and slipped the rock beneath the chain. Hopefully it would act as an anvil and channel the energy from the hammer into the chain. A moment later came the now familiar whack—only this time my wrists sprang apart.

I was free!

I held my hands before me. Old cast-iron manacles encircled each wrist. Two chain links dangled from each.

I turned toward Katja and gave her a huge hug. "Thank you!" I gushed, and planted a kiss on her cheek. To my surprise she smelled earthy and fresh.

I released her and lumbered to my feet. My body protested as if it were a hundred years old. I swooned and doubled over.

"Are you okay?" Katja asked, eyes wide.

I nodded. "Just dizzy." I buttoned and fastened my jeans that Katja had unfastened earlier and scooped up the hammer and the rock and told her to get the candle. "We need to help my friend now."

She glanced in Rob's direction. "But he's not awake."

"Yeah, he is. He woke up a little while ago. Right, Rob?"

"Yeah."

Katja stiffened at his voice.

"It's okay," I told her. "You can trust him. I promise."

Rob was on his back. I hadn't heard him move since Katja had entered the room, and I guess he had been playing dead. I helped him into a sitting position. His jaw was pebbly with a day's growth of beard shadow.

When he saw Katja's mutilations for the first time, I felt his body flinch, though he remained pokerfaced. "Hiya!" he said. "I'm Rob."

"It's a pleasure to meet you, Rob. I'm Katja."

Rob stared at her, and I smiled, an alien feeling right then. I told Rob to spread his hands behind him. I slipped the rock under the three-inch chain connecting his manacles, lined the hammer true, and brought the head down. The chain links exploded apart.

"Fuck, yes!" Rob cried, holding his hands in front of him as I had done.

"Katja," I said quickly, "we have another friend. A woman. Do you know where she is?"

She nodded. "I asked my uncles about her earlier. My father is keeping her in a room near his quarters."

"His quarters? Where are his quarters?"

"Where they always are."

"Yes, but—"

Rob asked, "How big is your home down here?"

"How big?"

She didn't have any conception of size, I realized. This section of catacombs was all she knew. She had nothing to compare it against.

"How long does it take you to walk from here to your father's quarters?" I tried instead.

She glanced at her wristwatch, as if it held the answer. "Ten minutes," she stated.

"And how far is it from here to the exit?"

"Ten minutes."

I frowned. Did she have no concept of time either? Or was it really equidistance to each location?

I drew a large circle in the dirt with the hammer claw and punched a dot in the middle of it. "If we are here, Katja, and that door there leads this way"—I pointed to the door a few yards away and marked a corresponding arrow in the dirt —"where are your father's quarters?"

She cocked her head to the side. "They would be...here." She pointed to a spot that would fall into the two to three o'clock wedge on a clock.

"And where's the exit?"

She pointed at another spot in the eight to nine o'clock wedge.

"Are there any other exits?"

"No, that's the only way in or out, and I've searched every tunnel."

"Can you take us to where our friend is being held without running into anybody else?"

"I think so," Katja said. "Most of my aunts and uncles stay in the Great Hall. They don't have their own rooms like I do. But we still need to be careful. They wander when they want to."

"We'll have to take our chances." I turned to Rob. "Ready?"

He looked pale but resolved. "Let's do it."

CHAPTER 57

DANIÈLE

Zolan stopped massaging Danièle's shoulders and slid his hands down over her chest. She clenched her jaw but didn't protest. He cupped her breasts and drew his thumbs over her nipples in small circles. She wanted to leap to her feet and run, but she forced herself to remain seated and relaxed.

He slid his hands lower over her abdomen, to the top of her groin. He pulled up her shirt. His hands touched her skin.

"You're cold," he said.

"A little," she replied, allowing a hint of throatiness in her voice.

He dug his fingers beneath the waistband of her pants, played them left and right along the top of her panties, pushed them farther, lower, but his hands wouldn't fit. He withdrew them, unfastened the button on her jeans.

"Stand up," he told her.

Danièle did so, turning, pressing her rear against the front of his desk. She did nothing to mask the fear and vulnerability she felt—it's what drove insecure sickos like Zolan; it fed their need for mastery, strength, authority. Marcel had been the same. He had wanted to control Danièle to assert his competency, and the more she resisted that control, the more she fought him, the more he enjoyed it.

"Don't be afraid of me," Zolan said, his eyes burning with desire. "I know what I'm doing. I'm good. You'll enjoy it."

A tear tripped down her cheek.

He brushed it away with his fingertip. "There's no need for that. You're going to like what I've got."

When he looked down, to undo his pants, Danièle reached for the bottle of vodka on the desk behind her. She grabbed the neck in an upside down fist and swung it around like a baton. Zolan glanced up at the last second and leaned backward. The bottle smashed his jaw instead of his temple. Blood flew in a fine spray from his mouth. He stumbled away from her and dropped into the chair she had been seated in.

Danièle swung the bottle again. It smashed into pieces against his forearms, which he had raised to protect his face.

"Fucking bitch!" he spat.

She darted around to the other side of the desk, almost slipping on the limestone floor in her haste. She planted her hands against the front of the desk. Zolan was holding his hand over his mouth, to slow the flowing blood.

Danièle shoved the desk. It was not too large and moved easily on the smooth stone. Zolan tried to push himself out of the chair, out of the way, but the desk caught him in the gut, knocked him back into the seat, and drove him into the wall behind him. There was a loud crack, which she hoped were his ribs fracturing. His breath burst from his mouth in a twisted gasp. He slumped forward, pinned in place.

She ran.

CHAPTER 58

W e had been moving for about five minutes, creeping from one passageway to the next, when Katja whispered, "Someone's coming! We have to hide!" She turned and hurried back the way we'd come, Rob and I sticking right behind her. We ducked into one of the corridors we'd just passed, and she pinched out the flame of her candle.

Darkness enveloped us.

"What if he comes down this way—"

She pressed her hand against my mouth, silencing me.

We didn't wait long. A few moments later I heard labored breathing and footsteps—fast footsteps.

We've been discovered missing.

The blackness at the mouth of the passageway lightened to gray. Then a shape darted past so fast I almost missed it.

"*Danièle!*" I hissed.

"Will?" Terrified.

"Danny!" Rob said.

She stood in the hallway, staring in our direction like a doe caught in headlamps, and I realized that was because she couldn't see us.

"Yeah," I said, "it's me and Rob. Katja—light the candle."

A match scratched. Katja touched the tip of it to the candle's wick.

Danièle cried out, shying away.

"It's okay!" I said, rushing forward. "She's helping us."

Danièle and I embraced, her body sinking against mine, as if suddenly emptied of all strength.

"Will…" she mumbled into my shoulder.

"It's okay," I told her. "We're getting out of here."

CHAPTER 59

KATJA

Katja didn't like the way Will put his arms around his friend. It made her feel squishy inside, and she glared at the woman angrily. But the woman wouldn't look at her so she gave it up and started off into the tunnels.

She couldn't remain angry for long anyway, because she was too excited. She was going to the surface! This was the most adventure she'd ever had. She felt like Dorothy in The Land of Oz on her way to the Emerald City. Dorothy had three friends to help her along the way, and Katja had three friends too. But Katja had it much easier. Dorothy had to battle wolves, crows, bees, Winkie soldiers, and winged monkeys. Katja only had to get past Hanns and the others.

And she had a plan for that.

CHAPTER 60

When Katja stopped abruptly, I thought she'd heard something again with her insanely acute hearing, and I whispered, "What is it?"

"We are almost there."

"Where?"

"The Great Hall."

She'd mentioned that before. "What's the Great Hall?"

"It's the room that leads to the exit. It's also where most of my aunts and uncles live, so we're going to have to trick them."

Trick them? I glanced at Rob and Danièle. They seemed equally skeptical.

I said, "How do we trick them?"

"Have you read *The Wind in the Willows*?"

"No, I haven't."

"I have," Danièle said. "Something about a frog getting into trouble?"

"Not a frog!" Katja said. "A toad. At one point Toad gets arrested—that means he can't leave Toad Hall—but eventually he gets bored and wants to leave. So do you know what he does? He tricks the Water Rat who is on guard at the time."

"How does he trick him?" I asked.

"He pretends to be sick!" Katja said proudly. "The Water Rat lets him go outside, and he runs away."

"I don't think pretending to be sick is going to get us past your uncles."

"No, you don't understand. You're going to hide. I'm going to tell them *my father* is sick, they have to go help him. That's when we will escape."

I thought this over. It was better than anything else that came to mind.

Rob said, "Where we gonna hide?"

"There." Katja pointed down a branching corridor.

"How far does it go?" I asked.

"Not far."

"What if someone comes down it? We'll be trapped."

"No one will come down it," she said.

▼

We huddled together in the darkness, listening. An icy mist swirled in my gut, and my heart thumped so loudly in my chest I wondered if the others could hear it.

"I hope you can trust her," Danièle whispered to me.

"She's brought us this far," I said.

"Why is she helping us?"

"She wants to go to the surface."

"Hey, Danny," Rob said. "How'd you get free?"

"Shh!" I said. "I hear them."

In the distance came what might have been Katja's voice, followed by several others, which were deeper, back-of-the-throat, masculine.

Danièle gripped my hand tightly.

A moment later someone holding a torch in one hand and a bone in the other passed the end of our corridor, less than fifty feet from us. Eleven people followed in a procession of broken-bodied gaits, three carrying torches, and all of them carrying bones.

After they had passed, and their guttural mutterings faded, a small light appeared and seemed to float toward us.

Katja stopped when she could see us and, with a delicate

index finger, indicated for us to follow.

▼

The Great Hall was appropriately named, as it reminded me of a great hall you might find in a medieval castle. Torches set in gilded sconces lined the walls at evenly spaced intervals. A solid-looking table, perhaps sixteen feet in length, dominated the center of the yawning space. Three silver candelabras stood on its chipped and stained surface, their gleaming spaghetti arms holding blood-red candles. Only a few chairs encircled the table, though they were high-backed, sturdy, and featured intricate woodworking and some sort of lion motif. My first thought was nobility, and I recalled what Danièle had told me about King Charles X and his morbid parties. Could this furniture have been scavenged from those party rooms?

Nevertheless, amidst the grandeur was smelly squalor. Grungy mattresses, either bare or topped with a mess of dirty sheets, lay haphazardly around the floor. Each was surrounded by a collection of boxes and baskets overflowing with the kind of stuff you saw bums pushing around in their shopping carts: soda cans, plastic bags, tin cans, plastic bottles, articles of clothing, other junk.

An overweight woman sat on one of those mattresses. She wore no clothes. Her large breasts drooped to her waist. Her belly folded over her waist onto her lap like an apron. Scabs covered her skin, some streaked with dried blood, some bleeding freely. She stared at us but didn't seem to see us.

Two others were curled up on the floor, apparently sleeping, while an old man with wild wheat hair and a craggy face and a puckered mouth shuffled toward us, arms outstretched, saying something I couldn't understand.

Katja didn't pay him any attention, which suggested he was not a threat, and led us quickly across the room to an arched doorway encrusted with human skulls. Then we were hurrying down a long stone tunnel, and even though we were still deep underground in a labyrinth from hell, right then I felt as free as if we were running across an open field with a spill of stars overhead.

We had escaped.

CHAPTER 61

When we reached the first T-junction I said, "Which way, Katja?"

She shook her head. "I don't know."

Rob's jaw dropped. "You don't know?"

"I have never been this far before."

We chose left at random, and Katja took the lead, holding her candle before her, one hand cupped around the flame so it wouldn't blow out.

A hundred yards on we stopped before a cat hole in the left-side wall.

I peered into it. "It's been carved out by hand," I said, "or at least the original fissure's been expanded. Either way, it was done for a purpose, so it must lead somewhere."

Rob nodded. "Maybe back the way we came—"

A high-pitched shriek cut him off. It warbled between sorrow and rage. Another joined it, and another, and more, all as shrill and degenerate as the first.

"They found Zolan," Danièle stated.

"Zolan?" I said, bewildered.

"My father," Katja said. "They will know we tricked them. They will come for us now."

"*Zolan?*" I repeated.

"What the fuck are you talking about, Danny?" Rob demanded.

A new, chilling howl reverberated through the tunnels. It

was close, not originating from behind us, but from in front of us, the direction we had been heading.

"Go!" I said, pushing Katja into the cat hole.

▼

Danièle scrambled into the fissure after Katja, and I was about to go next when I noticed a light down the hallway. It was approaching fast.

Rob saw it too. "Hurry the fuck up!" He shoved me forward. "Motherfucker, go!"

I ducked into the hole and scrambled ahead. My hands and knees slapped the stone ground, my back scraped the ceiling, my shoulders bounced off the rough walls, yet I didn't feel as if I was moving fast enough.

A wail erupted from behind us.

Rob cried out. Then: "Fucker's got me! Won't let go!"

"Kick him!" I shouted.

He crashed into my backside. "Go!"

I clambered onward.

Danièle tumbled out of the hole ahead of me. I flopped out behind her, somersaulting onto the ground, then whirling around to help Rob, my mind racing, thinking we were going to have to make our stand here, they would be bottlenecked, they couldn't overwhelm us, we'd take them out one by one—

"Fucker!" Rob yelled. He was on his back, kicking at whoever was behind him. "Let...me...go!"

I stuck my upper body into the shaft, grabbed Rob under the arms, pulled.

"Ow!" Shock, then squally, soprano anguish. "*Owwwww!*"

For a moment I thought I'd caused the pain and let go of Rob. He flailed like a skewered fish. I couldn't fathom what was wrong until I saw that his legs were on fire. A moment later the flames leapt to his T-shirt, the stench of burning pitch joined by burning flesh.

Screaming, Rob seemed to be attempting to brush the

flames off him. I tried grabbing him again, but he was thrashing too violently.

Finally one of his arms snapped past his head. I snatched it —his skin was hot and mushy; raw meat, I thought darkly— and yanked him as hard as I could. He came out of the shaft all too easily, and for a horrible second I was convinced I'd torn free his arm from the socket.

That wasn't the case, of course; he'd simply been released by whoever had been holding him.

I tripped and landed on my ass. Rob hit the ground next to me. He immediately began rolling back and forth. It was a futile action. He'd already become one big ball of fire. His face and neck and arms were pink and blistered and melting in places. His screams had stopped as well. I ceased thinking of how to save him and hoped he would die quickly.

A gleeful shriek pulled my eyes from Rob back to the hole. Through the reddish glow of fire and smoke I glimpsed Hanns. His was squirming out of the shaft like some ghastly gremlin, torch in one hand, bone-weapon in the other.

I shot to my feet just as Hanns extracted himself fully. I charged the bastard. He jabbed the torch toward my face. I batted it away with my arm, but I didn't see the bone that followed. It smashed my right knee. The pain was furious, though I didn't go down; he could have broken both my legs and I wouldn't have gone down right then. Instead I collided into him, bowling him into the wall. My hands locked around his corded neck. I heaved him off his feet with adrenaline-fuelled strength, pivoted, and ran him across the small room into the adjacent wall.

His head struck the stone with a brief, snappy sound, like billiard balls scattering on a good break. His body went limp. His disgusting mouth gaped open. His dark eyes dulled to sightless orbs. He was dead, but I wanted him *more* dead. I slammed his skull against the stone again and again and again.

CHAPTER 62

DANIÈLE

Danièle tried to save Rob. She tore off her shirt and beat it against his body. This did nothing to diminish the flames that consumed him, but she kept at it, not knowing what else to do. All the while she watched in horror as his skin went from blistered to pink to black. Worst were his eyes. They remained open the entire time, and she was sure he could see her doing nothing effective to help him. Then his rolling slowed and eventually stopped altogether. He came to a rest facedown. Thank God it was facedown. The flames continued to devour his body, but somehow they didn't seem as terrible now that he had gone still.

While Danièle's attention had been fixed on him, she was only partially aware of Will struggling with the zombie-man. Now she turned to them. They were across the room. Will held the thing around its neck like a ragdoll and was driving its head into the wall repeatedly.

She wobbled over to him and told him to stop, told him it was dead, and tried pulling him away from it. Finally he dropped the lifeless corpse to the ground and turned to look at her. His face was splattered with blood. A madness danced in his eyes and an aura of power radiated off him that she found both frightening and strangely desirable. He glared past her at Rob's still burning body, then at the thing at his feet.

He raised his shoe and stomped on its broken skull.

CHAPTER 63

KATJA

This wasn't what Katja wanted! This was making her sick! She didn't know Will's friend Rob well, and she'd never liked Hanns, but seeing them die, the way they died—it was never supposed to happen like this. She wished she could run back to her room and curl up on her bed and close her eyes and forget she had ever tried to help Will. But she couldn't do that, so she remained in the corner and kept herself as small as possible and waited for what would happen next.

CHAPTER 64

No time, I thought helplessly as I stared at Rob's burning body.

No time to put the flames out.

No time to bury him.

Hanns, it seemed, had been alone, wandering the tunnels and doing whatever he did down here by himself. But the others were coming. They would find us soon.

Once again I considered making a stand here and attacking each of our pursuers one by one as they wiggled out of the hole. But this, I decided, was not a good option. They wouldn't come through like lemmings. We might kill one, maybe two. But they would adapt. They would likely try to wait us out. How long could the three of us remain vigilant? We would have to sleep at some point. Also, that hole wasn't the only way into the room. A hallway extended from the opposite wall. They might know a dozen other ways to reach that hallway—and, consequently, us.

I picked up Hanns' torch and bone-weapon and turned to Danièle. She finished pulling her T-shirt back over her head and blinked at me with the eyes of someone who had just watched a tornado wipe out their home and all their earthly possessions. "We have to leave him," I told her. Then, to Katja: "Are you coming?"

She nodded mutely.

CHAPTER 65

T he hallway ran straight. We passed several small rooms on alternating sides of us. They were bare and led no-where. This discouraged me, as I had hoped to find branching passageways, which we could take at random, losing ourselves, and our pursuers, in the maze.

Seventy-five or so yards on the tunnel ended at a cavernous grotto. The ceiling must have cleared thirty feet. I couldn't be certain, because even with Hann's bright torch, it remained layered in thick shadows. The rocks walls were bulging and irregular, as you found in nature, leading me to believe this was some naturally forming underground pocket.

"Is that water?" Danièle asked me, her voice tight.

I had entered the grotto looking up, not down, and I hadn't noticed the ground before now. I took a few steps forward, sweeping the torch low. Danièle was right. Stretching ahead of us was a mirror-smooth pool of black water. It covered the entire ground save a narrow ribbon of land that followed the wall to the right of us.

"Must be some sort of reservoir," I said.

I was already moving along the ribbon, praying it linked to a connecting hallway. It climbed gradually, melding into the far wall, which rose in staggered sheets. I could continue left, jumping from one cleft to the next, like a mountain goat. But what was the point? It couldn't lead anywhere.

Cursing, I returned the way I'd come, running over our

dwindling options in my head. We had to head back down the hallway, back through the cat hole. If we could get there before our pursuers, we could continue the way we'd been going, the way Hanns had come from. When I reached Danièle and Katja, I said, "We have to go back—"

An enraged shriek shattered the hushed silence. A handful of others joined it.

"They found Hanns," Katja said softly.

"Shit!" I said, going cold with panic. It was too late. There was nothing we could do now, nowhere to go, we were as good as dead.

For a brief moment I wondered if I could take them all out. I was bigger and stronger than them, and I would be fighting for my life.

Nevertheless, this hope was extinguished almost immediately.

There were too many. They would overwhelm me.

I wouldn't stand a chance.

"Shit!" I repeated.

"What is that?" Danièle said. She was pointing across the water.

I didn't see anything. "What?"

"That! Look! The darkness!"

The darkness? But then I saw what she had indicated. A patch of black, where the far wall met the waterline. The torchlight didn't penetrate it.

A deep shadow? Another fissure? Perhaps if it extended far enough into the rock, it would conceal us. But that meant we had to cross the water...

Danièle searched her pockets and produced a book of matches. "Do not make any ripples," she told me. She popped the matches in her mouth, then waded carefully into the water. After three steps the water reached her waist. Another two it was to her neck. She swam silently forward.

I waded into the water reluctantly. The temperature was close to freezing, but that wasn't why my body was locking up, my stomach churning with dread.

A couple months after the boat accident on Lake Placid, I'd been with Bridgette on the ferry crossing New York Bay to Staten Island, to visit the zoo, and I'd gotten violently seasick, something that had never happened to me before. After that day, the mere sight of water, in any volume larger than what a bathtub held, made me nauseous until I looked away from it. I had not been on another boat, or swimming, since.

I glanced over my shoulder. "Follow me, Katja, we're going to hide."

She stood board-stiff. "I can't swim!"

I hesitated. We couldn't leave her behind. She'd give away that we came this way. Moreover, Zolan would grill her until she told him where we were hiding. "Climb on my back then," I said. "I'll carry you."

"I'll sink!"

"Not if you hold onto me. Hurry!"

She stepped slowly into the water and wrapped her arms around my neck. I disposed of both the torch and bone-weapon under the water. The flame went out with a hiss, and blackness swallowed us.

"I'm scared," Katja said, her breath warm on my ear.

"You'll be okay."

"Do you promise?"

"Yes," I said, slipping deeper into the water, trying not to think how far down the bottom was. "Now hold on." She tightened her grip around my neck, and I began to swim.

▼

The pool was roughly twenty-five feet in diameter. I crossed it quickly. When I touched the far rock I whispered Danièle's name.

"Here," she replied.

I followed the wall to the right. It curved into what I guessed was the fissure. Maybe ten feet farther on the ceiling pressed down until it was mere inches above my head. "Da-nièle?"

No answer.

"*Danièle?*"

No answer.

"Where is she?" Katja asked in a small voice.

"I don't know!" I said. "Danièle? Danièle!"

Something brushed my leg. I cried out, spinning, kicking. Katja tightened her hold around my neck, choking me. I struggled to stay afloat.

Then Danièle's voice: "Will! Quiet! Stop it!"

I pried Katja's arms from my throat enough so I could breathe again, but I continued to splash and pant, my eyes bulging. The water suddenly felt mawkish, like quicksand, and I knew I was going to drown.

"Will!" Danièle said. "Quiet!"

"*Can't!*"

"*Will!*"

Somehow I managed to calm myself enough to resume treading water—though it was a fragile calm that could still abandon me again at any moment. "Where were you?" I whispered, tilting my chin to keep my mouth above the surface.

"It continues underwater."

"What…the fissure? How far?"

"I do not know," she said awkwardly, and I realized she was speaking around the matchbook in her mouth. "I didn't go to the end. Are you ready?"

"For what?" I said, knowing exactly what.

"We have to follow it."

"No!"

"It might lead out of here!"

"Forget it!"

"You think Zolan and the others have not been here before? Of course they have! They will know about this fissure. They will search it."

She was right, I knew, and the dread in my stomach

bloomed to fill me completely, suffocating me from the inside out. I was nauseous with it. I couldn't dive beneath the water, beneath the rock, with no guarantee of surfacing again. I couldn't. I simply couldn't.

"Katja can't swim," I said.

"She does not have to. She only has to hold her breath."

"Danièle—I can't do this."

Faint light appeared, blacks edging to grays.

Someone had entered the grotto.

CHAPTER 66

DANIÈLE

anièle took a deep breath and sank below the surface of the water. She kept her eyes open, but everything was black as an eclipse. She swam forward with a breaststroke, her legs frog kicking. This made her think of Rob for the briefest moment before she blinked him out of her mind. The passage she followed was narrow. At the peak of her outswept arms her fingertips brushed the rocks walls.

She knew she could hold her breath for roughly two minutes—she and Dev used to time each other when they went to the Aquaboulevard on their birthdays as kids—which meant she had some sixty seconds to see where this passage led before reaching the point of no return.

She began to count.

CHAPTER 67

The light grew brighter. The grays bled into yellows. Still, our pursuers weren't making any sound. Did they know they had us trapped? Were they expecting an ambush? And where was Danièle? Had she emerged on the other side of the rock?

If I hesitated any longer I knew I would never be able to make myself follow her lead, so I whispered, "Take a deep breath, Katja—"

"No!"

"Yes!" She either came with me, or she'd have to let go: it was her choice. "One, two—three." I filled my lungs and sank below the surface just as Danièle had done.

The water slipped over my head and droned in my ears and immediately disorientated me. I didn't know up from down, left from right, couldn't recall which way I was supposed to go. I might have chickened out, crashed back through the surface, if I could find the surface, had it not been for Katja. She had not let go. Her thin arms remained wrapped around my neck. She was putting her complete trust in me, and I wasn't going to fail her.

I stretched my arms wide, touched the sides of the fissure, and began to kick. After a few yards I felt for the ceiling. It was submerged, confirming I had gone in the right direction.

A pressure began building in my lungs quickly—too quickly—so that soon my lungs felt as if they were about to burst.

I was going to have to turn back…but turn back to what? To Zolan and his mob? They would kill me. That was a given. The only question was how they would do it.

Likely slowly and excruciatingly, revenge for Hann's death.

Drowning, on the other hand, would be relatively painless. The TV depictions of swimmers flailing around in panic and agony underwater were wrong. That only happened to those who had not yet gone under (like me a minute before); it was their body's last-ditch effort to obtain air. The actual act of drowning was more often quick and unspectacular and silent.

Without oxygen reaching my brain, my body would shut down and I would lose consciousness. My breathing would stop. I'd go into respiratory arrest and sink. Then I would enter the hypoxic convulsion stage. My skin would turn blue, notably in the lips and fingernail beds, and my body would go rigid. Finally my heart would stop pumping blood, and I would be clinically dead.

That's what happened to Max anyhow; it had all been in the coroner's report.

▼

I could see Max and everyone else killed on Lake Placid gliding alongside me, phosphorescent shapes darting in and out of my peripheral vision. I could hear them too, their voices ghostlike echoes inside my head, telling me of all the things they would never able to do. Karen would never become a dentist and meet Mr. Right. Brian would never earn his MBA and prove himself at his father's investment management firm on Wall Street. Gina would never visit her older sister in Italy. Tommy would never bike through Central America. Eddy would never finish restoring the 1998 Porsche 911 Carrera he'd bought from a police auction, while Joseph, the sixty-three-year-old retired accountant who'd lived year round on the lake, would never catch the monster largemouth bass that had snapped his line and gotten away the summer before, and that, according to his wife, he had been hunting the night he died. And Max, of course, would never graduate the Manhattan School of Music, never play in Carnegie Hall, never achieve her dream of becoming a New York Philharmonic cellist—

The pressure around my throat lessoned.

Katja! I thought, momentarily clearheaded.

I snagged her wrists with my hands before she could float away and kicked on with my legs. I only managed to continue for another five seconds before my breathing reflex reached the breakpoint and I opened my mouth and took a futile breath. Water gushed into my stomach and lungs. I experienced the briefest moment of relief, followed by the faraway acceptance that I was about to die.

CHAPTER 68

DANIÈLE

anièle's knees and hands brushed rock beneath her as the ground angled upward. A moment later her head cleared the water. She wanted to whoop with relief. Instead she spat the matchbook from her mouth into her hand, took the candle from her pocket, and lit the wick on the second try.

The pool she stood in was tiny, only a few yards in diameter. The inky water came to her waist. She stared at the rippling surface, praying for Will and Katja to appear. The swim, physically, had not been very hard. It had taken her fifty-five seconds, and now that she knew how long the tunnel was, she could do it again no problem. It was the mental aspect, the doubt, which had been the tough part. At forty-five seconds she had begun to panic, but she'd told herself just a bit longer, a few more seconds. And thank God she had listened to that little voice. But what if Will hadn't? What if he hadn't even followed her? No, he would have. He knew as well as she did there was no choice. But he had Katja on his back. She would have slowed him down. Maybe he'd panicked or lost his nerve as she almost had—

Pale appendages appeared in the dark water in front of her, then Will reared to his feet, crashing through the surface with a sharp intake of air. Danièle caught Katja as she fell off his back and dragged her onto the dry ground. The girl was limp and unresponsive. Danièle felt for a pulse in her neck. She didn't find one—or was she doing it wrong? She put her ear to Katja's mouth. Nothing.

"She is not breathing!" she cried to Will, who was doubled over coughing and wheezing.

Danièle had taken a first aid course years before, but she couldn't remember the particulars of CPR. Different number of compressions for children and adults? More or less? How many breaths did you administer? Did it matter?

She placed the heel of one hand on Katja's breastbone, between her breasts. She placed the other on top of it, palm-down, and performed ten chest compressions. She covered Katja's nose holes with her hand, tilted her head back to open her airway, and blew into her lipless mouth. She performed more compressions. On the seventh one Katja coughed and spasmed and heaved water from her lungs. Danièle rolled her onto her side and slapped her back.

Will waded out of the water and collapsed beside them.

"Is she okay?" he asked.

Danièle nodded because she didn't trust herself to speak yet. Then, "Are you?"

"Yeah—" He commenced coughing.

Katja opened her eyes. It took a few moments for them to focus and for her to register their presence.

Will coughed a final time and gave her a forced smile. "Brave girl."

"Did I...fall asleep?" she mumbled.

"Sort of," he said.

"I hate...swimming."

"You and me both," he told her, kissing her affectionately on the forehead. "You and me both."

CHAPTER 69

W e started along the rock wall, searching for an exit from the new cavern, and after a short distance came to several scattered candles on the ground, a discarded torch, and a pair of old boots.

"Zolan's?" Danièle said.

Zolan! I had forgotten Danièle had mentioned him earlier. "Are you serious about Zolan being behind all this?" I asked her.

"Yes," she said simply.

"*Zolan* Zolan?"

"Yes!"

I pictured the old guy in my head: the green bandana, the missing teeth, the shark-tooth necklace, the bad BO. He was Katja's father? He was responsible for Pascal and Rob's death? Setting these absurdities aside for a later time, I said, "Well, if they're his boots, then that means he's been here before. He knows of that underwater passage. He'll be coming." I picked up the torch and sniffed the dirty cloth wrapped around the end of the stave. "Still smells of kerosene. Try lighting it with the candle."

Danièle obeyed and a flame whooshed into existence, dwarfing the candles. I looked away from the light until my eyes could adjust to the brightness—and found myself staring at an old foot ladder, affixed to the wall, less than ten yards away.

▼

I ascended the ladder first, climbing with one hand because I held the torch in the other. Thirty feet up the ladder reached the ceiling and continued through a shaft in the rock. I glanced down. Katja was only about five feet or so off the ground and seemed reluctant to go any farther. "Come on, Katja!" I said. "You need to move faster."

She looked up. "I'm scared."

"You'll be fine. Just keep coming. I'll wait for you."

Danièle encouraged Katja from below until she began inching upward.

"Good work, Katja!" I said. "Keep coming—"

Suddenly Zolan stood behind Danièle. He'd appeared so quickly I didn't have time to warn her. He bear-hugged her from behind, pinning her arms to her sides. She shrieked in surprise and kicked futilely. Then another figure emerged from the gloom next to him, and another, and another, the entire mob.

A male removed Katja from the ladder and set her on the ground.

"Will!" Danièle cried.

Zolan passed her, kicking and screaming, to a different male, who held her firmly against his body.

"Come down, Will," Zolan called to me. He held a hand against his stomach and appeared to be in some sort of pain. "There's nowhere to go."

I couldn't do as he asked, of course. It would be suicide. But what of Danièle and Katja? What was going to happen to them? I couldn't leave them—could I?

"What's wrong?" Zolan taunted. "You're not thinking of running away like a cowardly piece of shit, are you?"

"I'm going for help," I said, as much for his benefit as Danièle's. "I'm going to bring the police back here."

"You'll never find your way out."

"If I come down, you'll kill me."

"If you don't, I'll kill Danièle. If you do, if you act like a man, I'll let you live. It is your choice."

I winced at those words.

My choice.

"You'll let me live?" I said skeptically.

"We'll work out an arrangement."

"He is lying, Will!" Danièle yelled.

I knew she was right. Zolan would kill me immediately. But was he also lying about killing *her*, or was that an empty threat? I believed it was the latter. He was a man, and Danièle was a beautiful young woman. Why would he kill her when he could keep her as a concubine, albeit an unwilling one, with no risk of prosecution? And while that might be a horrible fate for Danièle, at least it wouldn't be death.

I tensed in anticipation of what I was about to do. It was despicable, but this wasn't a movie. I wasn't some heroic protagonist. I wasn't going to sacrifice myself for someone I'd met only a handful of times. This was real life, I didn't have a deus ex machina to bail my ass out, and I had to make a rational, calculated decision. One, I go down and get killed, and Danièle gets whatever she gets. Or two, I flee, Danièle still gets whatever she gets, but I potentially escape and bring back help. Really, option two was the best choice for both of us.

I climbed the ladder

CHAPTER 70

DANIÈLE

Danièle couldn't believe Will was leaving her! She didn't know what she expected him to do instead. If he came down, Zolan would kill him. Still, it was impossible to remain objective. She was overrun with emotions. Resentment. Injustice. Desperation.

He's leaving me behind.

CHAPTER 71

KATJA

G o, Will, Go! Katja urged silently. She knew her father was lying again. He wasn't going to work out an arrangement. He was going to kill Will just as Hanns killed Rob. And she didn't want that. Will was her friend.

She and Danièle would be in big trouble, they'd probably get locked up in the Dungeon for a while, but her father would eventually forgive them, and things would go back to normal—only better though, because she would finally have someone other than her father she could talk to, a big sister. Danièle could tell her all about the surface world, everything she needed to know to prepare her to live there, until Will returned with help to rescue them.

CHAPTER 72

As I scrambled up the ladder, Zolan shouted, "I'll kill her! Come back! I'll kill her right now! Come back!"

I climbed.

Moments later Danièle screamed: high-pitched, fevered, primitive in mindless agony.

"You're killing her!" Zolan said to me. "You are! You're killing her!"

I climbed.

Finally the shaft opened to a lateral hallway. The ladder continued up, through another shaft in the ceiling. I was tempted to keep climbing. Up was good; it was the direction I wanted to go. Nevertheless, I couldn't climb fast with the torch, and my pursuers were likely already gaining on me. Also, the shaft could lead to a dead end. I would be trapped.

Danièle screamed again, shrill but plaintive this time. The sound shattered me to the soul.

Then nothing.

I leapt from the ladder and began to run.

CHAPTER 73

ZOLAN

Zolan couldn't believe Katja had turned against him. He had thought Will and Rob must have coerced her to free them, to help them find Danièle and escape. But there she had been, climbing the ladder of her own freewill. He saw it with his very eyes. The treachery had been heartbreaking to witness.

He might not be her biological father—that would be Hanns, or *had been* Hanns—but he had raised her nearly since birth, and for all intents and purposes, she was his daughter.

She had been somewhere between eighteen and twenty-four months old when Zolan found his way here in 2000. Still, it had not been in time to save her from his father, who had begun performing the mutilations on all infants at as young an age as possible. Over the years it became less a deterrent to escape, he believed, and more a ritual to mark their inclusion into the community.

Zolan had been disgusted by these defacements, the general lack of hygiene and fetid living conditions, and his intention had been to kill everyone swiftly to free them from their miserable existence. Nevertheless, while he was researching lethal toxins and working up the courage to carry the poisoning out—mass murder was not something you undertook lightly, even if you had the best of intentions—Katja's innocence endeared her to him. Unlike the others, she was still a baby, not yet corrupted by the limitations of her environment and the primitive behavior of her family, and after exhaustive soul-searching he decided it wasn't his place to be her judge, jury, and executioner.

So Zolan left the lot of them to fare for themselves and vowed never to return. His resolve, however, lasted only two weeks. He was unable to stop thinking about Katja. He longed to hold her again, to look into her eyes, to have her fall asleep on his chest, and so he went back, time and time again. Each trip was supposed to be the last, a short visit to make sure Katja was doing okay. But after a few months of this he had fallen in love with her the way a father falls in love with his daughter. He was burping her, changing her, playing with her, watching her...and that he could do for hours on end...simply watch her. When she spoke her first word—"Papa"—he was thrilled. When she took her first step, he was ecstatic.

She became his savior and his curse. His savior because she taught him about fatherhood and responsibility and unconditional love—none of which he had experienced, or cared to experience, before in his life. Yet also his curse because she bound him to her unholy existence underground. He could not take her with him to the surface. Her pitiful appearance aside, there would be too many questions, too much explaining to do. So whenever he left for a fuck, or to pick up supplies, he made sure the only person allowed near her was her biological mother, Romy, and he set up a video camera and told Romy he was watching her every minute and played back recorded footage as proof.

When Katja turned three or so, Zolan began home-schooling her with songs and games before graduating to more formal lessons. And if his first mistake had been not to poison her when she was an infant, his second mistake had been to educate and civilize her. Because had he left her to grow up like her parents and aunts and uncles, had he left her to evolve into a savage animal (and despite what he'd told Danièle about his kin, they were little more than base animals, there was no doubt about that), then her innocence would have faded, he would have been able to distance himself from her, disown her, return to his old life.

But enlighten her he did, and like any enlightened child, she became curious about everything—but mostly about the aboveground world she'd come to know in her storybooks, the world that was so different than her own. He told her the same explanation his father had told him: Paris was destroyed in World War Two and the survivors had fled underground. Yet every question she asked forced him to build upon this simple premise until God forbid he could almost believe the elaborate tale himself.

He got lucky with her books. Originally he chose them carefully, only bringing her those published pre-1945 so they wouldn't reference modern history. Then one evening he had been reading *Swiss Family Robinson* to her and viewed the publication page. The novel was first published in 1812, but of course he didn't have a first edition, and the abridged reprint was dated 1992. It was a careless oversight, but no harm was done, and he removed all the publication pages from all her books before she became any the wiser.

Since then there had been a few other slipups, and he had begun to fear Katja was getting suspicious of her world paradigm. He had always known she would, and she would leave him, just as he had left his father, yet he had believed— wrongly, it turned out—that he still had a few years left with her.

Zolan climbed the final rungs of the ladder and poked his head into the lateral hallway. He aimed the beam of his flashlight at the chalky ground and spotted wet footprints disappearing into the dark.

▼

Alighting from the ladder, Zolan grimaced in pain. He figured Danièle might have broken one or two of his ribs with that desk stunt of hers. But it didn't matter. He could still move. And he had business to conclude.

He stared into the blackness in the direction Will had gone. His panic and urgency had subsided; there was no longer any need for haste. Although this section of tunnels spread for several kilometers, they were linear and led nowhere. If Will continued straight ahead, he would come to an impassable jumble of rocks five hundred meters onward. Likewise, if he turned right at the first and only branching passageway he would eventually come to another jumble of rocks. Both routes had once connected to the catacombs at large, but his father had sealed off each, to secure the perimeter of his domain against potential backdoor intruders.

Now only three entrances/exits existed that Zolan knew of, and they were all nearly impossible to uncover. In fact, since his arrival, he could count on one hand the number of intrusions there had been. The first was in 2004 when a lone cataphile stumbled straight into the Great Hall. Zolan was woken by the ensuing commotion, and by the time he arrived on scene the cataphile lay on the floor, motionless, one of the silver candelabras on the ground next to him in a spreading pool of blood. Hanns had been dancing and hollering like a lunatic under a full moon. However, the cataphile—a young Frenchman named Michel, according to his driver's license— wasn't dead, so Zolan chained him up in the Dungeon until he decided what to do with him. It was a pointless measure, as Michel didn't regain consciousness. Unwilling to nurse a vegetable, Zolan slit his throat and he and Hanns disposed of the remains in a distant chamber.

The second intrusion came a year later. Hanns and Jörg discovered two Frenchmen sleeping in the statue room above one of the many mass graves that littered this section of the catacombs. It wasn't a coincidence. Hanns and Jörg and sometimes Karl had taken to patrolling the deep tunnels and galleries, searching for interlopers. On this occasion it was the three of them, and they overpowered the two men (who had put up a fair fight, breaking one of Hanns' arms). They brought them back to the Dungeon, the way a cat sometimes brings the prey it catches to its master as an offering. Zolan would have preferred not to kill the men; they had professed to be husbands and fathers. But what else was he to do? He couldn't let them go. So he and Hanns dispatched of them as they had Michel.

The third breach in the security, if that was what these intrusions could be called, had been in 2008. Hanns and Karl crossed paths with an attractive couple, killed the female by accident, and brought the male to the Dungeon. Zolan was on the surface in one of the red light districts, and in his absence Hanns organized his first blood match. He won handily, and little remained of the cataphile when Zolan returned. Katja had been seven then, old enough to wonder about who the visitor was, and Zolan ordered her never to talk to any such people if they showed up in the future, because they were dangerous and would try to fill her head with lies.

Then there was the Australian woman named Tami from Perth. Hanns claimed he didn't touch her. She simply dropped dead when he cornered her. There had been no marks on her corpse, and Zolan supposed she'd suffered a massive heart attack.

Zolan hadn't known about any damn video camera then. If he had, he would have retrieved it—and he likely wouldn't have been in the mess he was in now.

Jörg emerged from the shaft, stormy-eyed and excited. With Hanns dead it seemed he had usurped the position of alpha male. Karl came next, then Lorenz, Erich, Leo, Franz, and finally Odo, the slowest and stupidest of the bunch, but as resilient as a pit fighter.

They milled about, shoving each other, making the noises they made, brimming with manic energy.

Pointing first to the wet footprints, then down the tunnel, Zolan shouted, "*Geh! Geh! Geh!*"

They took off like a pack of wild dogs on the hunt.

CHAPTER 74

They were dead. All of them. Pascal, Rob, and now Danièle—dead.

I tried not to think about this as I fled down the crumbling and rock-strewn hallway. I kept the torch ahead of me and above my head so the smoke didn't waft back into my face. The flames bounced shadows off the stone walls and filled the air with a sickening tar-like stench. The only sound was my labored breathing and my feet splashing through the puddles that dotted the chalky gray ground.

A passageway opened to my left, a gaping mouth leading away into blackness. I veered into it, hoping to zigzag ever farther through the underground labyrinth, praying it didn't lead to a dead end. If it did, I would be trapped. My pursuers would catch me. Smash my skull into bits like they did to Pascal. Set me on fire like they did to Rob. I couldn't fathom what they did to Danièle, but judging by her screams, I suspect she got it the worst.

I wanted desperately to believe that this wasn't the case, that Danièle wasn't dead, and for a moment I allowed my imagination to run wild with fanciful speculation, because I hadn't actually seen her die...

No—I *heard* her. She was gone, she had to be, and I was next, as doomed as the rest of them.

Still, I kept running, I kept putting one foot in front of the other. I was too afraid to accept the inevitable and give up and die, too hardwired to survive, even though there was nothing left to live for.

I opened my mouth and yelled. I hated the sound of it. It was shrill and broken and full of pain, what might come from a mongrel dog beaten to within inches of its life. My disgust with myself lasted only a moment, however, because seconds after the wretched moan tapered off, a riot of savage cries erupted from behind me.

So goddamn close!

The cries rose in a crescendo of frenzied bloodlust. Terror blasted through me, but I couldn't make my legs move any faster. They were cement blocks. I felt as if I were running in the opposite direction on a moving walkway.

Suddenly the ceiling and walls disappeared and a vast darkness opened around me. While looking up to gauge the size of this new chamber, I stumbled over unreliable ground, lost my footing, and fell upon a mound of rubble. The torch flew from my grip and landed a few feet ahead of me. I stared at the polished rocks illuminated in the smoking flame until I realized they were not rocks but bones. Human bones. Skulls and femurs and tibias and others. I grabbed the torch by the handle and thrust it into the air.

Bones and bones and more bones, for as far as I could see.

I shoved myself to my feet, took several lurching steps, as if wading through molasses, then sagged to my knees. A centuries-old femur splintered beneath my weight with a snap like deadwood.

The sounds of my pursuers grew louder. I refused to look back over my shoulder. Instead I clutched at the bones before me, my fingers curling around their brittle lengths, pulling myself forward, my legs no longer responding at all.

Finally, beyond exhaustion, I flopped onto my chest and lay panting among the thousands of skeletonized remains as a sleepy darkness rose inside me.

They don't smell, I thought, bones don't smell, funny, always imagined they would.

And then, absently, in a back-of-the-mind way: *I don't want to die like this, not here, not like this, not in a mass grave, I don't want to be just another pile of nameless bones, forgotten by the world.*

That video camera.

That fucking video camera.

CHAPTER 75

ZOLAN

Jörg and Karl and the others were waiting impatiently for Zolan at the entrance to the mass grave. Will had dried sufficiently and no longer left any footprints for them to follow, especially not over the pell-mell bone repository. They didn't know there was only one direction in which to proceed, because he had never allowed them to venture to this side of the pool before.

Zolan passed through their ranks and entered the vast chamber first, sweeping the flashlight from wall to wall.

Empty.

He started forward slowly.

CHAPTER 76

I lay perfectly still and listened. I heard my pursuers not far away. They sounded like feral animals. But what were they doing? Why had they stopped?

Suddenly a white light cut through the darkness. Footsteps followed, bones splintering. I held my breath.

Were they coming toward me?

Had they noticed where I'd dug?

I was a sitting duck.

I tensed, waited for one of them to cry out.

None did.

The footsteps passed close by, one set after the other, continuing in succession for what seemed like far too long. But then they began to fade.

I waited a full minute before shoving the layer of bones off me. I sat up and used Danièle's matches to relight the torch I had snuffed out. The room was deserted. I tried to stand, toppled over, tried again, and succeeded. I lurched through the bone field back the way I had come. As soon as I reached solid ground I stumbled on legs that felt like slats of splintery wood. I pinballed from wall to wall, believing the next step would be my last, or the one after that.

Abruptly a childhood memory appeared in my mind's eye. I was running along one of my favorite bike trails, carrying Maxine on my back, ducking overhanging branches, jumping roots, skipping over tire ruts.

I often biked there with my best friend, Stevie, but that Sunday afternoon in mid-August of 1997 Stevie bailed on me, so I invited Max along for the first time. Although the trail was in Ravenna Park, in the middle of U-District, it felt like it was in a sprawling, isolated forest, for conifers and old-growth trees towered above us, the canopy blocking out the sky, creating a premature twilight. With me leading the way, we weaved down into the ravine, spraying through foot-deep brooks and crunching over rotting deadfall. Some of the hills were a pain, and I was always puffing for breath when I reached the top. But, surprisingly, Max never walked her bike up them; she likely wanted to prove to me she could keep up, so she would be allowed to come back.

We were about an hour along the trail when the accident happened. I was zipping down a gradual incline, getting air on small jumps, glancing back to see if Max was doing the same. She wasn't; her tires remained firmly on the ground as she tackled each peak and trough. Even so, about halfway down, she picked up too much speed and lost control. Her front tire caught a rut, then hit a root. Her handlebars jerked, and she crashed through the thick vegetation for about twenty feet before plowing into a large tree. She suffered a greenstick fracture in her left leg, though all we knew right then was that her leg was bloody and bruised. She was crying, as much out of fear as pain, I suspected, but eventually I coaxed her onto my back. I must have carried her for two kilometers before we emerged from the park behind a 7-Eleven. The employee on shift called our dad, who picked us up and took Max to the hospital.

The memory left as abruptly as it came, and the stone hallway refocused around me. However, I must have gotten a second wind, because I was now moving at a good trot and arrived at the foot ladder a minute later. I took a moment to catch my breath, then gripped the ladder's uprights and shifted my feet onto the rungs. I climbed one step—and hesitated. I looked into the black shaft below me.

No, I thought. Danièle was dead. She had to be. I heard her screams. They were the screams of someone having a dagger plunged into their chest. She was dead.

But what if she wasn't?

She was. Had to be.

But what if she isn't? You left her once, you didn't have a choice, but you have a choice now.

"Fuck," I mumbled.

I stabbed out my torch on the wall and started down.

CHAPTER 77

DANIÈLE

anièle's left hand felt ten times its original size and pulsed with electrifying pain, as if it had been pricked with a thousand different needles. The skin on it was already bubbling with large, clear blisters, especially on the palm and between the fingers. She wondered if she'd ever be able to use it again, but that was only a passing thought, because she had much more immediate concerns.

Like the four zombie-bitches standing watch over her.

Two were overweight, one average, one skinny, though they all resembled each other. This wasn't surprising given they were related through inbreeding. Their ragtag clothing was filthy and torn, and their elbows were black, stained permanently, Danièle presumed, with dirt. These observations, combined with their undead stench, made her wonder whether they had ever bathed in their lives.

They watched Danièle, barely blinking. Their eyes shone with a dull luster—dull but not dumb, for they were cognizant enough to understand Zolan's orders to keep guard over her and Katja. They wouldn't even let her soothe her hand in the cool water of the pool. When she attempted to stand to do this, the skinny bitch shoved her roughly back to her rear.

Katja sat quietly next to her, staring at the ground for the most part, like a kid who knew she was in deep trouble and didn't want to make it any worse.

Danièle tried not to think about Will, but it was a futile attempt. She still couldn't believe he had abandoned her the way he had. She was so furious with him she almost wanted Zolan to catch him...almost. Because she knew she couldn't blame him. If their positions had been reversed, she would have done the same as he had—

Will emerged from the shadows like a wraith.

Were her eyes playing tricks on her?

Could that really be him?

Yes! Because Katja, gasping in excitement, saw him too. Yet before Danièle could tell her to shut up, she blurted, "Will!"

The four women whirled around, amazingly quick for such despondent creatures. They shrieked and raised their bone-weapons...and everything that followed happened very fast.

Danièle rocked forward, grabbed the ankle of the bitch closest to her with her good hand, and yanked. The woman lost her balance but didn't go down. Hopping on one leg, she attempted to kick free. Danièle tugged again, this time dropping her. She landed on her chest. Danièle scrambled onto her back. Her body, wiry and powerful, thrashed violently.

"Katja!" Danièle shouted. "Help!"

CHAPTER 78

KATJA

Katja didn't know what to do; she was frozen with conflicting loyalties. Danièle wanted her to help attack Toni. But she couldn't do that! Toni was her aunt. She'd helped raise Katja from birth.

Toni twisted and knocked Danièle off her.

Screeching, she raised her bone.

Katja leapt forward and grabbed the shaft, just above where she held it.

Toni whirled toward her, hissing her name.

Katja tugged the bone free and stumbled backward.

CHAPTER 79

I overwhelmed the two fat women with brute force, smashing through their raised femurs with mine and landing critical blows to their skulls. The skinny one, however, got behind me and leapt onto my back, her arms and legs locking around me. She bit me above the collarbone, tearing out a chunk of flesh.

Bellowing, I dropped the femur, reached over my shoulders, grabbed her with both hands by the greasy hair, and launched her into the wall. She hit it hard but recovered quickly, pushing herself to her hands and knees. I drove a foot into the back of her neck and heard a popping crack. She expelled a drilling shriek that splintered into something inhuman. She dropped to her chest and jerked her head back and forth, still shrieking, though unable to move her body from the neck down.

CHAPTER 80

KATJA

Katja knew Romy must be badly hurt because of the sounds she was making, but she didn't understand why her aunt was just lying there. Nevertheless, if she didn't quiet down, Katja's father was surely going to hear her and know they were escaping. He would come back with the others and catch everyone again.

Understanding this, Katja rushed beside Will and grabbed Romy's long hair in her hands.

"Get out of the way, Katja!" Will growled. He looked as angry as she'd ever seen anybody, and she knew he was going to stomp on Romy's head the way he'd stomped on Hann's.

Katja ignored him and began dragging Romy toward the water. She feared Will would stop her, but he was already turning his attention to the struggle between Danièle and Toni.

"Katja!" Romy hissed between her shrieks. "*Hilf mir!*"

Her German wasn't very good, not like Katja's father's or Katja's herself, she only knew a few basic words, and they were usually garbled by her pronunciation, but what she said now was easy enough to understand: "Help me."

Katja kept dragging her toward the water.

"*Hilf mir!*"

"I am!" she shouted.

Suddenly the cool water shimmered around Katja's ankles.

She backed up a few more steps until it was up to her knees.

Romy was shaking her head wildly, but she still wasn't moving her body at all. Her rounded eyes blazed and she hissed, "Katja—"

Katja released her hair and her head sank below the surface and her shrieks turned into bubbles.

"Go to sleep," she said softly.

CHAPTER 81

I didn't know what Katja wanted with the skinny woman, but I didn't care; the woman was a quadriplegic and no longer a threat. I turned to Danièle, who was grappling with the last remaining woman. I snatched up the femur and went to help. Danièle flipped the woman onto her back, pinning her to the ground.

Holding the bone with a wide grip, I pressed the middle of its length against the woman's throat and leaned onto it, crushing the cartilage in her windpipe and depriving her of air. She writhed and gasped and spat until she went limp.

"Will!" Danièle said when it was over, throwing her arms around me. We folded onto the rock together.

I couldn't believe she was in my arms, safe, *alive*.

"I'm sorry," I mumbled into her hair, squeezing her tighter.

"You came back."

"I left."

"You came back."

"Shit, Danièle," I said, noticing her hand.

"It is okay."

I sat up, easing her aside. "Zolan's still looking for me, he's going to come back. We have to go." I glanced around for Katja through a film of blurry fatigue. She was by the pool, crouched next to a pair of legs that extended from the water. *Had she drowned her own aunt?* "Katja...?"

She looked at me. "She isn't going to wake up, is she?"

"No."

She began to cry.

"Katja, I'm sorry. I didn't want any of this—"

"I didn't either!"

I glanced at Danièle. She shook her head. I got up and went to Katja and pulled her to her feet and shushed her and stroked her hair.

"It's almost over," I said softly.

She sobbed, and her body trembled.

"Can you climb the ladder?" I asked her.

"I—I don't know."

"You need to."

"I don't know what to do anymore."

"Just climb the ladder."

"I want this to end."

"Can you climb the ladder?"

"I…" She sniffed, nodded. "Okay."

"Faster this time?"

She nodded again against my chest.

Danièle had collected one of the discarded yet still-burning torches and joined us at the pool. She waded in, apparently intent on swimming back through the submerged passage. The mere thought of doing so made me shiver.

"Forget it," I told her. "I can't do that swim again. I won't make it."

"We have to. We cannot stay here—"

"We're going to take the ladder."

"The ladder!" she exclaimed. "That is the way Zolan went!"

"No—I got off it before I reached the top, so did Zolan, but it kept going up, through the rock. It might lead back to all those tunnels beneath Val-de-Grâce. We could easily lose Zolan in them, and we'd be closer to a way out."

Danièle frowned, contemplating this. "And if you are wrong, and it leads nowhere?" she said.

"I can't do that swim again," I said simply.

▼

I ascended the ladder first, carrying the torch, followed by Katja, then Danièle. At the lateral hallway, I half expected to find Zolan and the others, waiting to jump me, but it was all clear, and for the first time in...I don't know how long...I felt the nascence of hope.

We were going to do this.

We were going to escape.

These thoughts spurred me on, and I didn't realize I had left Katja and Danièle behind until I glanced down and all I could see was blackness.

"Katja?" I called.

"Coming!" Her voice was small and scared. Then she reached the torchlight. From my birds-eye angle only her forehead and eyes were illuminated—those captivating eyes of hers. Then the shadows covering her lower face peeled away, and a sadness welled inside me.

What was going to happen to her? I wondered. She thought she was going to be living with me and going on picnics and shopping for dresses. The truth was...what? The media would have a field day with her, that's what. She'd become a modern-day carnival sideshow. She wouldn't be able to go anywhere without attracting stares of pity and revulsion. She'd probably have to wear one of those burn masks to hide her face. She would never find love, never start a family. She would be doomed to a life of loneliness—what, ironically, I had naively believed I was saving her from.

No, that wasn't true. I never believed I was saving her from anything.

I had simply been using her.

She stopped at my feet. "Am I doing okay, Will?"

"You're doing great, Katja," I said.

Twenty or so rungs later the shaft came to an end. One moment nothing was above me, the next some sort of grate. With a sinking heart I placed my hand against the iron bars, positive they were going to be welded in place, and pushed.

They lifted away.

▼

The smell took me back to elementary school: wood polish and industrial cleaners and disinfectants. I turned in a circle and saw I was in some kind of small closet/office. Against one wall was a chair and desk on which sat a cup of pens and a stack of paper and a gooseneck lamp. The rest of the walls were obscured by shelves crowded with janitorial supplies.

Katja poked her head through the hole and her eyes widened in wonderment. I helped her out, then Danièle, who was right behind her.

"Oh God!" Danièle said, covering her mouth with her good hand. "We made it. Oh God, oh God, oh God. Will! *We made it.*"

I managed a nod. This felt too surreal. If I spoke, I feared I would break the spell and wake up back in the catacombs.

I went to the door. Turning the handle popped the push-lock. The door opened to a long hallway—one with waxed floors and painted walls and fluorescent lights set into ceiling fixtures.

Katja squeezed past me and gasped. "Is this Paris?"

"Almost, Katja," I said. "Almost."

▼

I snuffed the torch out on the floor and left it there, and we followed the hallway past several closed doors to a staircase. We ascended the steps and emerged in a room filled with a range of display cases lit by dimmed spotlights.

"Where are we, Danièle?" I said.

"It must be Val-de-Grâce."

"I thought Val-de-Grâce was a military hospital?"

"Originally it was a church. Then a convent was added to it. Then the convent was converted into a military hospital. Then a modern military hospital was built on the same grounds, and the old one was turned into a medical museum. So that is where we must be." She went to the closest display case. "Yes, see—I am right."

Katja and I joined her. On the other side of the glass was a primitive prosthetic hand that would have required the user to change the attachment—fork, spoon, tweezers—every time he or she undertook a different task.

"What is that?" Katja asked.

"A hand," I told her.

"A hand?"

"People who lost theirs stuck that on their arm." To Danièle I said, "Which way's the exit, do you think?"

She shook her head. "I have no idea."

We went in an arbitrary direction but didn't get far before Katja stopped at another display case.

"Katja," I said, impatient, "there's no time."

But she didn't move. When I realized what the exhibit was my stomach dropped. She was staring fixedly at several wax casts of human faces—those deformed by war injuries and those same ones put back together with reconstructive surgery. Katja pointed to one face in particular whose deformities bore an uncanny resemblance to her own. "What happened to him?" she asked.

"I don't know."

She indicated the post-surgery cast. "Is that what he looked like before?"

"No, that's what he looked like after."

"After?"

"There are medical procedures today…they can help…"

"Can they make me look like you?"

"I…I don't know…"

She frowned. "What happened to me?"

"Your father never told you?"

"He said my nose and lips fell off because of the radiation. But if there is no radiation, that can't be true."

"Will, hurry!" Danièle called softly. She was twenty feet ahead of us, beckoning us to follow.

"We'll talk about it later," I told Katja. "But we have to keep going. We're not supposed to be here, and we need to find help."

We passed a smorgasbord of other medical displays: colorful faience apothecary jars, paintings of medics at work on the battlefield (which made me think of *M.A.S.H.* circa 1814), scale models with old-fashioned dolls taking the place of patients, even a full-size reconstruction of a surgical anatomy lesson.

Finally we passed through a large wooden door and entered a long wide hallway. One wall was lined with marble busts and memorial tablets dedicated to medics killed in the field, the other a series of arched windows that overlooked a cloister and formal garden, though it was night and not much outside was visible.

We were halfway down the hallway when the door we were headed toward opened and a man dressed head to toe in black appeared.

CHAPTER 82

DANIÈLE

The military guard started at our sudden appearance before drawing his pistol and pointing it at us. "Who are you?" he demanded in French. "What are you doing here? The museum is closed."

"We were attacked," Danièle said. "We need help."

The guard came closer. He squinted at Katja's face and winced. "What's wrong with her?"

"She was attacked."

"Turn around. All of you. Hands on your heads."

Danièle obeyed. Will and Katja followed her lead.

"What's happening?" Katja asked softly.

"Just do as he says."

Danièle heard a burst of static. The guard reported a break-in and requested backup. Then: "Who attacked you?"

"A man," Danièle said. "His name is Zolan."

"Is he here with you?"

"I do not know. He attacked us in the catacombs."

"The catacombs?"

"We escaped up a ladder. It led us here."

"To the museum?"

"To the basement level. We were looking for a way out."

Silence.

"Please," she said. "We need help—"

"Have you been drinking alcohol tonight?"

"No!"

"Have you taken any drugs?"

Danièle shook her head in frustration. God! He likely thought they were a bunch of meth heads. She couldn't blame him. They were covered with dirt and sweat, her hand was a mushy pulp, Will's neck and face were smeared with blood... and Katja... Did he think they did that to her?

"Let me show you," she said.

"Show me what?"

"The ladder that led us here."

"The ladder in the basement."

"Yes."

He was silent.

"Well?"

"Quiet."

A minute later the door they had rushed through opened and two more military guards appeared. One of them had the cleft jaw of a drill sergeant, while the other was younger and sported dark stubble. They were both dressed in black uniforms with black folded side caps, black boots, and black ballistic nylon duty belts loaded with equipment.

Their pistols were trained on Will. When they saw Katja, they made no effort to hide their expressions of disgust.

"What happened to her?" Drill Sergeant said.

"I'm okay actually," Katja told him.

He ignored her. "They were just walking around in here?" he said to the guard behind them, outside of Danièle's field of view.

"They say someone attacked them in the catacombs. They climbed a ladder that led here."

"*Here?*"

"That is what they say."

Drill Sergeant crouched before Katja and said, "What happened to you?"

"What do you mean?"

He touched his nose.

"I don't know," she said.

"You don't know?"

She shook her head.

He glanced at Will, the bleeding wound on his neck. "Did you do this to her?"

"I don't understand," he replied in English.

Drill Sergeant blinked. "American?"

Will nodded.

Drill Sergeant stood, looked at Danièle. "And you?"

"I am French."

"Do you have identification?"

"Not with me."

"You," he said to Will in English now. "Passport? Residence permit?"

Will shook his head.

The three guards conversed with each other for a few moments, then they handcuffed Danièle's and Will's and Katja's wrists behind their backs. One of them got on the radio again.

"What are you doing?" Danièle protested. "We have done nothing!"

"This is a military facility," Drill Sergeant said. "You're trespassing."

"We need to see a doctor—"

"Relax, we're taking you to the hospital." He gripped her arm and pulled her to her feet. "But first you're going to show me how you got in here."

▼

Will and Katcha remained behind with the other two guards while Danièle led Drill Sergeant back to the basement level.

She pointed down the hallway. "It is that way."

"Show me."

She went slowly, feeling uneasy, suddenly convinced Zolan

was going to be in the room, waiting for them. But almost immediately she dismissed this worry. It was no longer the two of them alone in his quarters. Drill Sergeant was here. He was huge and had a pistol and Zolan wouldn't stand a chance against him.

Danièle stopped outside the door to the janitorial closet and said, "The ladder is in there. There is a hole in the floor."

"Step aside."

She did as he asked. He pushed the door open, reached inside, and turned on the light. The small room was empty. Danièle relaxed—until she saw that the grate was back in place over the shaft. She frowned, trying to recall whether they had replaced it. She knew she didn't. Katja wouldn't have. So had Will? She couldn't remember—she couldn't remember anything of those first few moments after exiting the shaft except for euphoria at escaping the catacombs.

"There," she said, pointing to the grate.

Drill Sergeant looked at her skeptically, then entered the room. He stood above the grate and peered down. She joined him.

Blackness.

He took a flashlight from his belt, flicked it on, and shone the beam between the bars.

Electric fear soldered Danièle to the spot.

Ten feet down, a horrible mutant face stared up at them.

"What the fuck?" Drill Sergeant said, aligning the pistol with the flashlight, so they both pointed into the hole. "*Don't fucking move!*"

Danièle sensed movement and spun to see Zolan burst from behind the door and swing his bone-weapon like a baseball bat at Drill Sergeant's head. Drill Sergeant turned just as the end of the femur cracked against his temple. He collapsed like a sack of flour. Danièle made to run, but Zolan pulled her against him and clamped his hand over her mouth.

"Don't make a sound," he whispered into her ear.

CHAPTER 83

I stared at the ground in front of me, fighting to remain conscious. My vision was blurring and my ears were ringing and every part of my body ached for rest, from the soles of my feet to the pads of my fingertips. But I wouldn't let myself pass out. Not here, not on the floor. I wanted to get to the hospital first, get looked over by a doctor, be told I didn't have any kind of traumatic brain injury. The latter worried me more than I cared to admit. I'd been knocked out cold by blunt force trauma twice. I could be suffering intracranial pressure, or cerebral bleeding—or something serious enough to turn me into a vegetable or prevent me from ever waking again.

Also, I needed to be around for Katja. The next few hours were going to be terrifying for her. She was going to come into contact with more people than she had seen in her entire life, while being inundated by sights and sounds and smell she wouldn't recognize or understand. She would likely be interrogated and locked up, perhaps even verbally abused and threatened.

And when our story was eventually verified, something that could take days, what then? Where would she be taken? Would she be dropped off at some almshouse and left to fend for herself? No, I decided. This wasn't the middle ages. She'd likely end up at an intermediate care facility or care house or whatever they were called nowadays—those places where people with physical or mental disabilities went. And...well, maybe that wouldn't be as bad as it sounded. After all, it couldn't be any worse than what she'd endured living with Hanns and the rest of her extended family. Also, there'd be care workers to help get her up to date with the world, help integrate her into society.

In fact, could it be that my earlier doom and gloom outlook for her future was misguided? Could she indeed live a full life? I recalled the look on her face when she saw the wax casts of the injured soldiers' faces: wonder and hope. I had not considered reconstructive surgery for her before, but could that be a feasible option? Medical technology has come a long way in a short time. Doctors have performed complete face transplants. Wasn't it possible then they could provide her some sort of artificial nose and lips? And the financial cost? Well, maybe there could be a silver lining to the inevitable media whirlwind. Surely when people learned what she had been through, donations would pour in. Plastic surgeons might even offer to work on her pro bono; the publicity and prestige if successful would be priceless.

This was all speculation, of course, but there was one thing I knew for certain: I was not going to abandon Katja. I would be a brother to her. I would be there for her every step of the way —

Someone on the other side of the door began whistling, a sad, windy melody.

One of the guards called, *"Qui est là?"*

"Je m'appelle Monsieur Lenoir," a voice floated back. *"Je suis le portier."*

"Le portier?" The guards exchanged glances.

Moments later the door opened and an old man in drab work clothes appeared pushing a mop protruding from a yellow bucket on wheels.

Zolan!

"That's him!" I said. "He's the one who attacked us!"

The guard closest to me yelled at me to shut up, but both he and his pal placed their hands on the butts of their holstered pistols.

"That's him!" I repeated, staring up at them. Then: "Katja, tell them! Tell them who that is."

"*C'est mon père*," she said in a small voice.

The guards seemed baffled. "*Votre père?*" one said.

She nodded.

They approached Zolan, speaking to him, giving orders. Zolan spoke back and held up his hands.

"Don't listen to him!" I shouted. "Whatever he's saying, he's lying!"

One of the guards yelled at me to shut up again, while the other resumed conversing with Zolan. I didn't know what Zolan was up to, but my carrying on like a raving lunatic wasn't helping any.

"Katja," I said quietly, looking at her. "We're going to have to run."

"Run? Where?"

I jerked my head in the opposite direction of Zolan and the guards. "Through that door."

"What's happening?"

"Just run. Don't look back. Okay?"

She nodded.

I moved from my knees into a crouch. Katja did the same.

"*Hé!*" one of the guards shouted. "*Arrêtez!*"

He started toward us. The other hesitated, then followed.

Zolan withdrew a pistol from beneath his shirt.

"Watch out!"

My warning was drowned out by the ensuing gunshot. The report rang through the hallway.

"Go!" I shouted to Katja, and we turned and ran.

A second shot sounded. A guard screamed. A third shot, and the screaming stopped.

Katja and I crashed through the wooden door and kept running.

▼

Danièle sat in the corner of the small room, a foul-tasting rag stuffed into her mouth, her hands still cuffed behind her back. Four zombie-men huddled together by the door while others continued to climb from the hole.

She almost wished Zolan had killed her along with Drill Sergeant. The fact he didn't meant he had other plans for her. These were not hard to fathom. He would take her back to his lair in the catacombs, only there would be no pretenses this time. He would imprison her, and he would rape her. She would become his go-to fuck. This knowledge filled her with a bottomless despair, a state of doom. She couldn't go back. She couldn't go through that.

Her only chance, she knew, was for the two remaining guards, or for Will, to stop him. This was possible, but Zolan now had Drill Sergeant's pistol—and the element of surprise. Danièle didn't know what his plan was, but he had changed into a janitor's uniform hanging on the back of the door and left with a mop and yellow bucket.

Did he really think this disguise would fool Will and Katja? Or did they not matter to him? Did he merely want only to get close enough to the guards to shoot them?

The last of the zombie-men emerged from the hole, seven in total. They stood shoulder to shoulder in the cramped space, ill at ease, restive, no doubt uncomfortable in the unfamiliar environment. Their collective stench was over-powering, making Danièle's eyes water.

Then one of them—the first one out of the hole, the one Zolan had called Jörg—tapped his bone-weapon against the door. He listened, then rattled the handle. He continued rattling it more and more aggressively until the push-button lock popped. He jumped backward, startling the others. Some moaned, some looked about wildly, but for the most part they remained quiet.

Jörg rattled the handle a final time, and the door clicked open. He grunted with satisfaction, stuck his nose to the crack, and made sniffing noises. He paused, sniffed, paused. Then he pushed the door farther open, wincing at the light. He glanced over at Danièle, his eyes calculating.

Apparently his curiosity trumped his obedience to Zolan, and he left the room.

The rest of the mob barked and groaned and bumped one another in what was either confusion or fear or both. Then one worked up the courage and left as well. Then another, and another, until Danièle was by herself.

She scrambled quickly to the fallen soldier and found the handcuff key in a belt keeper between the holster and baton. She stuck the key in the handcuff's keyhole and fiddled with it until the shackle jaw slid open. She brought her hands in front of her and unlocked the second cuff. Then she tore the rag from her mouth and sucked back air—just as a gunshot rang out.

▼

Katja and I dashed back into the museum proper, but there was no place to hide, no place to run. I heard the door bang open behind us and knew Zolan would be right on our heels. We turned one corner after another and ended up in the church Danièle had mentioned. The nave was capped by a sculpted ceiling and a cupola decorated with a fresco. A giant baldachin with distinctive twisted columns rose above the altar and a nativity scene.

"There!" I said, pointing down the left transept to a pair of giant doors.

We ran toward them, our feet slapping on the marble floor.

▼

For a moment Zolan had feared Will and Katja would escape into the gardens to the east of the museum and reach the military hospital, but instead they fled toward the adjoining church, the main doors of which would undoubtedly be locked at this hour.

He slowed to a fast walk with the SIG Pro held out in front of him and told himself this was all going to work out after all. In a few minutes he would be back in the catacombs with Will, Danièle, Katja, and the dead military guard in the custodial closet. Investigators would find the two men he'd shot, but that would be all. Suspicion would shift to the missing guard, yet there would be little to go on, and the case would go cold.

Safely underground once more, Zolan would not make the same mistake twice. He would kill Will immediately and then Danièle after he had his way with her, then he would finish what was long overdue. He would kill the rest of them: Jörg, Karl, Odo...Katja. It would break his heart to do so, but the time had come to end the insanity he had become a party to.

▼

After discovering that the doors of the church were locked, Katja and I had no option but to return to the nave—where Zolan was waiting for us. He aimed the pistol at me.

I froze, adrenaline roaring through my veins as I waited for him to squeeze the trigger.

"Papa!" Katja cried, stepping in front of me protectively. "Don't kill him! He's my friend!"

"Your friend?" Zolan chuffed. "He only used you to escape."

"He told me the truth about Paris! Something you've kept hidden from me my entire life."

"I did that for your protection, my mouse. This world is not for you."

She touched her face. "Did you do this to me?"

"No, of course not." He shook his head, and he genuinely looked pained. "Of course not."

"Then who did?"

"Your grandfather. He was a sick man. He did that to all your uncles and aunts. I was too late to save you, but I did everything I could for you. I raised you like my daughter."

"Like? I'm *not* your daughter?"

"This isn't the place for such a discussion, Katja," he said curtly. "Now, if you want Will to live, you will do as I say. Do you understand me?"

She looked at me for guidance.

"We should do as he says," I told her.

"Smart decision, Will." Zolan waved the pistol. "I want you both ahead of me, get going, that way."

He directed us back to the museum. My mind was racing to figure out what he had planned. The best I could surmise: he was either taking us to the catacombs again, where he would kill me, or he was taking us to the dead guards, where he would kill me. Neither option, of course, was acceptable, but there was little I could do. I was sure if I tried anything he wouldn't hesitate to put a bullet in my back. I said, "You're not going to get away with this."

"With what?" Zolan replied.

"You killed two guards."

"Three."

I swallowed. That had been my last hope—that the third security guard and Danièle were still alive. Nevertheless, I hadn't put much faith in this, for if they were, they would have heard the gunshots and returned by now. "And Danièle?" I asked, needing to know for certain what happened to her.

"Keep walking."

"Is she dead?"

He didn't answer me.

Katja glanced over her shoulder. "Are we returning to the homestead, Papa?"

"That's correct, my love."

"But I haven't seen Paris yet!"

"I will still show it to you."

"When?"

"Soon."

"Do you promise?"

"Cross my heart."

Katja faced forward again, and I thought she might be smiling. Her innocence, her blind trust, her forgiveness, were nearly incomprehensible to witness.

Suddenly a person darted from the shadows thirty feet ahead of us. I couldn't make out who it was in the dim lighting.

Zolan shouted and fired the pistol. The round shattered the glass of a display case.

I didn't think, I acted on instinct, spinning around and charging him, my shoulders lowered, trying to make the smallest target possible.

He fired at me. I felt the bullet whizz past my left arm. A second later I drove a shoulder into his gut. We crashed to the floor together. I lunged at him, trying to bite his face. He rammed the butt of the pistol against my skull.

Everything went hazy as I slid to the floor.

CHAPTER 84

ZOLAN

Jörg! Zolan thought. It was only Jörg! And who was that who followed him? Karl? And Lorenz and Leo and Odo and Franz and Erich... They were all there now, in the distance, all of them running around like headless chickens, wailing in excitement and fright.

They were ruining everything.

"Go back!" Zolan ordered them in German. "Jörg! Go back right now!"

He glanced Zolan's way but didn't obey him. Instead he shook his femur in the air, either in triumph or rebellion, then he was gone, around a corner, howling and smashing display cases.

Zolan fought his panic and thought: *There's still time.* He would have to skip his tryst with Danièle, and he would not be able to give Katja a proper goodbye and a painless death, but there was still time to burn the homestead and be gone by the time it was discovered.

He leveled the pistol at Will, who was folded into a crumpled heap at his feet.

"No!" Katja screamed, coming toward him.

Clenching his jaw tight, saying a silent prayer for her soul and his own, Zolan swung the gun at his adopted daughter and squeezed the trigger. The round struck her in the stomach, stopping her as surely as if she had hit an invisible wall. She fell to her side.

"I'm sorry, my mouse," he whispered. "I'm so sorry—"

His knees disappeared beneath him.

CHAPTER 85

The gunshot cleared the darkness from my vision, and for a split second I waited for the pain that would surely follow. When it didn't come, I realized I hadn't been shot. Then I noticed Katja, a few yards away, motionless on her side, like a wilted rose.

I brought my knees to my chest and kicked my legs out. My feet smashed into Zolan's kneecaps. He cried out and fell on top of me. The pistol struck the tiles and clattered away from us.

Zolan tried to reach for it. I locked my legs around his torso, but I could do little else with my hands secured behind my back. He swiveled toward me and kicked me in the groin. I groaned and released him.

He lumbered to his feet, took two lurching steps, swiped up the pistol.

Scowling, he aimed the barrel at my chest.

CHAPTER 86

DANIÈLE

D anièle burst from the stairwell and saw Zolan twenty feet away, about to shoot Will. She raised the gun and squeezed the trigger three times. One of the rounds clipped Zolan in the shoulder, spinning him around so he faced her. She squeezed the trigger three more times. A bullet smashed through his teeth, blowing away half his face in the process, and he collapsed lifelessly to the floor. She ran to Will. Katja was next to him, on her side.

Had Zolan killed her? The monster!

"Will!" Danièle said, rolling him over so she could access the handcuffs. Her hands were shaking so badly it took her several goes before she could get the cuffs unlocked.

"Katja…" Will said, crawling toward Katja. He held the girl's head in his hands. "Katja?" he repeated. "Katja!"

Her eyes fluttered open.

CHAPTER 87

I don't know how I managed it, I'd never felt so weak in my life, but I scooped Katja up in my arms and sprinted through the museum, searching frantically for an exit. After several wrong turns and dead ends I discovered a door that led outside.

Dawn was breaking, the sky an otherworldly red streaked with orange and lighting to pink in places. Across a sprawling, landscaped garden rose a large concrete building that had to be the hospital.

"Sky…" Katja mumbled.

I looked at her. "What?"

Her brilliant eyes were lidded but intense, staring past me. "Sky…"

"Hold on, Katja," I said. "We're going to get you help."

"Sky…" she said a final time.

Her eyes glassed over.

"No!" I said, and ran toward the hospital.

CHAPTER 88

THE SUNDAY TELEGRAPH, May 5, 2014

Five Dead in France in Val-de-Grâce Murder Mystery (LIVE UP-DATES)

Officials in France are scratching their heads after five people were killed at the Val-de-Grâce complex in central Paris, which includes a modern military hospital, a baroque church, and a former Benedictine convent that has since been converted into a museum dedicated to the history of military medicine.

The killings occurred in the museum.

Nine suspects have been arrested, but no charges have been made at this point. Speaking to reporters, a military spokeswoman said that all suspects are being held at the hospital to receive medical treatment for unspecified injuries.

According to one witness at the hospital, the suspects were "horribly disfigured" and "acted like mindless animals," stoking wild speculation on social media sites that the French military may have been conducting covert human genetic engineering experiments at the hospital.

This was immediately dismissed by a leading military official, who told French media outlets that it was "absolutely not true" and "ridiculous." He also dismissed claims that the killings were an act of terrorism. However, he refused to comment on a possible motive.

At the moment museum officials do not believe anything was stolen from the collection. The museum and church, which are popular tourist attractions, will be closed to the public until further notice.

1:54 PM – 05/05/2014

At an afternoon press conference, Interior Minister Alain Villechaize confirmed that the three soldiers killed were members of the National Gendarmerie, a branch of the French armed forces in charge of public safety with police duties among the civilian population.

Law enforcement officials say they are focusing their attention on a French national named Zolan Roux, one of two civilians who were killed at the museum. Mr. Roux, a welfare recipient, was unemployed at the time of his death. He had previously been convicted twice on first-degree murder charges and had served more than twenty years in state prison.

French news agencies, quoting sources close to the investigation, reported that Mr. Roux and his accomplices gained access to the facility via the catacombs. The network of ancient quarries beneath Paris have been closed off to the public for decades, but police have been locked in a game of cat-and mouse with underground urban explorers, who enter the tunnels illegally. Although once commonplace, most access points connecting the tunnels and public buildings have been sealed off, and it is unusual that one would go unnoticed in the basement of what is classified as a military facility. A French intelligence service has called for a complete security review of all of their military facilities.

According to the French newspaper *Le Monde*, the intruders

were armed with human femurs, presumably obtained in the catacombs, which is home to more than six million dead, and not firearms like some media channels have reported. "There is no evidence that they had their own pistols in their possessions," a spokeswoman for the Ministry of Defense said. "Instead, it is believed that Mr. Roux gained access to a guard's handgun...and after that he began shooting."

Despite the identification of alleged gunman Zolan Roux, many questions still remain, namely what prompted him and his accomplices to break into the museum in the first place.

11:45 AM – 06/05/2014

More details have emerged in the investigation into the killings at Val-de-Grâce early Wednesday morning.

Authorities have now confirmed that Zolan Roux and the other intruders accessed the former-abbey-turned-medical-museum through an underground tunnel that connected to the catacombs.

After a preliminary exploration into the tunnel, investigators believe that Mr. Roux and his accomplices lived permanently in the catacombs for what Paris public prosecutor François Duris says might have be a "substantial amount of time." He added that investigators are working around the clock to learn more about the suspects' motivations, backgrounds, and family environments. He also hinted that the death toll in this ongoing mystery could be higher than the five initially reported.

These revelations have led some news pundits to make comparisons to the "mole people" said to inhabit the abandoned subway tunnels and sewer systems below New York City. French police are downplaying this comparison amidst fear the sensationalism of the evolving story could encourage more people to illegally visit the catacombs.

On the French television channel i-Télé, police captain Vincent Reno warned potential adventurers to "think twice about entering the underground" and that "they did so at their own risk."

EPILOGUE

I was seated at a table in Manhattan's Chinatown McDonald's, sipping the dregs of my large cappuccino and thinking about Paris.

My mind drifted to those days often. I could be doing anything—standing in line at the bank, sitting in front of my computer at work, taking a shower—and then I would find myself in an imaginary conversation with Danièle, or running through the dark from Zolan, or listening to Katja tell me about the characters in her books.

It was crazy that those two days I spent in the catacombs could consume my thoughts so completely as to reduce the previous twenty-five years of my life to a footnote.

Time wasn't helping much. It'd been six months since I left Paris, and I wasn't sure I was any better now than I was then. I still had nightmares. I couldn't sleep without nightlights. And I was talking to myself more and more. I wasn't one of those guys you saw shuffling down the street cackling to themselves one moment and screaming obscenities the next. But when I was alone I'd occasionally find myself mumbling something that sometimes made sense and sometimes didn't. It would usually only be a word or three, such as "stupid" or "why the fuck," but it was occurring with enough regularity to start concerning me.

Although I had killed Hanns and two of the women I had attacked, and Danièle had killed Zolan, French authorities never charged us with any crimes. We cooperated with them fully, and they concluded the killings were justifiable homicides. We were released from custody after the statutory limit of seventy-two hours. I returned to my flat, but when the media began camping out front of it, I packed up most of my stuff, slipped out the back, and checked into a low-key motel, where I remained largely under the radar.

Rob and Pascal's funerals were held within two days of one another. Both were closed casket services for obvious reasons. I exchanged a few words with Danièle at the chapel where Rob's memorial was held, but that was all, as she spent the rest of her time with her sister, Dev, and Rob's brother and parents, who had flown to Paris from Quebec City. His two girls were gorgeous, both with blonde hair and blue eyes and dressed in frilly black dresses. They didn't leave their mother's side the entire time.

At Pascal's memorial, his brother broke down during his eulogy, and his sister and mother were a total mess, especially during the burial as the casket, covered in a spray of flowers, was lowered into the ground. I felt like an imposter being there to witness these intimate emotions, given that Pascal had never liked me, but Danièle had asked me to go with her, and so I went.

The city cremated Katja. I didn't want her remains to end up in storage somewhere, or a potter's field, so I purchased them from the coroner's office, and Danièle and I scattered her ashes in Pere Lachaise's Garden of Remembrance.

I returned to the United States the following week. It was hard to say goodbye to Danièle, but I couldn't remain in France any longer; I needed to get home. Danièle and I promised we would see each other again, but I don't think either of us really believed that. I flew to Seattle and stayed with my parents. I was immediately bombarded with media requests. Every national news network and major book publisher wanted the exclusive rights to my story. I don't know how people who've been involved in sensational murder sagas give tell-all interviews or write tell-all books. How could you cheapen what you had been through like that? How could you allow it to be turned into entertainment? Rob was dead. Pascal was dead. Katja was dead. I would never exploit their deaths for profit, not now, and not ten years from now.

Bridgette emailed me a number of times. I think she was worried about me, my mental health, though she didn't come out and say this. I always replied, though briefly. She wanted my phone number, wanted to talk. I told her I didn't have a US number yet, which was true. I was in no rush to get one either.

Danièle emailed too, almost every day at first, then a few times a week, then, over the last two months, hardly at all. I missed speaking with her, but I also believed it was for the best. She was an ocean away. We both had to move on.

One person I had been happy to hear from was my old boss. He emailed me one day to inquire when I would be returning to work. I thought he was kidding. I had assumed the travel guide company would have wanted to distance itself from someone who'd made the type of headlines I'd made. But my boss was serious. He said I could return whenever I felt up to it. I guess I shouldn't have been as surprised as I had been; he'd always been a friend as much as a boss. Moreover, since I've been back at the New York office, I've gotten the feeling he held himself partly responsible for what happened in Paris, given it was his idea to send me to France in the first place. That was nonsense, of course, but that was the type of guy he was.

I finished my coffee, dumped the paper cup and my half-eaten fries in a bin, and left the restaurant. It was late November and freezing cold outside. Snow fell in a kaleidoscope of flakes, leaving a white and bright layer over everything except for slushy brown tracks on the streets and sidewalks. Everybody had their heads down, their hoods up, against the chill. Several people carried umbrellas.

Manhattan's Chinatown was great for being anonymous. I was a six-foot-four Caucasian, but none of the Asians here recognized me, or if they did, they didn't say anything. This was not the case in other parts of the city, where I got "Hey, Mole-man!" and "Yo, Walking Dead!" and other stuff of a similar nature on a regular basis.

I made my way to my apartment building. It was on a warehouse street that even in the pit of winter smelled of dead fish. I greeted Jimmy, who acted as both doorman and concierge, then took the stairs to the fifth floor of the walkup. I stopped as soon as I entered the hallway. Someone was sitting with their back against my door, their knees pulled to their chest.

Another "fan?" Aside from the idiots who called me Mole-man, there were others, both men and women, who would come up to me and start a conversation. It didn't matter where I was—a park, a bar, a restaurant—they simply strolled over and started yacking it up. Most of them, I suspect, thought it was neat to be talking to someone of infamy. A few, however, were urban explorers who invited me to join them in the abandoned subway tunnels beneath New York City. I was blunt with the lot, telling them I wanted to be left alone. Their responses varied from polite and apologetic to indignant and offended, as if I was the one being rude for wanting to mind my own business. Nevertheless, they all eventually let me be—and no one had yet shown up on my doorstep.

I considered turning around, coming back later, but that was stupid. This was my apartment. I wasn't getting run away from my own home.

I walked down the hallway. The person stirred in response to my footsteps and lifted their face in my direction. It was a woman. For a moment—not longer than a heartbeat—I didn't recognize her. Then I said, "Danièle?"

She shot to her feet. "Will!"

We embraced, and I breathed in an unfamiliar jasmine-scented perfume. I stepped apart and grinned and said, "Wow."

She grinned back. Her hair was longer, but other than that she looked just as good as I remembered. "Are you surprised to see me?"

"Obviously. What are you doing here?"

"I was in New York...and I decided to drop by."

"You were in New York?" I said skeptically.

"Do not worry, Will, I did not come all the way from Paris just to see you. I am not a psycho stalker. I am here for other reasons that I will tell you about if you decide to invite me inside."

"Yeah, sure, right." I unlocked and opened the door.

She stepped inside, and I followed behind her. The unit had high ceilings, an exposed brick wall, a renovated kitchen, and newly refinished cherry wood floors. The rent was a bit more than I wanted to pay, but it was a block from the F train, which was what I took to work, and it had large corner windows that let in a lot of sunlight, which sealed the deal.

"I like it," Danièle said, moving to the brick wall, on which hung several oil-on-canvas paintings. "Hey!" she exclaimed. "That is my bicycle!"

I went to stand beside her. The painting depicted a woman riding a pink bicycle with white fenders and a wicker basket along a cobbled street. "Looks like it, doesn't it?"

"Yes, and even *she* looks like me."

The woman's face was turned away from the viewer, but she was thin and had short-cropped black hair.

"Where did you get this—?" She glanced at me, her eyes widening in understanding. "You painted it?"

I nodded.

"I did not know you painted."

"I took it up."

Danièle walked down the wall, studying the other paintings: a section of the Jardin des Plants I had particularly enjoyed, the tire swing hanging from the old maple at my parents' house, the view of neon and slummy anarchy outside my window.

"They are very good," she said.

"Thanks."

"And you painted me." She smiled. "That means you missed me."

"A little bit."

"Good. Because I do not know about you, Will. You stopped emailing…"

"You stopped."

"Because I always wrote first. You simply replied. So I stopped to see if you would write first. You never did."

"I'm sure I did."

"I am sure you did not."

"You were so far away…"

"Yes, I know, I know. You do not need to tell me one of your famous excuses." She looked around the flat. "Do you have any other paintings?"

"A few."

I led her to my bedroom and pointed to several canvases stacked against each other in the corner.

She flicked through them. "Oh, I like these too…" She studied one for longer than the others. "Is that…? It is."

She pulled it out and showed it to me, though of course I knew which one she was referring to. Katja's portrait stared back at me. Initially I had planned to paint only her eyes. I had wanted to capture them, their intensity and innocence, so I would never forget them. But then I found myself unable to stop there. I wanted to know what she might have looked like had she not been disfigured, and I ended up painting her entire face, unblemished, perfect.

I said, "I was thinking about her one day…"

"She is beautiful."

I nodded, but I didn't want to talk about Katja. "So where about are you staying?" I asked.

Danièle set the canvas back on the floor, stared at it for another couple seconds, then turned to me. "The Belvedere."

"In Hell's Kitchen."

"What a stupid name for a neighborhood, yes? Why would tourists ever stay in a neighborhood called that?"

"You did."

"Because it reminded me of you."

"Me?"

"Remember in the catacombs, when I showed you that inscription of the street name in the wall, and explained how an entire neighborhood had collapsed into a tunnel...?"

"Hell Street," I said.

"Yes. So when I saw a hotel located in Hell's Kitchen, I thought of you, and I decided it would be a good story to tell you when I arrived here."

I nodded. It made sense in a wacky Danièle-logic sort of way. "So what are you doing here?" I asked her.

"I am studying."

"Studying?"

"I was accepted to MIT's School of Engineering."

"Shit! Congratulations, Danièle!"

She beamed. "I told you I was not going to be a florist forever."

I shook my head. "So you're living, where, in Cambridge?"

"Yes, I have been there for about a month now. I wanted to come sooner to New York to visit you, but there was so much I had to do."

"Yeah, no problem, whatever, I—I just can't believe you're so close now. It's like, what, a three-hour drive?"

"The bus took me four hours."

"How did you know where I lived?"

"I called your work. Someone named Scott Swiercz-something gave me your address."

"He's my boss. Bastard never told me anything."

"I told him not to. I told him it was a surprise."

"Well...fuck, Danièle! I'm blown away. Do you want a drink? We should celebrate."

"How about dinner? I worked up an appetite sitting outside your door."

"Did Jimmy just let you up?"

"The doorman? Yes—I told him not to say anything either."

"Great security, huh? Let me get my jacket. There's a good —"

"I thought we could eat in," she said. "You promised to make me a French dinner. Remember—you, me, and your hot twenty-year-old neighbor."

"Madame Gabin, right." I shrugged. "Okay, French home cooking it is. Um—do you know any recipes?"

We inventoried my refrigerator and cupboards, Danièle decided I had the ingredients to attempt a beef bourguignon, and we spent the next two hours preparing and cooking it, polishing off two bottles of Cabernet Sauvignon in the process.

I didn't have a dining table—I usually ate at my computer —so we spread out a picnic on the thick-pile rug in the middle of the living room. It was the most fun I'd had since…since I could remember.

At some point we ended up leaning against the sofa, folk music playing from the stereo system, Danièle's head resting on my shoulder. Outside the windows dusk turned to night, and the room filled with shadows. When those shadows threatened to blend into a unified blackness, the nightlights switched themselves on.

"You have nightlights?" Danièle said, her voice startling me. I had been half asleep and had thought she'd been too.

"Yeah…a few…" I said.

"Me too."

"Really?"

"I'm afraid of the dark."

"Get a place with big windows."

A chuckle. "Will?"

"Yeah?"

"I missed you."

"I missed you too."

"Did you really?"

"Yeah."

"You do not have to fake it—"

"I'm not faking anything."

"Will you visit me in Cambridge?"

"Of course."

"Good…" She snuggled closer.

Just as I was drifting off once more, she said, "Will?"

"Yeah?"

"Hold me."

I wrapped my arm around her shoulder and held her.

Made in the USA
Columbia, SC
27 May 2020